LUCK BE A LADY

Before she could respond to his cryptic words, Jake grabbed her shoulders and lowered his head to hers. His lips pressed against hers with an energy she'd never felt before—an energy that raced through every square inch of her body.

Her mouth responded as if completely separate from her mind, because certainly this wasn't a good idea, but damned if she could remember a reason why not. His lips parted and hers went right along with him, their tongues mingling in a sensual dance that made her moan.

Suddenly, he dropped his hands and stepped away. The desire on his face was plain as day, and Mallory could tell his self-control was as precarious as her own, body warring with mind in the endless battle of whether this was a good idea or a really bad one that felt like a really good one at the moment.

He stared at her for a moment, indecisive, then shoved the sliding door open and slipped inside, never even looking back.

She watched him, the heat from her body still radiating out every pore. She ought to have been angry, but instead she smiled. Jake McMillan had thought he'd grab a quick kiss to ensure a run of bad luck this afternoon. He'd thought he was being sneaky, but he'd gotten far more than he bargained for.

Other books by Jana DeLeon:

RUMBLE ON THE BAYOU

Unlucky

Jana DeLeon

LOVE SPELL NEW YORK CITY

To my grandma, Elizabeth Mae Heyse (1909–2002),
the strongest woman I've ever known.
Your faith humbles me even today.

LOVE SPELL®

November 2007

Published by

Dorchester Publishing Co., Inc.
200 Madison Avenue
New York, NY 10016

ISBN-10: 0-505-52729-4
ISBN-13: 978-0-505-52729-5

The name "Love Spell" and its logo are trademarks of Dorchester
Publishing Co., Inc.

Printed in the United States of America.

10 9 8 7 6 5 4 3 2 1

Visit us on the web at www.dorchesterpub.com.

ACKNOWLEDGMENTS

To my husband, Rene, for all of your support and for continuing to believe in me absolutely. To my incredible friend and critique partner, Colleen Gleason, for pushing me along when this book had me stuck and for always reminding me that I really can write— you are the best! To my friend Sarah Fogleman, for reminding me that this business couldn't kill me or my loved ones—even though it might have felt like it. To my critique partners Cari, Cindy and Kelly, for supporting my crazy story ideas and helping me polish them into publishable material. To the Non-Bombs, Diana, Wendy, Colleen and Elly, for your continued support. To my parents, Jimmie and Bobbie Morris, for all your support and marketing efforts—and a special thanks to God for looking out for my dad and ensuring he didn't get arrested for accosting strange women in Walmart and telling them to buy my book. To my brother, Dwain, for being a chip off the old block and taking the same show to Barnes & Noble, and his wife, Donna, and my beautiful niece, KatiAnne. To my fabulous agent, Kristin Nelson, for helping make this book so much stronger. To the incredible art department at Dorchester— your covers are the absolute best on the market! To my wonderful editor, Leah Hultenschmidt, for ensuring that everything from the manuscript to the cover copy is absolutely perfect. And finally, to all the booksellers with an unfailing support of romance, and romance readers everywhere for making this the most popular genre in fiction.

Unlucky

Chapter One

Exhausted after a long day of work, Mallory Devereaux entered J.T.'s Bar on Thursday night intending to have a cold beer and a bit of relaxation. Then some misplaced Yankee challenged Father Thomas to a round of pool.

She had barely gotten the door closed behind her when her bayou neighbor, Scooter Duson, grabbed her arm and dragged her into the corner for consultation.

"I've got two hundred on Father Thomas to win this game," he said. "Those Yankees been taunting him most of the evening."

Mallory stared, certain Scooter had lost what was remaining of his rapidly disappearing brain cells. "Father Thomas has never played pool in his life. Why in the world would you put money on him?" She eyed the group of men in the far corner of the bar—midforties, beer bellies, cheap haircuts (on what hair was remaining), polyester shirts. They looked more like a bunch of out-of-work plumbers than the stockbroker image she had of the northern U.S. residents. The Yankees. "Those guys are probably hustlers. You know better."

Scooter had the decency to look a bit embarrassed. "I know, but damn, I couldn't just let them get one over on Father T. What kind of Catholic would I be if I didn't come to his defense?"

"The kind with two hundred dollars in his wallet?"

Scooter nodded, her sarcasm lost. "Exactly. That's why I need your help. I know you can turn it to the Father's favor."

She glanced one more time at the men in the corner and smiled. They *were* Yankees, after all, but did she really want to tackle something like that tonight? The energy she'd have to spend on this kind of project was probably better saved for something more important. And definitely better looking.

"What's in it for me?" she asked, not about to turn on the juice for nothing, especially when Scooter had gotten all the way in this one by himself. "Flirting with ugly guys should be worth something," she continued. "Besides, I'm probably going to have to touch him to ensure bad luck." She shuddered.

Scooter cast a glance back at the Yankee and grimaced. "Half," he said instantly. "A hundred for you, a hundred for me. Just fire your death ray or whatever it is."

Mallory laughed and headed toward an empty spot at the bar, signaling to J.T., the bar owner. She shrugged off her denim work shirt, exposing the tight white tank top underneath. She gave the thin, clingy cotton a good yank down, just enough to expose about an inch of cleavage, then pulled off her steel-toed work boots. Reaching up with one hand, she grabbed the pair of FMPs that J.T. had retrieved from behind the counter, where he kept them in reserve for just this kind of occasion. She eased on the shiny black shoes with the five-inch titanium heels, careful not to scratch them on the worn-out wood of the counter, and tugged down her jeans until they sat just a little bit lower on her hips, exposing the tiny silver hoop that glittered in her belly button.

Her outfit complete, she turned to the bar where J.T. had already supplied two ice-cold beers for her job. "Thanks," she said, and gave the older man a wink. She grabbed the drinks and sashayed across the bar, chest out and full hips swinging.

"Go get 'em, killer," J.T. shouted behind her.

She could already sense the anticipation in the room as all the locals waited for her to perform her magic. It was better than Friday night at the movies.

"What's such a good-looking group of gentlemen doing in a place like this?" Mallory asked, and set the extra beer down in front of the ringleader and pool challenger. "I know you're not from around here. Too much class for a joint like this." She gave him her sexiest smile and leaned over to his ear, allowing tendrils of her long, glossy black hair to brush gently against his neck. "And far too good looking," she whispered, then raised back up.

The guy's eyes widened, and he grinned with almost comical elation. "You got that right, darlin'," he said, and glanced around the bar. "This isn't exactly the caliber of place I'm used to, but now that you're here, I guess it will do."

She squeezed into the chair next to him and tried not to roll her eyes. The guy was definitely a total loser, but a Yankee? Somehow he didn't sound like one. "So where are you from?" she asked, and put one hand on his leg, causing him to twitch with anticipation.

"Up Ferriday way," he replied. "We're here for a store meeting at the port-a-john plant." He puffed up his chest a bit and gave her a huge grin. "I've got my own store. Biggest one in the district."

She nodded and took a huge gulp of her beer, trying not to groan. Not only were they *not* Yankees, they were port-a-john salesmen, which was almost worse. Ever since Walter Royal had figured out the need for portable potties and built his manufacturing plant, the town of Royal Flush had never been the same. Hell, it hadn't even been called Royal Flush at the time, but one of the city council members decided to get cute over a bucket of beer at Lucy's Catfish Kitchen and the rest was history.

A history that had turned Royal Flush into the butt of far too many Louisiana jokes.

"That's wonderful," she said, and squeezed the man's leg, really laying it on thick. Father Thomas was going to need all the bad luck she could muster. "I've always been impressed by businessmen. You're all so smart." She took another gulp of her beer, emptying her glass, and wished she'd asked for a double.

The salesman's eyes widened when she downed the beer, but he didn't say a word as he pushed his still-full mug over in front of her. The idiot probably thought she was going to get drunk and he was going to get lucky. No way was that happening. Not even with a double.

"Go ahead," he offered. "I've already had my limit. Empty calories, you know?"

Mallory stared at him for a moment. "Empty calories?"

The salesman nodded. "Yeah, no protein, too many carbs, then alcohol that turns to sugar. Not good for the diet."

Mallory did another once-over of the man next to her, just in case she'd missed something relevant, or gone partially blind. Nope. The ruddy skin, sagging triceps, and protruding belly were still there. She wondered for a moment exactly what he saved those empty calories for but was afraid to ask.

"So how exactly does one get into the business of containing crap?" she asked, and gave him a sexy smile. "Most of the people I know are more satisfied spreading it around."

The salesman guffawed and winked at his buddies. "A sassy woman. I like that."

Good God. Mallory reached for the second mug and took a big drink, not impressed with the compliment. This guy would probably like anything just short of dead.

The salesman gave her a huge grin and dropped one hand down to her leg, running it over her knee. Oh goodie, he was moving in on every woman's erogenous zone. For thousands of years no woman had been able to resist a good squeeze to the knee. She cast a single glance at his hand, and it was all she could do to hold her sexy smile in place. The thin white line around his third finger told the entire story.

The King of Crap had a queen sharing the throne.

No hitting the customers, she reminded herself, even though a good elbow to the crotch was the least the cheater deserved. But making the man temporarily lame wasn't exactly the best way to get the pool game won. She took a peek at the clock on the wall and decided her work here was almost complete. If it didn't work, Scooter would just be out two hundred. Hell, she couldn't work miracles and spending another minute at the table with the King of Crap was going to require one.

Giving him her most winning smile, she placed her hand over his hand on her knee and wrapped her fingers in between his, gently stroking them up and down. With the other hand she downed the remainder of the beer and held the mug in the air, hoping that either Scooter or J.T. was paying enough attention to rescue her from the louse.

Her mission was accomplished. The toilet salesman

was just leaning in for a kiss, God forbid, when Scooter interrupted them, pulling her by her shirt. "No time for this nonsense." He pointed to the port-a-john guy. "You've got a game of pool to play. You can chase snatch on your own time."

The salesman sobered instantly and put on his focused face. "Sorry, darlin'," he said, and gave her a wink, "but we'll have to finish this in a bit. I've got to win some money off these hicks." He rubbed one finger down her bare arm with the sexual prowess of a fifteen-year-old, making her hope the Queen of Crap had a good-looking and very skilled pool boy back at home.

"By all means." She motioned to the pool table. "Can't have those hicks ruling the world, right?" She rose from her chair and made her way back over to the far corner of the bar, Scooter in tow.

"What kind of moron are you, exactly?" she asked Scooter as she took a seat at the bar. "Those guys aren't Yankees. They're port-a-john salesmen from north Louisiana." She narrowed her eyes at Scooter. "You *do* know where the Mason-Dixon line is, right?"

The blank expression on Scooter's face said it all.

She waved one hand in dismissal. "Never mind. Just get over there and get Father Thomas to the pool table. He looks like he's going to need help walking."

Scooter cast a glance at the priest, who was currently hanging half-on, half-off a bar stool, and groaned. "Oh hell. I hope he can stand well enough to play."

Mallory motioned for J.T. and pointed at Father Thomas. "You'd better stop the beer and start the coffee. The pool game I can handle, but there's no way I can do Mass on Sunday."

J.T. glanced at Father Thomas and hurried to the back, most certainly to put on a pot of coffee strong enough to strip paint off a car bumper. Scooter doused the fallen priest with a glass of ice water, and he awoke with a start, sputtering water across the bar. "Is it raining?" he asked, gazing wildly around.

"You're in the bar, Father Thomas," Scooter explained. "You have to play pool now. Remember?"

Father Thomas thought for a moment, then his face cleared a bit. "Oh yeah, damn Yankees!" He slid off the bar stool and staggered toward the pool table. "And the Lord sayeth verily unto me that his will shall be done in J.T.'s Bar as it is in heaven!"

"Good Lord." Mallory shook her head and followed Father Thomas to the pool table, wondering if this situation was beyond even her capabilities.

The bar was crowded for a Thursday, and every single patron was within viewing distance of the pool table. But as she approached the crowd, they bumped and nudged each other until they created a path for her right up to a front-row seat. Taking a seat on a bar stool next to the dartboard, she nodded to the King of Crap, and he gave her a broad smile and a thumbs-up. With any luck, that thumb would fall right off and settle this nicely, she thought, barely managing a smile before turning her attention to Scooter, who was flipping a quarter to decide the break.

There were a couple of boos and more than a few curse words when the break went to the salesman, but the noise level dropped to nothing as soon as the crap king took his place at the front of the pool table and lined up for the break. You could have heard a pin drop as he drew back the cue, then released the shot with a bang.

The cue ball hit the racked balls like lightning, and they began to scatter across the table. One dropped, then another and for a moment, Mallory was afraid that even she had not been enough to swing this one in the right direction. But then the murmuring began, and she realized the cue ball had banked against one side and was now traveling the length of the pool table, headed directly for the corner pocket.

If it had enough steam to make it.

The ball seemed to hesitate a millisecond just in front of the pocket, then tumbled over the side with a clunk.

Father Thomas rose from his chair and raised both hands in the air. "Praise God and pass the peanuts."

The crowd went wild and Mallory hopped off her stool and headed back to the bar. This one definitely deserved a beer. Maybe even two. And since she was still four beers short of her six-pack limit and the night was young, things were looking good all the way around.

"Not bad, huh?" she said as she took a seat in front of J.T. and bent down to replace the high heels with her work boots, happy she'd made it all the way across the bar twice without breaking one of the thin daggerlike spikes. But her glory was brief.

"How'd you like the reinforcements in the shoes?"

"What are you talking about?" she asked, and studied the shoe she'd just removed. "What reinforcements?"

The older gentleman winked at her. "Look in the heel. Scooter got some sheet metal screws and secured the heels. Nothing short of a hurricane is tearing those babies off."

She held the shoe closer and looked inside. Sure enough, the flat head of a screw sat flush with the sole and directly above the titanium spike. Obviously Scooter had been "borrowing" from his construction site again. Smiling, she pulled off the other shoe, tugged on her work boots and turned back to the bar. You had to love having friends who really, *really*, knew you.

J.T. twisted the top off a cold one and slid it across the

bar. "No charge," he said. "I already pulled you a couple from stock. Worth it to see that shitter salesman go down."

She smiled and took a swig of the beer. "Been digging into the stock already, huh? How did you know it was going to work? Father Thomas is pretty far gone."

J.T. waved a hand in dismissal. "Please, I've known you since you were a kid. No offense, Mallory, but you're like a twenty-first-century Typhoid Mary. Hell, I'm surprised you made it all the way across the bar with mugs."

"Such flattery." She laughed and tapped the side of the plastic beer bottles J.T. stocked just for her. "You make a woman all warm and fuzzy."

He grinned a moment, then sobered. "What I got to say next probably won't hit the warm-and-fuzzy meter."

His tone and expression were so serious that she knew immediately something was wrong. Not much in the world got to J.T., so if her friend was stressing over something on a Thursday night, it was major. "What's wrong?"

"It's about Harry."

Mallory sat upright so fast a single stream of beer sloshed out of the bottle and across the counter. "What about Harry? What's going on?"

Harry Breaux, owner of Royal Demolition, was her employer and more importantly, her friend. He'd given her a break in the construction industry and had schooled her over the years until she held the top title of foreman in his company. And being the kind person he was, he'd overlooked the stock she came from and had invited her into his home when she was a teenager. He and his wife, Thelma, had treated her as family, something she'd never had before.

"What, J.T.?" she asked again, every muscle in her body tense.

"I heard the IRS has been sending him notices. Real

regularlike and with bold print, if you know what I mean."

She took a deep breath, trying to make sense of what J.T. said. Anyone with a brain knew better than to mess with the IRS, and Harry was far from stupid. "So maybe there was a mistake or something. He'll work it out." He had to work it out. Whatever it was. There wasn't another option. "Maybe—"

"The mistake was not paying his taxes, and it's all on Harry, not the IRS," J.T. interrupted, a miserable look on his face. "He owes them a lot of money, Mal. Upward of fifty Gs."

"Fifty thousand dollars! You've got to be kidding me."

"'Fraid not. Rumor has it they're going to take the business and sell off the equipment unless he can cough up the money and real fastlike. Rumor also has it that the tax note may be for sale if there's an interested buyer, and it so happens that there is . . . Walter Royal."

She tossed back a huge swallow of beer, trying to calm her nerves and think. It couldn't possibly be true, could it? Sure, Thelma's cancer had cost a lot of money, even now that she was in remission. The treatments and checkups and tests had seemed a part of her everyday life. But could Harry really have shorted the IRS fifty thousand dollars?

And Walter Royal? Heaven help them all. The man was already the Donald Trump of Royal Flush, but at the rate he was buying up property and businesses, the town would soon cease to exist and become a principality instead. Buying the IRS out of Harry's tax debt would be a quick, cheap way to pick up a business he'd had his eye on for years.

"This whole situation sucks," J.T. continued. "You know as well as I do that if Royal gets his hands on Harry's business, he'll fire everyone local and replace them with his useless relatives just like he has all the other businesses in this town he's managed to buy."

"Where'd you get this information anyway?" she asked.

He pointed across the bar to Father Thomas just as another round of cheers went up from the locals. Father Thomas's voice boomed above the crowd, "And God saw that Adam was lonely and sent him beer!"

Mallory shot a glance across the bar and shook her head. "Your source is Father Thomas? Please tell me he wasn't given this information in confidence. Besides, I thought Harry stopped going to confession after the last time Father Thomas blabbed." And if this was any indication of the church's position on confidential information, she'd just made her last confession too, at least locally.

"Wasn't Harry that confessed."

Mallory studied the man for a minute then sighed. "Stanley's been reading mail again, hasn't he?"

J.T. shrugged. "You know how Stanley is. Leopard ain't gonna change its spots."

"Good God, he's been a postman for over thirty years. Doesn't he have any appreciation for federal law?" Not to mention the privacy issue. She made a mental note to change the mailing address on a recently placed order for a "personal item" she'd bought from a "specialty" store in New Orleans.

"I swear, J.T.," she continued, "I sometimes wonder why our government spends so much money on war. If we really wanted to cripple the intelligence of other countries, we'd just send the two of them over."

She was just trying to recall anything damaging or otherwise embarrassing that she might have mentioned to Father Thomas the week before when Scooter clapped her on the back and dropped a hundred in front of her.

"No problem collecting?" she asked. "I figured he'd argue for a rematch."

Scooter grinned. "Idiot claimed his hand went to sleep, then cut out of here with the rest of those Yankees. I asked if he wanted your number, but he didn't even look at me." He poked Mallory in the ribs with his elbow. "Guess that means your date is off." Laughing hysterically at himself, he motioned to J.T. for a beer.

J.T. grabbed a bottle, popped the cap and slid it across the bar to Scooter, then leaned on the bar in front of Mallory. "So if the tax note goes on sale, are you going to buy?"

She downed the remainder of her beer and picked up the hundred-dollar bill Scooter had dropped in front of her. "Fifty thousand dollars? Father Thomas would have to challenge the rest of Louisiana to a pool match for that to happen. Even with all my savings, I'm about ten grand short and no assets for a quick sale, none I can do without, anyway."

J.T. nodded. "I hear ya. Ten Gs is a wad of cash, especially to come up with in such a short time frame."

Scooter turned around on his bar stool and gave her a curious look. "You short on cash, Mal? You can have my other hundred. I was just going to buy new lures with it anyway."

Mallory smiled at Scooter, his offer confirming her opinion that her neighbor was silly as a goose but had a heart the size of the Gulf of Mexico. "I appreciate it, Scooter, really I do, but I need a lot more than a hundred."

Scooter scratched his head for a moment, his eyebrows scrunched together in obvious concentration. "There is probably one way you can make a lot of money fast—next week, as a matter of fact."

Mallory stared at Scooter. "I'm not doing anything illegal," she said, bringing up the only thing she could imagine Scooter would come up with. "Besides, ten grand in two weeks is a lot, even for a New Orleans prostitute. And I don't have the enthusiasm for the job anyway."

J.T. laughed. "She got you there."

Scooter stared at her, a dumbstruck expression on his normally jovial face. "Good God Almighty, Mallory, I never said you should do anything of the sort. I wouldn't even think it."

She narrowed her eyes at Scooter, still waiting for his suggestion. "So if it's not something illegal then why don't you just come out with it?"

Scooter glanced both directions, apparently making sure they couldn't be overheard, then leaned over closer to Mallory. "Your uncle is hosting a high-stakes poker tournament. I bet he'd cough up a pretty penny for you to cool for him."

J.T., who had leaned in to hear what Scooter said, jerked back from the bar, his jaw set in a hard line. "Hell no, Mallory. You're not working that tournament for your uncle. Even if I have to padlock you in the storage room to keep you from it."

Mallory stared at J.T. in surprise, trying to process what Scooter said and the bar owner's unexpected reaction. "What in the world has gotten into you, J.T.? I know Reginald flies on the wrong side of the law sometimes, but I've cooled for him before and you haven't had a problem with it."

"Damn it." J.T. grabbed a rag from the bar and shook it at Scooter. "You want to ask your genius neighbor how he knows about this tournament? Because he's been doing construction at your uncle's floating boat of fun. And do you know what he's been installing, specifically for this tournament?"

"Forget I said anything," Scooter mumbled. He slid

off his bar stool and slunk across the bar, away from J.T.'s wrath.

J.T. tossed the rag on the bar and ran one hand across his balding head. "That idiot you live next to has been installing metal detectors at the casino, that's what. This unorthodox tournament of your uncle's is a chance to beat the house. Dealers have been flocking from all over the state to try out for a spot."

"Why would dealers care?"

"Because they're playing on the casino's behalf. They put up ten grand for the spot and get to keep half their winnings, less what Reginald kicks in. Reginald is matching the ten with another forty. He's got several hundred thousand at stake."

Mallory frowned. "Okay, so putting up his money isn't the smartest thing Reginald's ever done, but how do metal detectors fit into it?"

J.T. leaned across the bar, his voice low. "The tournament is invitation only. There's a couple of locals invited for good measure, I suppose, but the rest . . ."

"The rest what?" Mallory prodded.

"Oh hell," J.T. said finally. "Your uncle has assembled a group of heavy hitters—Mafia, drug dealers, politicians, crooked law enforcement—and not a single one of them worth pulling out of the bayou if they were drowning. He's putting together a floating boat of criminals—hardcore, no-conscience-having, bad guys."

Mallory sat back in her chair and stared at J.T., stunned. "You're sure about that?"

"Not a doubt in my mind. The teller down at the bank said Reginald's been in there every day for the past week, depositing cash in fifty-thousand-dollar increments. He listed the name of each player on their deposit, so the teller was real clear on that. This tournament is going to happen all right—they've already bought in."

"What in the world is Reginald thinking?"

J.T. shook his head. "I don't know, and I don't think I want to. Word on the street is that he's into a New Orleans loan shark for a wad of cash. If this is his best idea for getting repayment, I'm afraid Reginald has finally lost his mind."

"Then I guess asking him to loan me the money is probably out of the question, and that was actually my original plan. But if he's really in that much of a bind over money, I'd be a sure bet for him to get a hunk of it back. I bet he'd pay a pretty penny for that guarantee."

J.T. sighed, knowing he was losing the battle. "But at what cost? Cooling for a bunch of bored husbands or businessmen is one thing, but this is an entirely different kettle of fish. Your uncle has been pretty good to you over the years, but that doesn't change what kind of man he is. Do you really want to get in the middle of one of Reginald's schemes—especially if he's as desperate as it appears?"

Mallory stared out the window of the bar, the billboard for Royal Port-A-Johns seeming to taunt her from its roadside perch. "I don't have a choice, J.T. It's the only way."

Chapter Two

Jake Randoll looked across the poker table at Reginald St. Claire and hoped like hell the man wasn't holding a flush. Trying to pull an inside straight with the cards he held was risky, but then some might say that most of his choices were. Securing the lead dealer position at St. Claire's poker tournament was a huge gamble, but it was also his only option—his last chance to take down a money launderer who kept getting away. He also hoped to find out what had happened to his partner, Mark, who had been working undercover for the money launderer and had disappeared more than a month ago.

Which left Mark's frantic wife, Janine, and his young son with no answers. And that wasn't good enough for Jake.

Nothing short of beating St. Claire at this round of cards would give Jake the coveted dealer's slot at the lead table—a seat across from the money launderer, Silas Hebert—and he was willing to risk anything for that position.

St. Claire studied his hand with the intensity of a trained pit bull monitoring an intruder. At one time his beefy frame had probably been muscular and toned. But with St. Claire on the other side of fifty, what used to be firm and hard hung loosely on his arms and created jowls on his neck. His face was completely blank, his dark piercing eyes focused on the cards he held, never once even glancing across the table at his opponent. Which was perfectly fine by Jake. He hoped the casino owner was distracted enough by the game to forgo looking too deeply into Jake's background. Oh, he had the usual cover-ups in place, but anyone with determination and a little cleverness could always get through them.

And of all the things people had accused Reginald St. Claire of being, stupid definitely wasn't one of them. Jake didn't for one minute consider St. Claire as anything less than a formidable opponent, despite his less-than-stellar physical fitness.

Jake pulled a single card from his hand and discarded it. Time to let his talent flow. He'd been holding back just a bit from the onset, keeping a low profile to ensure that St. Claire didn't get *too* interested, but it was time to take the rest of the man's chips and collect his dealer position. Time to get the answers he'd been searching for so that he and Mark's family could face the truth, then get on with the rest of their lives.

He held his breath as he pulled the card Reginald dealt him across the table. Had he misread the other man? Had his card-counting ability lapsed and he'd taken a chance he shouldn't have on the straight? He didn't think so, but there was only one way to find out. Gripping the edge of the card, he turned up the corner, all the while maintaining the blank look he wore so well.

Bingo!

He tossed in a couple of chips, careful not to look St. Claire in the eyes or show any change in expression or body language. A real poker player never gave away his hand.

He could feel Reginald's stare and knew the man was studying him, knowing that a one-card pick usually implied a straight or a flush, and right now, St. Claire was using his considerable people-reading ability to try and determine if Jake had hit his intended mark.

The casino owner must have bought his charade because he upped the bet by over half of his chips and stared at Jake, his calculating eyes taking in every nuance of Jake's expression. Jake pretended to consider the up for a moment, trying to decide if he could increase the stakes one more time but ultimately deciding against it.

He let out a bit of a sigh. Not overly theatrical, because then St. Claire would know for sure he was shamming, but just enough for the man to think it had slipped by unintentionally. Finally, he picked up the chips from the stack in front of him, shook them in his hand for a moment, and tossed them onto the pile in front of them. "Call," he said, knowing this hand was played out and upping the bet any further would be an amateur's mistake.

St. Claire smiled and lowered his cards to the table—a pair of kings and a pair of twos.

"Not bad," Jake said, and returned the smile, "but not enough to beat a straight." He fanned the cards across the table and had the luxury of watching St. Claire scowl at his hand. After a moment, the casino owner looked up at him with begrudging admiration.

"That was smooth," St. Claire said. "I was sure you hadn't pulled the straight."

Jake nodded. "Good. That's what you were supposed to think."

St. Claire narrowed his eyes and cocked his head to one side, studying Jake with an intensity that made him worry for a moment that he'd taken things a bit too far with his last comment. The casino owner was the kind of man who would appreciate confident but probably not cocky.

With any luck, St. Claire would let his suspicions ride long enough to take advantage of Jake as a dealer, because there was no doubt in Jake's mind that St. Claire was in desperate need of some professional-level card handlers. Jake had no earthly idea what had possessed a man like St. Claire to put up his own money for a tournament of thieves, but he didn't care, either. This was the golden opportunity Jake had been waiting for.

"You said you deal in Atlantic City, right?" St. Claire asked finally.

Jake nodded. He lived there, anyway, so at least the geography wasn't likely to trip him up. "I'm visiting a friend in New Orleans who works at a casino downtown. He turned me on to this game. Thought it sounded like a good chance for me to pick up some quick cash."

"Why didn't he come himself?"

"He runs a craps table. Cards aren't his skill set."

St. Claire nodded and sat back in his chair, arms folded across his chest. "If you have the buy-in amount, I can offer you the lead position. But I'm warning you now, you'll be up against some of the best Louisiana has to offer."

Jake smiled, trying to keep a calm, collected appearance, which was hard with so much riding on this poker tournament. "Ten grand?"

"Yeah. Ten, all up front. I'll spot you another forty on the first day. You better make it last—or more importantly, you better make more."

Jake pulled the wrapped set of hundreds from his backpack and handed it across the table to St. Claire. "Oh, I'll make more," he said with conviction. "You can bet on that."

St. Claire studied him a moment more. "I thought I just did."

"I don't want to hear it, Mallory," Harry Breaux said before she could even get out of her truck. He shot a dirty look at Scooter, who was perched on the passenger seat, then continued toward the dilapidated building at the far end of the parking lot.

"Aw, hell," Mallory said as she jumped out of her truck and hurried after Harry. She'd wrestled with Harry's plight and how she could fix it all day Friday until finally making that all-important call to her uncle late that evening. And as much as she would liked to have called in sick or claimed to be taking an impromptu vacation, Mallory knew there was no way she could carry out her plan without telling Harry first. Still, knowing good and well what Harry's reaction was going to be, she'd been in no big hurry to speak to the man and had put the entire conversation off until Monday morning at the last minute possible.

Since she hadn't even gotten a word in before Harry had stalked across the parking lot, obviously someone had tattled on her before she had gotten around to talking to her friend. Probably J.T., since Scooter had been uncommonly quiet after the thrashing he'd taken from the bar owner for blabbing about the tournament in the first place.

With a sigh, she grabbed her hard hat and hurried across the parking lot, falling in step next to Harry, who was systematically checking dynamite wiring surrounding the building. "I'm not here to argue, Harry," she said as she followed him through the inside of the structure. "This is something I want to do. Don't ask me to back out. You would do the same thing if the situation were reversed and it was my business at stake."

Harry stopped and turned to face her, looking her straight in the eyes. "I always intended to sell you my business, Mallory. And if it hadn't been for Thelma's cancer, I would have retired years ago, but the fact is, we needed more income for the doctors than retirement would bring." He shook his head and frowned. "But I will not take money from you this way. It's not worth the risk, and you're too important to me and Thelma."

Mallory sighed. "I don't have a choice, Harry. The reality is, no one else will ever take the chance on me that you did. Not with my reputation. Without your company, I have no future."

Harry lowered his eyes. "Damn it, that's not fair."

"I wasn't aiming to be fair, just honest."

Harry shook his head and waved her outside, away from the building. "You can always start your own business."

"With forty thousand dollars, no equipment and no business credit? I don't think so."

"There are other ways." Harry handed her a headset, then put one on himself, making further discussion impossible.

Reaching down with both hands, he pushed the lever to set off the dynamite, and the ground underneath them shook with the blast. It took several seconds for the dust to clear well enough for them to see a huge section of the building still standing.

"Shit!" Harry threw off his headset and walked into the dust storm toward the building, Mallory close behind.

"Let me handle this." Mallory said as she surveyed the remains of the building. "You'll be way into overtime hours if you have the guys re-rig it."

Harry looked at her and shook his head. "You've got to

stop taking these kind of risks, Mallory. One of these days, it's going to come back and bite you."

"Maybe. But we all take chances. Mine are just different than most."

She put on her hard hat and motioned to Harry to step back. Once he was clear, she entered the building, hurrying through the half-fallen structure as quickly as the debris allowed. She'd barely made it three steps out of the building when what was remaining collapsed behind her.

Harry watched as the rest of the building crumbled, unable to hide the pride and amazement he always felt when watching Mallory in action. "You're as stubborn as they come, Mallory Devereaux."

"I learned from the best."

Harry stared at her for a moment, the hint of a smile hovering on his lips. Finally, he nodded. "Go ahead then with the poker tournament, but there is one thing that is not negotiable."

Mallory felt relief wash over her. "Whatever you want."

"If you win the money and bail me out of trouble with the IRS, I'm transferring controlling interest of the business to you. No arguments, no discussion. That was always my plan and by God, I'm going to get one thing my way before I die."

Mallory smiled. "I guess this one time is all right." She stood there for a couple of seconds just looking at Harry, not wanting to ask the next thing on her list.

"What now?" Harry said, and narrowed his eyes at her. "I know that look, Mallory. You want something from me, and I'd say you're about maxed out on favors."

Mallory felt her face flush and for a moment, she felt like a kid all over again. "It's T.W.," she began, and Harry started shaking his head before she could finish her sentence.

"Oh no," Harry said, and held up one hand. "You are not leaving that fleabag of yours here with me."

"C'mon, Harry," Mallory pleaded. "You know T.W. doesn't have any fleas. I don't want to leave him alone all day. He might get bored."

"Bored! All that damned dog does is eat, sleep and shit. Why the hell can't he do that at your house?"

Mallory put on her best sorrowful face. "He can't hear a darned thing anymore, except for the dynamite blasts. Coming to the site during the day at least allows him to hear something. Do you really want to deny one of God's creatures in his senior years?"

"Ha! You're not getting me with that one—I *am* one of God's creatures in his senior years. Last time I checked, God wasn't calling on me to babysit any of his dogs."

"He won't be any trouble, I promise. And you can drop him off at my place on your way home. I'll drop him off every morning before the tournament. C'mon, Harry. It's not even a mile out of your way."

Harry stared at her, trying to keep a stern look on his face, but Mallory could tell he was crumbling. "Oh, crap," he said finally. "Bring me the damned mutt. I guess five days won't kill me."

Mallory grinned and signaled to Scooter to get T.W. out of the truck. "I really appreciate this, Harry. And T.W. does too." She turned toward the truck just as Scooter placed the ancient, three-legged basset hound on the ground. He looked around for a moment, somewhat confused by his surroundings, but finally spotted Mallory, then sort of limped/trotted in her direction, his tail wagging just enough to throw him off balance and force his trot sideways.

Mallory slipped the leash from her pocket and cut off the wayward dog before he could veer too far off to the right. Leash in place, she walked him back over to Harry, who was shaking his head.

She placed the leash in Harry's hand before he could change his mind and hurried across the parking lot. "There's dog food in my office, under the desk. I'll come by Friday night—when I have the money."

Harry nodded and waved. "Be careful, Mallory. Please."

Scooter gave her the thumbs-up as she jumped in her truck. "That was way cool with the building, Mallory. There's nothing over a foot left standing. You're getting better."

Mallory grinned at her friend and turned her key over in the ignition. "I think we have a casino to board," she said, and tore out of the parking lot onto the highway.

It was a ten-minute drive to the casino that she made in seven. As she screeched to a stop at the docks, she stared at the boat and frowned. "What the hell happened to the casino?"

"Hurricane Katrina."

Mallory looked at the floating disaster and didn't even bother to try and hide her distaste. Paint peeled from every square inch of the boat and since the original colors were bright green, gold and purple, the whole thing now resembled a Mardi Gras float with the mange. "Reginald had insurance. What the heck did he do with the money?"

Scooter looked over at the casino and scratched his head, his brow scrunched in concentration. "I'm not sure exactly. I mean, there was this rumor about a street performer in New Orleans and a midget." He shrugged. "Who knows with your uncle?"

Mallory stared at Scooter for a moment, not even sure where to go from there but positive she wasn't pursuing the midget angle any further. "I thought we were cruising for this tournament. Does that thing even run?"

Scooter nodded. "Oh sure, the engine is still pretty sound. I mean, there's a problem from time to time, but that's why Reginald has me on board for the tournament. You know, just in case something breaks."

Great. She was about to board a boat of criminals that would pull away from the dock and cruise the Gulf for the better part of the day, and Scooter was the only hope she had for returning.

"You thinking of backing out?" Scooter asked, cluing in on her hesitation.

"No way," she said immediately. Granted, cooling cards had never really set well with her since she essentially saw it as her uncle's way of cheating people out of what was already an unfair advantage to begin with. But in this case, the players had plenty of money and no scruples. "This is my only shot at Harry's business. It might not be ideal but at least it pays well."

Besides, there was no cause for all the worry, she argued with herself. This was just another job. Five days of being hit on by nasty men with even nastier employment records.

But no matter how much she tried to rationalize it, the job made her a little uneasy, and for a woman that lived alone on the bayou and imploded buildings on a daily basis, that worried her. She could have handled a "watch your back" feeling, but the "run like hell" that had washed over her when she parked at the docks was stronger than any she'd felt before.

"You know," Scooter said, "if you really don't want to

go through with this, I can probably get you on with my construction company when Walter Royal fires you."

Leave it to Scooter to cut straight to the heart of the matter. "I appreciate it, Scooter, but with my track record, do you really think anyone in Royal Flush is going to hire me to build things?"

Scooter frowned. "I guess not." He brightened a bit and smiled. "I definitely wouldn't want you installing glass, anyway." He pointed to the casino. "There's always cooling for a living. You don't have to do it here. You could move to New Orleans, or heck, go all the way to Vegas. That would be awesome."

"To hell with that," she said, and grabbed her duffel bag from the backseat. Demolition may not have been her first choice when she was slugging through college but damn if it wasn't what she was best at. "Let's get this over with."

Scooter nodded. "And don't worry about a thing, Mallory. J.T. ripped me fairly good over telling you about this. I promised him I wouldn't let anything happen to you. If things get out of hand, I can always shoot somebody with my nail gun." He pulled the tool out of his backpack and shoved it over to her for inspection. "It's a real beauty—magnesium housing, adjustable exhaust, and double cams."

Mallory smiled and jumped out of the truck, waving at her neighbor as she headed across the dock. What the heck—a boat of criminals versus Scooter and a nail gun. They weren't the best of odds, but they were the best she was going to get.

She put on her poker face as she walked through the sliding doors and into the casino. Might as well get her game face on now. But as she rounded the corner to the ladies' room, her cool and collected plans fell apart in an instant.

The woman who hurried out of the restroom and collided with her didn't even look old enough to be in an R-rated movie, much less in a casino. "What in God's name are you doing here, Amy?" Mallory used her duffel bag to push her friend toward a private corner of the lobby as more attendants emerged from the ladies' room. "Do *not* tell me you signed up to play in my uncle's poker scam?"

Amy's bright blue eyes widened at the tone of her voice and she shook her head with the innocence of a five- year-old, her honey blond bob swinging around her face. "I'm not a player, exactly—I'm a dealer. I tried out last week." She squirmed and stared at the floor. "I was going to tell you, Mallory, I promise." She looked at Mallory with a pleading expression. "It's for my thesis. You knew I was going to do something like this eventually. What's wrong with now?"

Mallory felt her back tighten and she clenched her duffel bag until her hand ached. "I thought you would finish your thesis by playing a nice round of cards with some businessmen at a large casino in New Orleans. Not sign up as a dealer for my uncle, a man of questionable legal status at best, and certainly not against the players he's lined up."

Amy blinked, then stared at Mallory in obvious confusion.

Mallory tossed the duffel bag onto the couch next to them and threw her hands up in exasperation, causing Amy to jump. "He didn't tell you, did he?" She tried to keep her voice low but barely succeeded.

"I guess not."

"Damn it to hell!" Mallory ranted, and the other

women in the lobby stared at them. Before she caused a scene in front of witnesses, she pointed to the exit, giving Amy no choice but to head outside. "My uncle has lined up a bunch of criminals, heavy hitters, for this tournament," she continued once the doors slid shut behind them. "He's up to something and it can't possibly be pleasant. You have absolutely no business getting in the middle of it."

Amy's eyes widened. "Oh, my God."

"You have to back out," Mallory said, and yanked her cell phone from her pocket. "Either you call or I will. Pretend you never showed up and get the heck out of here. There's no way I'm letting you back on that floating prison block."

The expression on Amy's face went from frightened to pure misery in under a second. "I can't back out. I used my tuition money to buy in as a dealer. If I don't make it back, I can't graduate."

Mallory groaned. "How can someone as smart as you constantly do things as stupid as this? It's like you manage to find the one thing you should never be involved in and you're the first in line to sign up."

"I'm a math genius, Mallory. I guess that doesn't translate to street smarts, so I'm sorry to have offended your redneck rules of play for criminal activity. This wasn't exactly something my instructors covered in finishing school."

"They didn't cover it because you were supposed to be married off at twenty to some rich doctor or lawyer or politician and spend the rest of your life folding napkins into swans like your parents intended."

"My parents don't have a clue what's important to me and never have. And don't tell me I should have fallen into their plans. You, with a master's in engineering, and you only use it to tear things up."

Mallory opened her mouth to protest but Amy held one hand up to stop her.

"Let me finish," Amy said, and pointed at Mallory. "You've spent your entire life making your own way exactly how you wanted to and that's why I admire you so much. I'm not going to believe for a moment that you think I should give up my dreams and marry some short, fat, balding man twice my age just to have a 'good life' and please my parents."

Mallory shoved her hands in her jeans' pockets and studied the dark wood floor planks for a moment before raising her gaze back to her friend. "I didn't say you should follow your parents' way, Amy, but c'mon, poker at my uncle's casino? Isn't there another way to prove your genius besides pissing off men who probably won't deal with things by quitting and having a beer?"

Amy waved her hands in frustration. "You think I haven't already tried? I can't make it through two or three hands at a casino table before everyone leaves. One of the dealers in New Orleans said men generally don't like to play with a woman."

"Probably not," Mallory conceded. "Especially if the woman looks like she's twelve and is whipping their butts at cards."

Amy grinned. "They're all going to be very sorry when I'm running the country one day."

Mallory stared at Amy in surprise. "What the heck are you talking about? You thinking about running for president?"

"Please, the president doesn't run the country, his economic advisor does. He who controls the money has the power."

Mallory laughed. "You want to be Alan Greenspan, Jr.?

Good God, Amy, it would probably be easier to be elected president."

"Exactly. Which is why this tournament is not an option. I have to finish my thesis by the end of next semester or I can't apply for PhD candidacy. And that will be a little hard to do without the money to pay for school." Amy shot her one final belligerent look, then shrugged. "Besides, I hate swans. And napkins."

Mallory was unable to stop the smile that quivered on her lips even though her world had just gotten even more complicated than she'd ever thought it could. "Fine, so you'll deal at the Criminal Poker Tournament of the decade." She stood up straight and stared down at her friend, pointing one finger at her. "But you *will* be careful—painfully so—and you will not incite any anger whatsoever in these men."

Amy relaxed visibly as she realized Mallory wasn't going to push the issue beyond a butt-chewing, at least until the tournament was over. "You really ought to be nicer to me, you know."

"Oh, really? And why would I want to do something like that?"

Amy grinned. "Because if I wanted, I could be your aunt. Reginald proposed to me after I took him at cards."

Mallory smiled. "Probably a sure thing compared to that whole Alan Greenspan plan. Let's face it—with the company he keeps, sooner or later someone is going to pop dear Uncle Reginald. And you could inherit all this." She waved a hand at the dilapidated casino.

"Yuck," Amy said. "Even if your uncle was like, the Robert Redford of Royal Flush, do you really think I'd give it a moment's thought after that whole midget thing?"

Mallory stared at her friend. "Am I the only person who doesn't know about the midget?"

Amy laughed. "Probably, but if you Google—"

"I don't even want to know. You're already in this neck-deep. Don't make me change my mind by giving me the gory details of what a perv my uncle is."

"You're one to talk," Amy shot back. "You stand here telling me to walk on eggshells but since I know you're not here for a demolition that can only mean you're working, too."

Mallory frowned and shook her head. "It's not the same for me."

"Why not?"

"I know how to manipulate criminals. I was raised by them."

Chapter Three

Since her run-in with Amy had set her a bit behind schedule, Mallory hurried into the ladies' room and changed her outfit with lightning speed. Fortunately, Reginald hadn't been overly picky about the dress code—any combination of black and something else would do as long as it was thin, clingy and short.

She still had a black spandex micromini from her prior cooling days, and the skirt coupled with a thin lacy tank top and short cropped black jacket did quite nicely. Add to that the reinforced stilettos from the bar and she was ready for action.

In the looks department anyway.

She did a quick study of herself in the full-length mirror of the bathroom, then grabbed her long black hair and twisted it into a knot on top of her head. Turning from side to side, she viewed the effect and decided she was satisfied. She could always pull the pin out and let her hair down later if a bit of distraction was needed for the players. In the meantime, she enjoyed the cooler air on her with the thick mass lifted. The early morning humidity was already taking its toll on her skin.

She stuffed her jeans and T-shirt along with her makeup bag into the duffel bag. But as she lifted the bag from the bathroom counter, the strap broke completely off one side and everything dumped onto the floor.

Cursing both the handle and the zipper, which had stripped this morning as she was packing, she retrieved her items and tossed them into an open locker along with the semidestroyed bag. She took one final look in the mirror—dusted some face powder off her shoulders and straightened her skirt hem—then slammed the locker door shut and strode out into the lobby, ready to take on the world.

Or Reginald St. Claire.

Her uncle stood just outside the ladies' room and in her rush to make it to the casino, she'd almost run into the cigar he was never without.

"About time you got out here," he said, frowning. "I need a word with you before we begin. Wanted to make sure we're clear on your payment terms."

Here we go. Mallory fixed her uncle with a hard stare. "I don't believe I stuttered one bit when we talked. I shut down the table, you pay me ten grand. I don't shut down the table, you pay the same as the other attendants." It wasn't the greatest deal in the world. In fact, it pretty much sucked. But according to Reginald, it was the best he could offer, and Mallory got the feeling that he was telling the truth.

"I don't have a problem paying the money if you deliver the goods. Hell, you'll save me ten times that. That's not the problem." He puffed once on the cigar, then yanked it from his mouth, his face starting to redden.

"That asshole Silas Hebert is here. I'm putting you on his table and I don't care if you have to stab him with a kitchen knife. Just keep him from winning any of my money."

Mallory felt as if she'd just been sucker punched. Her hands involuntarily clenched, and she could feel her lower back starting to tighten. Certainly, she'd been prepared for something to go wrong—this was Reginald St. Claire she was dealing with. But Silas Hebert? How in the world had her uncle allowed that to happen? Surely, he was pulling her leg. But one look at Reginald, puffing his cigar like an asthmatic on an inhaler, let her know he wasn't joking.

"Why in God's name would you invite Silas Hebert?" Mallory asked.

Reginald waved his cigar in the air. "I didn't—" Reginald stopped abruptly. "That's not really your concern," he said finally, squaring off his shoulders and pulling himself up to full height. "I'm just giving you warning. I'm not the least bit worried about the rest of the players. You could cool them in your sleep. But Silas Hebert better not leave my casino a winner."

He shoved the cigar back in his mouth, spun around as fast as his large frame would let him and waved at her over his shoulder. "Come with me. You need to meet your dealer."

Mallory stared at him for a moment before following. Silas Hebert? Silas Hebert was the closest thing Louisiana had to a professional gambler, and he was all the way at the top of the ladder of professional crooks. Not to mention that her entire family hated the man for reasons she'd never known and never wanted to.

Why in the world would Silas be at her uncle's tournament?

She followed Reginald across the casino toward the

card tables. He'd started to say something. *I didn't.* Didn't what? Didn't invite Silas?

But that would make no sense. If Reginald hadn't invited Silas, he could just ask him to leave. After all, this was a private game. And if he had invited him, why did he seem so angry about it now when he should have known it was coming for weeks?

I didn't.

She stared after her uncle and shook her head, somehow knowing already that whatever Reginald *didn't* do was going to be an enormous problem.

From his blackjack table across the room, Jake stared at the set of legs attached to the woman talking to Reginald St. Claire and decided they were a work of art. Lean but toned, tan but not that rusty-looking tan. No, this lady had spent some quality time outdoors in regular sunlight. The stiletto heels made the muscle in her calf ripple as she shifted her weight from one foot to another and it pulled all the way up into her rear, the muscles of her nice, round butt flexing as she repositioned.

"Whoo boy!" the voice of another dealer sounded right next to him. "That's enough to get a Cajun in some serious trouble."

Jake tore his eyes from the goddess leg display in a flash and started restacking his chips. "They're all right, I guess," he said, trying to cover his blatant ogling. The last thing he needed was trouble and given the length of her conversation with St. Claire and the proximity of their bodies as they talked, the owner of the sexy legs was potential trouble.

"You guess so?" The other dealer, Brad, jabbed him in the side and laughed. "From the way you was staring, I thought you was on the verge of proposing."

Jake stopped stacking the chips and stared at Brad, wondering already how he was supposed to concentrate on his work within ten feet of a man whose biggest ambition seemed to be getting his next beer. "The only thing I'm proposing I do is win some serious money."

Brad grinned and shrugged. "Ain't no one saying you can't win some money. Hell, win it all." He glanced over once more at the woman talking to St. Claire. "Might buy you some time with sexy legs there."

Jake sighed and forced himself to play along. "Yeah, money might buy some time." He shrugged. "I don't know, though. The better looking they are, the more trouble they bring."

Brad nodded. "Got that one right. I met this hot little number a year ago—hell, next thing I knew she'd got me to spending most everything in my savings and once I even thought about selling my bass boat." He shook his head, a chagrined look on his face. "Can you believe it—my bass boat? What the hell was I thinking?"

Jake held in a smile. Lifetime companionship with a hot little number versus a bass boat. He could definitely see where the problem would lie. "So what happened?"

"She took off with a lawyer from New Orleans. He had a ton of money and no fishing habits." Brad smiled. "It was a near miss."

Jake nodded in agreement. "That it was." He inclined his head toward sexy legs. "That's exactly why I might look at those legs from across the room, but don't want to be any closer than this or know any more about the woman attached to them than I already do."

Brad looked longingly at the legs again and sighed. "Yeah, you're right. Anyway, St. Claire would probably kill us for messing with the help, especially if he thinks it will affect our playing. Damn shame, though."

Jake just nodded. Yeah, right. Avoiding women seemed like the best idea in the world when he considered the collateral damage Mark's disappearance had caused. Damned if he was going to put a woman and child in the same position as Mark's family. Damned if he was going to put them in the same position as he and his mother had been all those years ago.

"Hey." Brad jabbed him in his ribs again and broke into his thoughts. "She's turning around. Check it out."

Despite his better judgment, Jake looked over at the set of legs just as the owner swung around. Jake tried to put on his poker face but knew he was giving everything away.

St. Claire walked around her and continued across the casino floor, pointing in Jake's direction. The vision with the legs walked beside him, an aggravated look on what was an otherwise gorgeous face.

Her features were strong, high cheekbones, wide-set eyes that he was positive were going to be light green before he even saw them. Her hair was a black, glossy mass, all twisted on top of her head, small tendrils brushing the sides of her cheeks and her neck. And the rest of the body—wow. Curvaceous hips were offset with an ample chest in a perfect balance of flesh. The waist was tiny and as they closed the distance, Jake could see that the firm and muscular condition of her legs extended to all other parts of her body.

He'd bet she even had a six-pack, and for some ungodly reason, he had an overwhelming desire to see it.

"They're coming this way," Brad said, yanking Jake from his thoughts. "Guess I better get back to my station."

Jake watched as Brad hustled over to his table, casting sideways glances at the woman while trying to appear he wasn't looking at all. And for the first time that day, Jake could hardly fault Brad for acting like a teenage boy. He needed to get a grip on his own thoughts and focus on the game.

He looked up just in time for St. Claire and the woman to step in front of his table. He gave them a nod and St. Claire pointed to him. "This is Jake McMillan," he said to the woman. "You'll be working his table. Jake's a ringer from Atlantic City."

The woman turned to St. Claire in a flash. "You hired a Yankee to deal to Silas?"

St. Claire paused for a moment, and Jake could tell this was an angle he hadn't thought of. One that didn't please him to think of now. Damn the woman. She was going to get him removed from the tournament before he even got started. Trouble. Women were always trouble.

"I don't really have Yankee tendencies," Jake said, trying to smooth things over and convince St. Claire and the woman, who obviously pulled some weight with the casino owner, that he was the right man for the job. "I don't have much of a northern accent and no one has to know where I'm from."

The woman didn't look convinced, but St. Claire studied him for a moment, obviously considering his words. "He's probably right," St. Claire said finally. "He doesn't sound much like a Yankee and probably no one will ask. They'll be concentrating on cards."

The woman shook her head and frowned. "Silas will ask."

St. Claire threw his hands in the air. "Hell, Mallory, so the old bastard will ask. Let him."

"I don't see what the issue is," Jake said, trying to keep the irritation out of his voice. "Why should it matter who's dealing?"

Mallory gave him a frustrated look. "Because Silas hates Yankees, and Reginald is well aware of that fact. I'd prefer not to start off this tournament by unnecessarily antagonizing the best poker player in the state. And if you think these men are going to sit quietly and concentrate on the cards, then it just proves my point that you know nothing about the South."

Jake shrugged. "So I'll have to talk a bit. Sports are an easy topic. I still don't see the problem."

Mallory laughed. "Sports are easy, huh? Well, Mr. McMillan, if I were fishing in the big saltwater tournament next weekend and I were to ask you which reel you recommended, what would you suggest—the Quantum or the Mudbug?"

Jake frowned. Who the hell cared? But from the look on the woman's face, she cared, and she thought Silas would care. "I guess the Mudbug," he said, figuring he had a fifty-fifty chance of picking the right one and the latter of the two seemed to match the description of the dirty bayou the casino floated upon.

Mallory shook her head and sighed. "The correct choice was the Quantum. You just suggested I enter the tournament using a crawfish as a reel." She turned back to St. Claire. "Good Lord, Reginald. You've got to give me something better than this to work with. He probably doesn't even watch NASCAR."

St. Claire jammed the cigar back in his mouth and studied Jake for a moment, the uncertainty in his eyes clear as day. Jake felt his insides clench. To hell with manners, he finally decided. He had nothing to lose at this point and everything to gain.

Jake turned to face the woman. "Excuse me, miss, but isn't Mr. St. Claire paying *you* to distract the players? Or should I assume that the practically nonexistent skirt and the push-up bra is your normal dress?"

Mallory locked eyes with Jake, her expression hard, the green eyes studying him like a lab rat. And for a moment, Jake decided he had underestimated this woman, but in a matter of seconds, her expression cleared into a fake smile.

"Of course that's what he's paying me for, Mr. McMillan," she said. "Whatever was I thinking?"

St. Claire laughed, but she ignored him and continued to smile at Jake. "My name is Mallory Devereaux. It's a pleasure to meet you." She stuck one hand out and Jake lifted his own, wondering what she was up to now. But before he could get it across the table, St. Claire grabbed his arm and yanked it down.

"You'll want to watch touching my niece," he said.

His niece? "Of course," Jake said, trying to process this bit of information and decide how it affected his plans. "I didn't mean to offend anyone."

St. Claire laughed. "You didn't offend me, boy. I'm just saving your ass. Mallory's a cooler. One touch of her hand and your playing would be reduced to that of a five-year-old." St. Claire shook his head and pointed a finger at Mallory. "You know better."

Mallory shrugged and tried for an apologetic look, but Jake knew she had been deliberate. "Sorry, Uncle Reginald," she said. "It slipped my mind."

St. Claire narrowed his eyes at her. "Well, don't let it slip again. Remember our agreement." With that, St. Claire turned and stalked off across the casino.

Mallory cast one final cutting look at Jake. "For the record, Mr. McMillan, I don't even wear a bra."

Mallory sat on her stool at the end of the poker table, wishing for the first time in her life that she smoked. Right now, something to take the edge off would be wonderful, and a beer at nine o'clock in the morning was pushing it unless you were fishing. This situation was much more complicated than she had planned when she'd agreed to cool, and the players hadn't even entered the room yet.

She looked across the room and saw Jake McMillan talking to her uncle—probably trying to figure out a way to get rid of her. Mallory had seen the look he'd given her when Reginald had announced her card-cooling ability. Skeptical was a polite way of putting it. Mallory got the impression Jake would prefer a dim-witted, big-boobed blonde working his table. A mute Pamela Anderson.

Which was a shame, really, because Jake McMillan wasn't a bad-looking man, and in different circumstances, Mallory might have considered taking a shot at him.

He was taller than the other men she'd dated since college—well, all two of them—lean legs, broad shoulders and a muscular build that could be seen even beneath his white button-up shirt and black slacks. His face was rugged, a man's man sort of face, with brown hair cut in one of those short "ready for action" sort of cuts that suited him well. She'd felt a small jolt when he'd first turned his amber eyes on her, studying her with the precision of a cat stalking prey, and she couldn't help wondering how a dealer from Atlantic City had found his way to Royal Flush and her uncle's tournament.

She was just starting to wonder when the players would arrive, when the double doors to the casino opened and Louisiana's Most Wanted began to enter the room. Studying them carefully, she tried to place who they were, what they did for public record, and what they were suspected of doing otherwise. After the first ten or so had received their seating placement from the hostess and headed toward their tables, Mallory decided Reginald had been wise to put in the metal detector.

Five of the first ten had been suspects in murder investigations and the fact that one of them was a current Louisiana politician didn't deter her from believing the man would do anything to get what he wanted, public eye or no. She cringed for a moment as the men made their way across the casino and hoped like hell she got a murderer instead of the politician.

Even in Louisiana, a girl still had standards.

A smile played on her lips as the politician headed to Amy's table. How appropriate. He might as well get used to her now since she planned on running the country in a few years.

The politician stood at the edge of the table and stared at Amy as if uncertain how to proceed. Amy gave him a dazzling smile and extended her hand. The politician narrowed his eyes at her and said something that Mallory couldn't hear from across the room. Amy looked bewildered for a moment, and then her expression turned to irritated. She yanked her purse out from under the table and presented the politician with her driver's license.

It was all Mallory could do not to laugh.

Served Amy right for putting herself in a situation like this. Certainly Mallory didn't doubt her card-playing ability. Amy had blown her mind with some of the tricks she did with numbers, and it wasn't exactly like Mallory was a slouch. Most engineers were fairly adept at math but she wasn't anywhere near Amy's league.

She took one final look at her friend and shook her head. If she hadn't been trying so hard to be sneaky, Mallory could have given her a bit of advice concerning high-stakes poker playing. Starting with, a black skirt with white daisies and a ruffled white lace blouse were not exactly dealer dress standard. And you never, ever shook hands with the players. Stern nods were the most common fare.

A man sat down at the far end of her table and Mallory

gave him a nod and a smile, trying to get a feel for him from his looks alone. He reminded her of someone she'd seen before and it took her a minute to realize that she'd seen him on television and not in person. An evening news item. Banker fired for suspected embezzling of funds, but the whole story had disappeared as quickly as it had hit the public eye, making Mallory wonder exactly which judge or upper law-enforcement figure the banker had on his private payroll.

Not a bad first player. An overweight businessman whose weapon of choice was a computer didn't pose much threat to her as she saw things. Peering at the doors, she wondered if she'd fare as well on the second round.

She did a double take when the next man to walk through the doors was none other than her nemesis, Walter Royal. Her mouth went dry, and she clenched her fists as he smiled at the hostess and tipped his cowboy hat. The idiot was always wearing that damned cowboy hat, even though she'd bet all of her forty thousand that he'd never even touched a horse, much less ridden one.

Immediately, she was angry with herself for not seeing this one coming. J.T. had told her straight off that some locals were included in the mix. Walter Royal was an important man in Royal Flush, whether she or anyone else liked it. Her uncle would have been remiss not to include him in the players' list. Not to mention that only a handful of people in Royal Flush could afford the stakes of this tournament.

Still, she hoped her uncle had been wise enough to place Royal far, far away from her, where she couldn't be distracted from play by thoughts of dumping him overboard somewhere in the middle of the Gulf of Mexico. She let out a sigh of relief when the hostess pointed her enemy to the far side of the room to a table next to Amy's.

With that momentary concern alleviated, number two for her table was bound to be a breeze. She could hardly contain her relief when Two turned out to be a small-time mob man for the Monceaux family out of New Orleans. She'd seen him numerous times on the news. Always smiling, always touting his innocence. Apparently he was right, since he was still walking around and playing poker. Or he had even deeper pockets than the banker. Either way, he was mostly wanted for racketeering and hadn't had any violent offenses that she'd heard of.

But as the third player approached the table, Mallory felt a chill run through her. Silas Hebert. And for just a moment, her confidence wavered.

Silas Hebert was no small-time racketeer or foolish banker. The man was tall, almost imposing, and there was none of the flab to his body like her uncle. This was a man who worked out and worked out hard. His black hair was thinner than the pictures she'd seen of him when he was younger, but the eyes were the same, the same shade as his hair. And his glare could cut right through you.

There was no denying it—Silas Hebert was a force to be reckoned with.

Mallory sucked in a breath and tried to calm her nerves. *You can handle this. He's just a man. So what if he's a professional gambler and he's usually wanted for very scary stuff? He's here to play poker, not kill someone, and you're not even playing. He'll never even suspect you're involved with his run of bad luck.*

She hoped.

Because for the second time that day and probably only the third or fourth time in her entire adult life, Mallory felt a small quiver of fear pass through her. Her flight instincts were kicking into overdrive and she knew that

44

before this was over, she'd probably have wished a thousand times she'd never come.

She nodded briefly to Silas as he took a seat in the stool next to her at the end of the table. She stiffened a bit as he chose a position so close to her but quickly realized the advantage that presented. Sometimes close proximity wasn't quite enough to ensure a real run of bad luck. At least this way, Silas was near enough for an accidental brush of the hand or foot. And it would be far less obvious than traipsing around the table, patting grown men on the heads like an adult version of duck-duck-goose.

She reached down to fiddle with the strap on her shoes, and could feel Silas's gaze on her. She didn't want to look him straight in the eye. Not yet. Not until she had reached a calmer place. If Silas even suspected for a moment the fix was on, there would be hell to pay, even if he couldn't prove a thing.

"Good morning, gentlemen." Jake's voice sounded next to her and she rose up a bit surprised that she hadn't heard him approach.

Jake looked around the table and nodded to the men, then glanced at the remaining empty stool. "I'm told our fifth has been slightly delayed but should be here any moment. Perhaps Ms. Devereaux would like to begin with drink orders."

Mallory stopped her sideways assessment of Silas when Jake said her name and rose from her stool, irritated that the dealer had to point out her job because she was too busy trying to size up Silas without him noticing. Looking around the table at the men, she gave them a broad smile. "Would anyone like some coffee this morning? The kitchen also has a nice selection of fruit and Danish if that interests anyone."

She pulled out her pad and pen, ready to write, but not a single player said a word. In fact, they weren't even looking at her. They were all staring at Jake.

"You a Yankee?" the banker asked.

Jake looked at the man in dismay, then scanned the other players, but it was obvious the banker had asked the one thing on everyone's mind.

"I'm from Atlantic City," he said finally.

"A Yankee," the mobster confirmed. "What the hell kind of insult is St. Claire going for here?"

Jake blinked once and stared at the man, obviously unsure how to proceed. He glanced over at Mallory and she shrugged. She'd tried to warn him.

"I assure you, gentlemen," Jake offered, "that I am well versed in poker and you will find nothing lacking in my dealing capabilities."

The mobster glared at him. "Ain't nobody worried about your 'capabilities,' stiff shirt. The fact is, this tournament is full of important men. We got our reputations to protect."

"I was born in Oklahoma City," Jake offered. "Does that help?"

The mobster shook his head. "If it's north of Interstate 10, you're still a Yankee."

Mallory bit her lip to hold in a laugh. Although she was enjoying Jake's discomfort more than she should, it was time to reel the situation back in or Reginald would let her have it. "C'mon, guys," she said. "His chips play like everyone else's. Besides, Reginald's the only one who needs to worry about looking foolish here. He's the one who put up his own money for a Yankee to play with. Why should you care who you take it from?"

There was dead silence for a moment, and all the men

continued to stare. Finally, the banker shrugged. "Whatever."

The mobster studied Jake a minute longer. "I guess I'll live with it." He pointed one finger at Jake. "But you're not allowed to start any topic of conversation, understand? I know what y'all do up in those big cities—ballet, theater—bunch of girly stuff. If it doesn't involve a racing engine or killing something, I don't want to hear a word out of you except cards."

The beginning of a flush started at the base of Jake's neck, and Mallory could tell he was losing patience fast. His jaw set in a hard line and she couldn't stop herself from thinking that he looked sexy when he was mad.

Unfortunately, a fight, verbal or physical, was not going to move either of them toward their goals. It was time to wrap this up and get on to the business of playing cards. "Mr. Hebert," she finished roll call, "you in or out?"

She tensed a bit, waiting for his response, but Silas surprised her by giving Jake an amused look and waving one hand for him to proceed. "See," Mallory said. "That wasn't so hard. Now if you'd like to give me your drink orders, I'll get those started for you."

There was a momentary pause, apparently none of the buffoons wanting to be the first to speak, but finally the banker barked out his order and the rest followed suit. All coffee, all black. Mallory shoved her pad back into her jacket pocket. Didn't take a genius to remember four black coffees.

"Mr. McMillan?" She turned to Jake before leaving. "Can I bring you anything?"

He continued to stare at the players and for a moment, Mallory wondered if he was going to answer at all. The expression on his face was an interesting mixture of aggravation and disbelief. Apparently Jake McMillan had run into far more than he bargained for in southeast Louisiana, and he was having a bit of difficulty adjusting.

Finally, he turned his gaze to her and his expression shifted to one of mild appreciation. "A bottled water would be great," he said, and gave her a nod, apparently his way of admitting that she'd been right about the whole Yankee thing.

Mallory smiled at him and couldn't help wondering how much that tiny acknowledgement had hurt Jake McMillan's ego. She turned to leave when the double doors to the casino opened and Father Thomas walked through. Kind of. It was a bit more of a stagger, but it managed to propel him into the casino.

"Blessed are the poor in wallet, for theirs is the King of Hearts," Father Thomas shouted, and Mallory stifled a groan. A quick look at the other tables, all filled with their requisite four players plus dealer, let her know in a heartbeat that the drunken priest was their latecomer.

She shot a look over at Amy, who was trying, quite unsuccessfully to hide a smile as she watched Father Thomas make his way to Mallory's table. Laugh it up, underage girl, Mallory thought and turned her attention back to the priest. It could have been worse, she decided. He was wearing his ceremonial robes in black, collar and all, which was enough to stand out, but the camouflage sweat pants, purple and gold socks and red sandals completing the bottom of his outfit were a bit of a worry. Not to mention where he'd gotten the cash for this kind of tournament in the first place.

How drunk is he? She pondered for a moment over whether she should speak to her uncle before the priest managed to get all the way across the casino and take a seat. Why in the world would Reginald put a local, someone who knew everything about her, at her table?

She scanned the room for Reginald, who was at a table in the far corner of the casino. Just as she was about to cross the room and confront him, Father Thomas caught sight of her.

"Mallory, my child," his voice boomed across the casino. "I was hungry and you gave me food. I was thirsty and you got me Jack Daniel's."

"What in God's name," Jake said, and stared at Father Thomas, a confused expression on his face.

"I believe that's our final player," the Mafia guy said, and smirked. "This ought to be fun."

"Surely not," Jake said, and looked over at Mallory, apparently hoping she would explain away the nightmare crossing the casino.

Mallory shrugged, not about to let her own doubts show. "Father Thomas likes his card games. I guess he was invited."

Jake stared at Mallory, then looked back at Father Thomas. "But he's clearly drunk, and it's not even ten A.M." He stared at the priest, dumbfounded. "It will be a miracle if he stays awake for the game."

Mallory gave the priest a quick assessment and shook her head, his drunkenness actually a plus for her given the situation. "Nah, he's really not that bad considering everything he drank this weekend. The miracle will be if he spends one day sober."

And if he doesn't give away my cooling ability by lunch.

Chapter Four

By the time Mallory managed to get the swaggering priest onto the bar stool and facing the poker table, she'd lost sight of Reginald and needed to get the drinks. She wanted to spread her ill will as soon as possible, and the appearance of the priest at her table made expediency even more important.

Damn it, what had Reginald been thinking?

Pushing through the doors to the kitchen, she almost ran headfirst into Scooter.

"What's the hurry, Mal?" Scooter asked as he grabbed the door before it could slam into him. "People can't want a drink that bad. It's not even ten o'clock yet."

Mallory pointed to the beer in Scooter's shirt pocket. "Then what's that for? The fish?"

Scooter grinned. "Hell, I'm not most people. Besides, Reginald told me I could have all the free food and drink I want if I would stay on the boat for the whole thing. It's just like one of those all-inclusive vacations to Cancun. 'Cept no one's naked and I ain't gotta speak Mexican. Anyways, I plan on getting my money's worth on the drinking part since I'm sorta missing out on the whole naked thing."

Mallory took one look at the grinning Scooter and held in a sigh. She wasn't about to explain that he could hardly get his money's worth since not only wasn't he paying—he was being paid to take the ride. And since most of the poker players were men—unattractive, older men—she didn't think he was really missing much on the naked end of things, either. "That's great, Scooter. Listen, I need to find Reginald and I'm kind of in a hurry. Did you see which way he went?"

Scooter nodded. "He said he was going back to his suite for a shower. He'll be back after that."

Crap. They were right back to the old, unattractive, naked man thing. The bathroom was probably the only place Reginald could go that Mallory wouldn't follow, but she didn't have the time to wait on Reginald to finish showering.

Mallory motioned Scooter over to a corner of the kitchen and glanced around to make sure no one would hear. "Something's not right here, Scooter. This list of players is all wrong. My uncle is so mad about some of them being here, and that doesn't make sense. It's almost like he didn't make up the invitation list. Do you understand what I'm saying?"

Scooter scrunched his brow for a moment, then nodded. "Yeah, I guess it's kinda weird that he would put Father T at your table. Heck, Father T blabs everything people say in confession, and he's supposed to have a contract with God on keeping that a secret. He's probably already told everyone you're a cooler."

Mallory nodded. "That's what I'm afraid of. I figure I can pass most of it off as him being drunk, but I don't know that it can last for a week."

"So what are you going to do about it now? It's too late to change everything."

"For now, I'm going to keep him drunk, which shouldn't be difficult. But if I knew what my uncle was up to, I'd have a much better idea of how to play this out long-term." She thought a moment more, then looked Scooter directly in the eyes before she could change her mind. "I need you to do something for me."

"Anything for you, Mal, you know that."

"Good. I need you to stay as close to my uncle as you can without him noticing. Remember everything he says, even if it doesn't sound important. Whatever he's up to is bound to be a huge problem, and I have no intention of being caught in the middle."

Scooter's eyes widened and he gave her a big grin. "You want me to play Sherlock Holmes? That's the coolest thing ever."

Mallory stared at Scooter in surprise. "You read Sherlock Holmes?" Surely not. In the seven years she'd lived next to him, Mallory had never seen Scooter read anything but road signs or advertisements for a sale on beer. Well, and that one time she'd caught him in his bass boat with a copy of *Penthouse*, but neither of them spoke of the matter and she did her best to keep it in the far back reaches of her mind.

"Of course, I read Sherlock Holmes," Scooter said. "Spent most of junior high with a book under my desk instead of listening in history—I mean, who cares about dead people? Heck, Mallory, every boy wanted to be Sherlock Holmes—or Dale Earnhardt."

"That's great, Scooter. You play Sherlock Holmes, then. We'll save Dale Earnhardt for a car chase, if it comes to that."

Scooter scratched his head. "Um, Mal, I don't know

how to tell you this, but Senior ain't driving anymore since the accident and all. If you want a car-chase person, then I might have to be Junior."

"Junior, it is."

Scooter rose to his full height and stiffened his posture. "'My name is Sherlock Holmes,'" he said, in the worst British accent Mallory had ever heard. "'It is my business to know what other people don't know.'"

With a nod, Scooter flattened his back against the casino wall, glanced both directions, then slowly crept toward the hall. When he reached the end of the wall, he pulled his pocketknife from his jeans, opened it and stuck the blade into the open walkway, apparently attempting to use it as a mirror.

Mallory gave a silent prayer of thanks that no one had been entering the kitchen when Scooter had decided to stab at the open doorway and watched in dismay as he gave her a thumbs-up and inched sideways through the opening.

Mallory hesitated a second or two but finally strode off toward the coffeepot, already regretting having put Scooter up to anything requiring stealth and finesse. It didn't take a genius to know this was going to be a disaster.

Jake shuffled the cards again while stealing glances at Mallory as she served the drinks to the players. The woman was a complete anomaly—clearly smart enough to rein in the Redneck Lynch Mob that the players had formed against him this morning, but not smart enough to figure out that all that incidental touching she managed to do while serving was a complete waste of time.

And Reginald St. Claire was only making the situation worse by encouraging her ridiculous beliefs. Jake noticed that Mallory was the only attendant not carrying her own tray. A kitchen worker had trailed behind her with the drinks and placed them on the serving table, then reminded her to call him for pickup before dismissing himself. Jake surmised Mallory was encouraged not to carry anything breakable. At least not in mass quantity.

Why in God's name she'd brought the drunken priest more alcohol, Jake didn't even want to know. At this point, the priest was the least of his worries. Based on the players' lack of reaction to Mallory, women were obviously not going to be a distraction and that clearly put all the responsibility on Jake. They had barely even looked at the mound of partially exposed breasts as she leaned in to place drinks in front of them. They were too focused on the game, which was a real shame. Breasts that stood at attention with no bra, *if* she'd been telling the truth, were worth at least a glance.

He was just trying to decide if there was a tan line buried somewhere in that shirt when he felt someone's eyes on him. He lifted his gaze to the table beside them and saw Brad smiling at him. The other dealer gave him a thumbs-up and grinned. Jake held in a sigh and turned back to his table. His only objective at this tournament was to fly below the radar until he was ready to bust Silas, and twice already Brad had caught him acting like a horny sixteen-year-old.

If he didn't get his act together, Brad might want to hang out or something equally as painful. Drinking beer, entertaining loose women and watching NASCAR. Or, even worse, one of those fishing shows. If it was hunting season, he'd probably be expected to kill something and wear a funny hat.

He waited until Mallory had taken her seat at the end of the table to start dealing. The first hand had gone well. Silas had won a bit of money, and Jake had been smart enough to bow out early. If he continued to play smart, he might have a chance. All he needed was one exchange of cash.

At least he hoped that would be enough.

Finished with the deal, he pushed the card shoe over to the left and lifted the edge of his cards from the table. No fucking way. The handful of hearts seemed to smile up at him. A royal flush on the deal? The odds of pulling a royal on the deal were less than him actually knowing those NASCAR drivers, like Mallory had suggested. Granted, a royal flush wasn't as bad as drawing five of a kind, but neither hand was believable.

Before he could stop himself, he glanced over at Mallory. She was staring directly at him, the briefest of smiles on her face. No fucking way. She could not have made this happen. But it was obvious from the amused look on her face that Mallory knew he'd drawn a good hand.

Disgusted, he glanced around the room, wondering if St. Claire's security people were closely watching the camera that showed his hand. He needed to ditch a card but couldn't afford for one of St. Claire's flunkies to see it happen.

He raised one hand to stroke his jaw and tried to clear all expression from his face. If he dropped one card, Mallory might think he'd pulled a straight on the draw and was gambling the last card on the royal. What the hell. It was early in the game and he could always defend his choice by saying he had to take the chance. It might not be the most brilliant or conservative of moves, but no one would be able to fault him for trying it.

If St. Claire's goons were watching the cameras, he could always say they were mistaken. He seriously doubted they were recording everything, so unless he kept tossing away winning hands, he shouldn't have a problem.

Mind made up, he yanked the ace out of his hand and tossed it on the pile of discards. The worst thing that could happen is she would assume he was a risky gambler. The last thing she should guess is that he was intentionally trying to throw the hand.

Pulling cards from the shoe, he dealt replacements to all the players and dropped a single card with the rest of his own, praying for anything that didn't make a winning hand. And frustrated at himself for fearing the worst. He had nothing to worry about and that was just reality. The shoe contained six decks to help cut down on the card-counting ability of some of the better players. So even though the card existed in the decks another five times, the odds of him drawing another ace of hearts were incredibly minute.

Even so, he found himself clenching his jaw as he lifted the edge of the card off the table.

When the red "A" made its appearance, it was all he could do to hold his blank expression in place. He blinked once to make sure he was seeing clearly. A second glance revealed a red diamond, and he slowly let out the breath that he'd been unaware he'd been holding. It wasn't the loss he'd been hoping for, but it wasn't another royal flush, either.

He turned his attention back to the table and waited for his turn to bet. Silas had opened with five thousand, so Jake knew he was holding something worthwhile. The man next to Silas folded and it was on to the drunken priest.

The priest studied his hand for a moment, then swayed a bit in his chair, studied the cards again, took a drink of Jack Daniel's and cleared his throat to speak. Jake steeled himself for the onslaught of garbled scripture but the priest elected to butcher the shortest verse in the Bible.

"Father Thomas wept," he said and tossed his cards, facedown, onto the table.

The man next to Father Thomas gave a sigh of relief, and despite himself, Jake almost smiled. On the previous hand, they'd gotten the entire 23rd Psalm. Sort of.

The other player folded also, so it was left to Jake to bet. He knew what he should do—what he would do if he were playing for real and for keeps—he'd see the five and raise it another. Hell, if he were playing for keeps, he'd have run the table on the royal, but winning some cash wasn't his primary objective. In fact, it wasn't an objective at all. It was only necessary to win enough to keep him in the game and force more money out of Silas.

Mallory knew he had drawn a good hand and if he folded, she'd be able to tell something wasn't right. Then she'd run straight to her uncle.

Damn it.

Call or raise? It should have been simple, and by God, it was. He grabbed some chips off the stack in front of him and tossed them onto the pile.

"I'll see your five and raise you five," he said, and lifted his gaze to the hard stare of Silas Hebert.

Silas studied Jake's face for a moment, then tossed in the required chips. "Call."

Jake laid his cards on the table and watched Silas carefully for any change in expression. Silas seemed momentarily surprised with the display, but finally nodded and flipped his cards over, displaying his own straight, six through ten, but not the same suit.

"You almost pulled it," Silas said to Jake.

Jake nodded. "Would have been a first."

Silas studied him again. "Would have been the first time in over thirty years of card playing that I'd seen it."

Jake met the man's eyes, forcing himself not to look

away, but he felt his confidence drop. Silas was issuing the challenge. He had his doubts Jake had drawn the hand fairly and was letting him know he'd be watching very closely from now on.

Jake reached across the table for the spent cards and put them with the other discards. No problem, he thought. The royal was a fluke, a freak of nature and statistics colliding to give him a heart attack. He wasn't cheating, so there was nothing Silas could catch him doing. From now on, the cards would flow normally, and he'd have to rely on his own playing ability to control the table. He could do this. He'd been preparing for years.

As he reached for the shoe, he looked over at Mallory, perched sideways on her stool, her long legs seeming to flow endlessly from the seat. As his gaze moved up the long lines of her body to her face, she gave him a smile, then winked.

It was going to be a very long day.

It seemed to Mallory that lunch would never come. The play on the table was definitely swinging to Jake's advantage, and she couldn't be happier with the results. That first hand was almost overkill, but since then, things had settled down to a steady stream of chips in Jake's direction. Not that Mallory believed for one moment that Jake gave her any credit for his growing pile of chips. Hell, based on the way she was dressed for the tournament, Jake probably didn't give her credit for an IQ higher than her bra size.

And for absolutely no reason she could explain, that bothered her.

She knew he found her attractive—had caught him eyeing every square inch of her body outright. And the blush that crept up his neck when she winked had clinched it. But the reality was, Jake McMillan probably thought she was a two-bit hustler, like her uncle. He had no real cause to suspect differently, and definitely no reason to attribute to her an advanced degree or a high IQ.

Which should have been nothing new, really. Certainly men, especially men in Royal Flush, rarely acknowledged intelligence in a woman. Of course, they would have had to be smart enough to recognize it, but that was another issue. The reality was, in Royal Flush intelligence wasn't exactly what men were looking for in a mate. A late-model truck with good tires and a bass boat got you a heck of a lot more mileage than a college education.

Not that Mallory was in the market for a man. She'd dated a couple of guys since college but always with the same result—one disaster after another.

Guy #1 had been really sweet and tried desperately to work around the issues. Fortunately for him, he'd only run the gamut of car repairs, failed watches and one twisted ankle while dating her. Well, and that one incident with his suede jacket and a trout, but that could have happened to anyone. Still the jacket had been the last straw, and Guy #1 had waved a hasty good-bye from the parking lot of J.T.'s Bar, his car already loaded with his belongings. Apparently, it wasn't enough to just stop dating her. He'd decided leaving the state was required, and just like that, he was gone.

Guy #2 had been a whole other story. Brash and cocky, loud and egotistical, he was exactly the kind of man she would usually have avoided. But she was younger then and year after year of being without the company of a man had left her lonely and ripe pickings for the first guy with the balls to ask her out—and hey, he still had one of them, right? After she'd put Guy #2 into an ambulance, she'd learned that he'd only dated her on a bet. Apparently, there had been some kind of betting pool about how long a man could date her without acquiring an injury requiring medical attention.

Guy #2 had lost that bet and something a little more important, but that was hardly her fault. She'd told him not to put a loaded gun in his pants pocket and that snake wouldn't have bothered him besides. It certainly hadn't been any reason to panic and shoot off a body part.

She let out a sigh and focused back on the game in front of her. Her life was what it was, and nothing she could do would change it. God knows she'd tried.

"We have time for one more hand before lunch," Jake's voice broke into her thoughts.

She took in a deep breath, hoping to clear her mind, focus on the game in front of her, but the musky smell of Jake's cologne wafted through her nostrils and caused her vision to blur momentarily. Such a tiny thing, that scent, so sensual and masculine all at the same time, but it seemed to draw her toward him, mind and body.

Turning her gaze to the table, she watched as Jake deftly dealt the cards across the table, making note of the way his strong hands operated with a light touch and exact precision, pulling and placing each card with finesse and accuracy. Long fingers, too. Lots of uses for long fingers.

She sat up straight on her stool and lifted one hand to study her nail polish. Where the hell had that come from? Of all the men in the world Mallory had come in contact with, Jake McMillan had seemed the least interested of all. Why in the world was she working the most important event of her life and having a fantasy about the fingers on a man that most likely thought she was a bimbo, or even worse, a criminal?

This would never do. She needed to regroup her thoughts, remember who she was and what her future was—concentrate on shutting down the table before the end of the week so she could get the hell out of Jake's line of sight as soon as possible. Emotionally, she may not have been in the market for a man, but apparently no one had sent her body the memo.

She made a mental note to pick up new batteries on the way home. It was definitely time for new batteries.

Jake looked up from his cards and locked his gaze on hers. She felt a blush start to creep up her neck at being caught ogling him, and she had little doubt that he knew exactly what she was doing. It was probably written across her forehead.

Giving her a slow sexy smile, he winked.

It was going to be a very long day.

Chapter Five

Mallory waited until the last hand of the morning was played out, careful to avoid any more concentrating on fingers or hands or anything else long and hard, then counted the men's chips and gave them each a slip of paper with the tally. Slips of paper in hand, they all headed out of the casino and into the restaurant with Jake close behind.

With her focus back on the game, Mallory had sensed that something was off. Yet she couldn't put her finger on exactly what. Certainly, given the players, there was any number of possibilities for the "off" category, but as she turned her attention to the men, one by one, she finally had to admit that the feeling was coming from Jake.

But damned if she knew why.

His play seemed to be aboveboard. A bit on the conservative side, but perhaps that was just his style, or maybe he was a bit nervous and would loosen up more as the tournament went along. With the run of luck he'd had, he should have been a bit more confident, but not only had he remained somewhat reserved, he'd seemed almost hesitant about most of his betting.

She looked at the table, the final round of hands still faceup in front of each player's seat, then cast her gaze to the card shoe. She glanced around the room, ensuring it was empty, then lifted the top card from the spent pile in the card shoe before she could change her mind. This card should be the one Jake threw on the last hand.

But what she saw didn't make sense at all.

If this card were indeed the one Jake had thrown, then he'd tossed out a full house and ended up with only three of a kind. Sure, he'd still won the overall, but there was no logical reason for a player to throw a full house, and Jake McMillan had not seemed the least bit stupid. Well, if the dealer didn't have the table under control, at least she did. Besides, it was very possible the cards had been placed in the shoe in a different order than discarded.

She returned the card and started across the casino to the kitchen. At the moment, her biggest worry was finding out what Reginald had gotten himself into.

As soon as she stepped inside the restaurant, Mallory scanned the room for Scooter, wondering if he'd had any luck tracking Reginald. She hadn't caught sight of her uncle the rest of the morning. What could the scoundrel find more important than overseeing his own tournament? At this point she was willing to try anything to get information. Even Sherlock Scooter.

She heard her name and turned toward a small table in the corner of the room where Scooter was standing on a chair waving his arms at her like he was trying to direct a plane. Amy sat quietly next to him The expression on her face was an interesting combination of amusement and horror.

Mallory lifted one hand to Scooter, hopefully giving him the signal to get off the chair and stop drawing attention to the table. Scooter shot her a huge grin and hopped off his chair, banging his knee against the table, which, in turn, caused a glass of water to tip over. Amy jumped up from the table before the worst of the flood could reach her and glared at Scooter as she mopped at her skirt with a table napkin.

Mallory tried not to smile. She wasn't the only one that could make a mess of things.

By the time she reached the table, the glass of water was righted and Amy's skirt would probably survive the experience, although based on the look on Amy's face, Scooter's fate was questionable. Mallory was also happy to note that the tables surrounding them were unoccupied, which made not being overheard a heck of a lot easier.

"Hi, guys," she said, and slid into her seat. "How's the tournament going so far?" she asked Amy.

Amy nodded and her expression cleared from scowling to enthusiastic. "It's going great! I think I'll be able to take out one of my players after lunch. That makes one down on the first day."

Mallory stared at Amy, a bit surprised. She'd known her friend was brilliant, but running a player out in less than a day, especially the players at this tournament, was nothing short of a miracle. "That's incredible, Amy. Not that I doubted your skill, but a day? Wow!"

Amy gave her a huge grin. "The idiot made it easy. He hates women and refuses to believe I can play cards. So no matter what indicators there are that I'm holding a ringer, he won't fold. Even the politician called him stupid."

Mallory smiled. "You've reached an all-time low when

a Louisiana politician starts demeaning your intelligence. I guess you didn't bother to mention to the politician that he'd be working for you someday?"

Amy shook her head, the grin still in place. "It hasn't come up, but I might give him a heads-up when he's leaving."

Mallory was about to reply when she saw Amy's grin fade as quickly as it had come. Amy's eyes centered on something directly behind her and based on the look of disgust she now wore, Mallory knew it couldn't be anything good. Turning around in her seat, she looked straight into the fake smile and huge, annoying cowboy hat of Walter Royal.

"Mallory," he said, with his booming voice, "I see you're trying to establish a new career before the bottom drops out of Harry's business. Smart idea." He gave her an apologetic look. "I know you're a good foreman, but my wife has an unemployed nephew from New Orleans that we really need to do something with. Hell, he don't know the correct width of a two-by-four, but then what do you really need to know to tear shit up?"

Mallory's entire body tensed and she started to rise from her chair, her fists already clenched in anticipation of knocking the bastard out cold. Then she felt the sharp point of Amy's heel stab her directly in her big toe. She glared at her friend, who gave her the barest shake of her head, everything in her expression telling Mallory not to do what she'd been planning.

Mallory bit her lip and unclenched her hands. As much as she hated to admit it, Amy was right. Hitting Royal wouldn't solve anything but to get her a night in the tank for assault—hardly a good way to win the money she needed—and now more than ever, Mallory wanted to keep Royal from owning Harry's business.

"You think it's easy to work demolition?" Scooter stared at Walter Royal like he had lost his mind. "Demolition's harder than construction. Hell, you can bend wood to fix just about anything, and what you can't bend you can hide with molding and caulk, but if you rig dynamite wrong, you blast up a city block."

Royal gave Scooter a look of dismissal and waved one hand. "I never said I was replacing everyone at the company—just the foreman. It's a management decision. I wouldn't expect someone like you to understand."

Scooter leveled his gaze on Royal, his voice calm and strong. "I understand being screwed, Mr. Royal. It always looks the same."

Mallory saw Scooter tense and knew he was about to stand up and finish what she'd started to do earlier. Holding one hand up to put Scooter at bay, she gave Walter a fake smile. "I guess I'll be looking at my other options, then." She extended one hand toward Royal. "I appreciate the heads-up. It will give me an opportunity to start checking on some firms in New Orleans."

Royal stared at her for a moment and she tried like hell to form her expression into the model of sincerity. It must have worked because he finally gave her a broad smile and extended his hand. "I knew you'd see reason. It's nothing personal, after all. It's just business."

Mallory shook his hand and gave him a nod. "Of course." She released his hand and turned around to face the others, knowing Amy would let her know when her archenemy had vacated the area.

"Asshole," Amy said, and Mallory knew Royal had retreated to his hole under a rock.

"Is his back to us?" Mallory asked, itching to turn around and see what would befall her nemesis.

Amy nodded. "Yeah, it's safe to look."

Mallory turned slightly in her chair and watched as Royal crossed the dining area. Just as he stepped in front of the double doors to the kitchen, someone inside swung one of them open and plowed him right in the face. The force of the blow had Royal staggering backward into the nearest table where the occupants had just been served the lunch meal of spaghetti and meatballs.

The occupants jumped from the table as Royal fell backward across it, a shower of spaghetti and red wine shooting up from the table and raining down to cover him. The door-slinging waiter stared in horror, then rushed into action, helping Royal off the now-broken table and trying to wipe at the stains on his shirt.

"Stop touching me, you moron!" Royal yelled, and shoved the waiter away from him. "I'll be talking to Reginald about this. You *will* be buying me a new suit." Royal gave the waiter a final glare, then stomped across the dining area to the lobby exit, leaving a trail of spaghetti in his wake.

It was all Mallory could do to hold in her laughter until he'd made his exit. Amy's face was beet red and she had her napkin pressed over her mouth. Scooter was doubled over on the floor next to the table, giant tears streaming down his face.

When the door slammed behind him, the three of them collapsed in laughter. The other players stared for a moment, then started to join in by smiling or letting out a chuckle or two. After all, it *was* funny, and Walter Royal wasn't exactly the most popular man in Louisiana.

"I can't believe he was stupid enough to shake your hand," Amy said as she dabbed at the corner of her eyes with her napkin. "What was he thinking?"

"Royal is too self-absorbed to know anything about the locals," Mallory said. "Even if someone had warned him about me, he would have immediately dismissed it. His imagination would never stretch that far."

Scooter pulled himself up from the floor and slid back into his seat. "That was great, Mal," he huffed, still trying to get his breath back to normal, "but you still should have let me hit him."

Mallory grinned at her friend and shook her head. "I appreciate the desire, Scooter, and certainly have no doubts about the outcome, but you have to admit, the challenge isn't really there. It would be like shooting alligators in the game preserve."

"I guess," Scooter admitted somewhat grudgingly. "But I'm not above an unfair advantage as long as it's mine."

"Neither am I." She lifted one hand in the air. "It was handled the best way possible for the time being. Besides, I need you here watching Reginald. Royal wouldn't hesitate to file charges against either of us for hitting him and what we need to do can't be accomplished from jail."

"Why is Scooter watching Reginald?" Amy asked, a confused expression on her face.

"Because," Mallory explained, "I want to know what my uncle is up to before it comes back to bite us all in the ass."

Amy gave her a slow nod. "Okay, while I might agree in theory, do you really think it's a good idea to have Scooter following your uncle around?" Translation: *Won't Scooter make an ever-living mess of this the way he does everything else?*

Mallory shrugged. "He's the only one available, and Reginald will be more likely to say something important in front of Scooter than others." Translation: *Reginald thinks Scooter's an idiot and won't watch his words when he's around.*

Amy nodded her understanding, then turned to Scooter. "So did you find out anything?"

"Nothing to find," Scooter said. "He spent almost the entire morning back in his storeroom doing inventory. He came into the kitchen about twenty minutes ago and told me he was going to grab a bite to eat then take a shower and if I needed anything, he'd been in his office after that."

Mallory narrowed her eyes at Scooter. "I thought you told me he was taking a shower earlier this morning."

Scooter scratched his head and looked momentarily confused. "Yeah, I did. I mean, he did. At least, that's what he said." Scooter paused for a moment. "That's an awful lot of showering for a guy who spent his whole morning carrying around a clipboard."

"It certainly is," Mallory agreed. "Unless he isn't really showering."

"So what do you think he's really doing?" Amy asked.

"I don't know," Mallory said, a million ideas running through her head. Finally she turned to Scooter. "Is there any way to hear what happens in Reginald's office? I mean, how thick are the walls?"

Scooter shrugged. "The walls ain't all that thick, but if you're wanting to listen to Reginald take a shower, that's even easier to do."

"How's that?" Mallory asked.

"You see," Scooter explained, "Reginald had me put that shower in after the fact, guess he didn't think about it before, and there was no way to vent it through the floor—no room with the ducts for the air conditioning for the two levels of casino. I tried to get him to install it on an outside wall so we could vent outside the casino, but he didn't want to block his view." Scooter gave them a satisfied nod, like what he'd just said explained everything.

Mallory absorbed his ramblings for a moment, then smiled. "So you vented the bathroom into the hall, right?"

"Exactly."

Amy frowned. "So anything Reginald does in the bathroom is vented into the hall? That's gross on so many levels I'm not even going to get into it."

"It's not so bad," Scooter said. "His office is on a dead-end hallway between the storage rooms." He grinned at Amy. "No one really has any reason to be back there, and the stock probably won't complain if Reginald eats beans for lunch or anything."

"That," Amy said, "was entirely too much information."

Mallory laughed but then grew serious as she thought about the conversation Scooter had overheard. "I think a trip to my uncle's vent may be in order. Scooter, why don't you pay the kitchen a visit and see if Reginald's left yet."

"No problem." Scooter rose from his chair and ambled off into the kitchen. A minute later he poked his head out and gave them a thumbs-up.

"I guess that means Reginald is done eating," Mallory said, and rose from her chair.

"Or that he's still in the kitchen knee-deep in a twenty-ounce steak," Amy said. "What if Scooter misunderstood?"

Mallory shrugged. "It's a chance I'll have to take. Besides, what's Uncle Reginald going to do? Fire me?"

Amy pulled her napkin from her lap, folded it into four equal squares, and placed in on the table next to her plate. "Then I'm going with you."

"Oh no—"

Amy held up a hand. "Don't even argue. I've put you in a bad position by being here at all. The least I can do is help out. Besides, I'd like to hear firsthand what I've gotten myself into."

The hallway to Reginald's office was dimly lit and at the very back of the casino, which suited Mallory just fine, since it cut down on the chance of being seen. She slipped down the hallway, Amy close behind, and hoped that whatever Reginald had retired to his office for was still happening when they got there.

Directly to the right of her uncle's office door, Mallory spotted the vent Scooter had mentioned. It was too high on the wall to stand next to, but there were several empty wooden crates stacked across the hallway next to the warehouse door. Mallory snagged one and placed it below the vent, then kicked off her shoes and stepped carefully onto the platform, placing her ear against the vent.

It took her a second to realize that noise she heard was a shower running. Then she heard a series of beeps, like someone punching in numbers on a phone. Someone was definitely in the bathroom. Someone who was making a phone call while pretending to shower. Someone she hoped was Reginald.

She motioned to Amy to step onto the crate and moved over to the side to ensure her friend could join her on the platform without making any physical contact. Amy nodded and stepped gently onto the crate, carefully balancing herself on the other side.

Someone coughed on the other side of the wall, and Mallory heard Reginald say, "I'm getting a bad feeling about this. I don't think it's going to work."

She wished they could hear both sides of the conversation and not just the one.

"I've got everything I own and some things I don't riding on this," Reginald said. "If it doesn't come off like you said it will, I'm a fifty-four-year-old man with no viable skills, legal ones anyway, starting over in life."

Amy stared at Mallory, her eyes growing wider as Reginald spoke. Mallory placed one finger on her lips.

"No, God damn it!" Reginald shouted, and Mallory sucked in a breath.

"I don't prefer the alternative," he continued, "as that leaves me with nothing, too. What I prefer is to go back to my life the way it was before you showed up and ruined it."

Mallory pressed closer to the wall until she was almost flattened against it, but not a peep came from the bathroom except for the spray from the shower. Several seconds passed and Mallory was just about to motion to Amy to leave when she heard an explosion of plastic against tile. Assuming her uncle had thrown the phone against the shower wall, Mallory decided about right now would be the perfect time to get the hell out of there.

She motioned to Amy, who carefully backed off the crate. Mallory waited until she was clear, then took one step away from the wall and directly onto a section of rotten board. The board split instantly from her weight and her foot went crashing through, scratching the heck out of her ankle as it went. Amy gave her a horrified look as Mallory tried to yank her foot out of the crate.

It took two tries before she pulled it free, and already she could hear Reginald yelling in his office. Any second now, they were going to be caught.

Without a moment to spare, Mallory pushed open the storeroom door and Amy ducked inside. Mallory spun around to face her uncle's office just as he yanked open the door and glared.

"What the hell are you doing out here, Mallory?

Sounds like you're tearing shit up. This ain't one of Harry's sites, you know?"

Mallory took a quick breath and tried to regroup. "I needed to speak to you about a couple of things and banged my foot on one of those crates when I walked up." She twisted her foot to the side, hoping her uncle wouldn't notice the tiny trickle of blood running down her ankle.

Reginald glanced down at her feet, then shook his head. "You shouldn't be walking around without shoes on. Jesus Christ, Mallory, you weren't raised in a barn. So what do you want?"

"I'm a little concerned about my table."

"What's the problem? Your table is running fine."

"For now. But just how long do you think Father Thomas is going to make it without telling everyone at the table, or the tournament for that matter, that I'm a cooler?"

Reginald pulled a cigar from his shirt pocket and lit it. "Father Thomas gave me his word he wouldn't say anything about you. It was the only way I would agree to let him play at your table."

Mallory threw her hands up in frustration. "His word? For Christ's sake, Reginald, he made a promise to God not to repeat things said in confession and he does that on a regular basis. Why in the world would you think he'd keep this a secret just because he promised you? And why would he want to be at my table anyway? He's got to know he's going to lose if I'm there."

Reginald puffed once on the cigar, then yanked it from his mouth, his jaw set in a hard line. "The old fool wanted a crack at beating Silas Hebert at the poker table, so that's what he got. You were part of the deal and he knew it up front. I'm not going to waste any more time on this conversation. Just do your job and your table will be fine."

Mallory narrowed her eyes at Reginald. "I'm trying to do my job, although I'm beginning to wonder if you even want your dealer to win. What the hell have you gotten yourself into, Reginald? This whole tournament seems too much, even for you."

"What I do in my casino is none of your business."

"It is if the fallout is on me—and Amy and Scooter. I've already got a bad feeling about all this. I need to know exactly what I'm worried about."

Reginald stared at her for a moment as if trying to decide what to say. Finally, he puffed once more on the cigar and shook his head. "The only thing you have to worry about is shutting down Silas Hebert. The rest will take care of itself. And believe me, you and your friends are perfectly safe in the casino. You have no idea just how safe." That said, he stepped back into his office and slammed the door behind him.

What the hell? Mallory stared at the closed door, not knowing what to think.

Finding a new job was starting to look less complicated by the minute.

Jake stood on a balcony just off the back of the restaurant and pulled out his cell phone. There was a cool breeze blowing off the Gulf and he leaned over the railing, hoping to catch a bit more of the refreshing air. He had two phone calls to make—one he was dreading and one that he hoped would be good news.

He decided to bet on the good news first. The phone had barely started ringing when the young man he had been hoping to reach picked up the call.

"Jake, is that you? Man, I been trying to find you. You out chasing the ladies?"

Jake smiled. "Hello to you too, Brian. And to answer your question, no I'm not chasing ladies—I'm out of town on business."

Brian laughed, fully aware of Jake's job and what his "business" probably consisted of. "Man, you make it sound like a bankers' convention."

"As far as you know, it is. I don't have very long, but I wanted to check in with you, see if you had some news yet."

There was a couple of seconds' pause and Jake could feel the energy from young man, even across the phone line. "Yeah, I guess you might call a full scholarship to Georgetown some news."

Jake felt the grin spread across his face. "That's fantastic! I hate to say I told you so—"

"I know, I know. But you gotta admit, it was a long shot for a guy like me."

"It was never a long shot. You just didn't believe that."

"I know, but you believed enough for both of us. And Mama prayed enough for all the saints to hear. I appreciate what you've done for me, Jake. Helping me see the things I could accomplish without the risks I was running. Let's face it, I was headed down a whole different road before I met you."

"Maybe. Or maybe you were just taking the scenic route."

Brian laughed. "Yeah, it didn't look so scenic from the backseat of a police cruiser, but since I won't be taking a chauffeured ride with the Atlantic City PD again, I'll just have to live off the memory."

"Maybe that's a memory better forgotten."

"No way, man. That ride plopped me straight down at

the youth center and on the other side of your desk. You are one hard dude, but you're making a difference here."

Jake's voice caught a bit. "I sure hope so."

"And I know so. You better get back to catching those men that I'm never going to become thanks to you."

Jake felt his pride in the young man swell even more. "You got it."

"And Jake—be careful. I'd like to have you around when I get that diploma."

"I wouldn't be anywhere else."

He pressed the "end" button and scrolled down to the number he'd been putting off for the last few days. Taking a deep breath, he forced his mind into a calm, collected state.

"Jones—it's Randoll," he said as his captain answered.

"Is it safe for you to talk?" Jones asked.

Jake looked out across the miles of open water. "Unless you're worried about the fish overhearing, it's as safe as cell phones get."

Apparently satisfied, his captain launched into his Q&A routine. "Is everything in place? Did you pull Silas's table? Is the bastard there? Why the hell haven't you checked in before now?"

Jake took a deep breath, forming answers to the onslaught of questions, his hope of finishing this phone call in time to grab some lunch evaporating in an instant. "I got the dealer slot at Silas's table, and yes, the bastard is most certainly here. Smug as ever. And I haven't checked in before now because I wasn't sure about player placement and there hasn't been a way to call without being overheard since the tournament started."

"Did you get the money scanner past the metal detectors?"

"Yes, sir. Security thought it was a regular laptop, just

like I thought they would. I'll keep it in my locker. Testing the money in the dressing area shouldn't be a problem. No one's in that room except for first thing in the morning and right before we leave.

There was a pause on the other end and Jake knew his boss's mind was whirling with every possible scenario this sting could take on—both good and bad.

"Why do I get the idea you're not telling me everything?" his captain finally said. "Your voice is strained."

Damn it. The man could pick up tension in a corpse.

"There's nothing here I can't handle, sir," Jake said.

"Why don't you let me be the judge of that," his captain shot back. "What's the problem?"

"There is no problem. Merely a small inconvenience, and I'm handling it."

"What inconvenience?" his captain asked, not about to let it go.

Jake gritted his teeth, knowing he was about to have the very discussion he'd been hoping to avoid. "St. Claire's niece is the attendant at my table so I have to be extra careful with my actions. And before you ask, there's no getting rid of her. St. Claire detests Silas and doesn't want him to win a dime. St. Claire put her at my table specifically to shut down Silas. This niece and St. Claire both have some nutbag idea that she can cool cards."

"Can she?"

Jake paused for a moment, not even sure how to reply. "Sir, you're not serious. There is no paranormal ability to cool cards that I've ever heard of in my life."

"I didn't ask if you'd heard of it. I asked if she could do it. How many hands have you won so far?"

"All but one," Jake mumbled. *Not counting the three I threw.*

Jana DeLeon

"What? I can't hear you. You're cutting out."

"All but one," Jake shouted.

"And you think that's normal?" his captain asked. "I don't care if she's clouding his judgment with perfume or goosing him under the table. Results are everything and sounds to me like she's getting results."

Jake shook his head in disbelief. "Sir, she's not getting anything but rounds of drinks. You can't possibly buy into this bullshit."

"I didn't say I was buying into anything, except the fact that whatever she's doing is apparently working. The key to success here is figuring out how to turn everything to your benefit."

"As far as she's concerned, I'm already benefiting," Jake said, unable to keep the frustration out of his voice. "If Silas doesn't win a hand or two soon, he will guess the fix is on and leave before I can get an exchange. Even if I were going to believe that this woman has some kind of supernatural ability, she's not helping me at all."

"Well, then I suggest you start by getting on this niece's good side. Treat her with that can't-be-bothered attitude you take toward most women and you're likely to create a problem you can't fix. I don't think I have to remind you what's riding on this. Or that this is our last chance."

Jake clenched the balcony railing with one hand and stared out over the glistening water. "No, you don't have to remind me."

"If you were any other single agent, I'd tell you to romance her, but you take avoiding women to new heights. So I suggest you start with being friendly. And don't tell me you can't. I know your mother, and I'm certain she raised you with manners or you wouldn't have seen adulthood."

"Yes, sir," Jake said, trying to figure out how the hell he

was supposed to be friendly to a woman that frustrated him with her odd beliefs as much as she stirred other feelings in him that he'd shut down long ago. It wasn't possible. Keeping Mallory Devereaux at a distance was the only way this was going to work for him. Just the fleeting thought of having her closer to him had his mind swimming, unorganized, unfocused, and that was something he couldn't afford regardless of his captain's advice.

"One more thing, Jake," his captain said. "That hand you lost—was the niece at the table then?"

The line went dead, and Jake flipped the phone shut and shoved it in his pocket. He leaned over the railing again, letting the cool Gulf air blow across his face. It didn't mean anything that she wasn't at the table.

Not a thing.

It was about ten minutes before play would start again, and Jake stood at his table, removing cards from the shoe and shuffling them, his boss's words still ringing in his ears. He was just trying to make up his mind how to approach the afternoon of play—and Mallory Devereaux—when the object of his thoughts stepped into the casino and headed for his table, her full hips swinging as she walked.

"Hi there," she said as she stepped up to the table.

Was it possible that her top was lower cut now than it had been this morning?

Jake held back a frown and managed an unenthusiastic "hello." Being friendly to Mallory Devereaux just wasn't going to be possible—not without his train of thought wandering to things best left alone.

Her smile faltered a little at his weak greeting, but she pointed at the stack of chips in front of him, by far the largest stack on the table, and tried again. "It was a great morning, huh?"

"Oh, yeah," Jake muttered. "It was a fantastic morning." *If you consider that Silas Hebert thinks I'm cheating and is probably planning to cash in his chips and leave.*

Mallory frowned at his sarcasm. "Surely you weren't expecting to take them all the first day? That would take a miracle. I'm good, but I don't do miracles."

Jake stared at her a moment, an idea forming in the back of his mind. Sure, the whole card cooling thing was bullshit, but what would it hurt to test it out? "Then maybe you should talk to your friend, the drunken priest. Anything he could work up would make as much difference as you do."

Mallory's face flushed with anger. "You still don't believe, do you? Even after almost every hand this morning went your way. Even though some of the hands you pulled on the draw go against the laws of nature."

Jake shrugged, knowing it would only goad her more. "Whatever you say."

Mallory threw her hands up in exasperation. "You don't honestly think you're *that* good of a player, do you?"

Jake stared at her for a moment, then held out one arm. "Prove it."

"What?" Mallory looked down at his bare arm. "Are you insane?"

Jake laughed. "As far as I'm concerned, my sanity is not the issue here. Your touch is supposed to bring doom and gloom, so prove it."

Mallory shook her head. "No way. My job is to shut down this table. I can't do that with you losing."

"You say I will lose. I say it won't make a bit of difference." He looked her straight in the eyes, challenging her. "So assuming you're right, what's the worst that can happen? I lose a few hands before you switch things back

80

the other way? What's the big deal? Unless of course, you're lying."

Mallory bit her lower lip, the indecision on her face clear as day. He knew she wanted to prove him wrong and by God, for the first time since the tournament started, he hoped she could. If only she'd touch him. Just one tiny touch. Enough to keep Silas around for another day.

"Okay," she finally agreed. "But only with one finger and just for a second. Less. Less than a second."

Jake nodded. "Whatever you say."

She stepped toward him, studying his bare arm like he might be an incendiary device. Hesitantly, she reached over with her index finger and barely brushed it over the top of his wrist.

Jake felt a tingle where her finger grazed his skin and his heart began to beat a bit faster, making him wonder if this had been such a good idea after all.

No sooner had she made contact with his skin, she yanked her hand back, almost as if burned, and looked over at him, a frightened expression on her face. She really believed. The thought struck him hard even though she'd maintained her position from the beginning.

He held his arm up in front of her. "See. It's fine. No sprain, no rash. It's not going to make a difference. You're worrying for nothing."

Apparently tired of being ridiculed, Mallory shook her head. "We'll just see about that."

Chapter Six

Before Jake could formulate a comeback to her cryptic response, the players began to arrive, and Mallory pulled out her pad to start the afternoon drink orders. When they were all seated, Mallory scanned the room and sighed. Where the hell was Father Thomas?

"I'll find him," she assured Jake.

"He's got twenty minutes to get back to the table or he forfeits half his chips to the house—your uncle's rules." Jake gave her a brief nod and turned back to the other players. "What do you say we go ahead and start? Maybe we can get in at least one hand without the Old Testament involved."

Mallory shoved the pad into her pocket and headed across the casino, hoping Father Thomas wasn't far from the liquor cabinet.

She'd been searching for the wayward priest for almost ten minutes when she finally got a lead from one of the dishwashers. "I saw him walk out the back doors onto the deck," the man said.

Good God. She hurried to the double doors at the rear

of the restaurant, hoping Father Thomas hadn't pitched off into the Gulf. Pushing the doors open, she stepped outside and scanned the deck for the priest.

He was hard to miss.

Father Thomas stood on top of a lawn chair, both arms fully extended above him, one hand clutching a Bible. "Seek first a glass of Jack Daniel's and its righteousness, and if you can't find one then seek a bottle of beer."

Mallory looked around, but there was no one to be found. Either Father Thomas was hallucinating or he thought the fish needed praying over or a drink. "Father Thomas," she said. "The game is starting. You need to get inside."

Father Thomas turned to face her and pitched backward off the lawn chair, his robes floating around him like a warped version of Batman. He hit the deck with a thud and Mallory hoped to hell he hadn't broken something or killed himself. She hurried over to the priest and bent down to see if he was alive.

Father Thomas groaned and managed to sit up. He rubbed the back of his head then gave Mallory a grin. "Must have been a heck of a homily for Satan to toss me off the altar like that."

Mallory nodded. "The absolute best, Father Thomas. In fact, it was so good that God is rewarding you with an afternoon of poker. How does that sound?"

Father Thomas gave her a huge grin. "The Lord giveth and he giveth my way." He struggled to rise from the deck and Mallory grabbed one arm to steady him, figuring she might as well give him the afternoon dose of bad luck while helping him upright. Once he was standing she guided the priest back into the restaurant and into the casino.

"It's the table in the far corner," she said, and pointed to their spot. "Do you remember? You played with them this morning."

A look of confusion momentarily crossed Father Thomas's face, but it quickly cleared and he smiled. "Oh yes, I remember," he said, and stumbled off in the direction of the table. "Praise God and pass the chips!"

Mallory watched for a second or two, just to make sure he wasn't going to fall over or stop at the wrong table; then she spun around and hurried into the restaurant for drinks, not wanting to be away from the table any longer than absolutely necessary. She knew she shouldn't have touched Jake but he was the one who'd asked for it.

The desire to prove that she wasn't the nutbag he thought she was had won out over good common sense. The only thing that made her feel a little bit better was that the touch was slight and shouldn't cause a lot of damage. Plus, Jake's argument was correct—as soon as she returned to the table and made her pass with the drinks, it would far outweigh the miniscule touch she'd given Jake.

She hadn't been gone long, but still she felt the overwhelming need to hurry back to the table to turn the luck the other way.

And to gloat.

The gloating was definitely going to be the highlight of her day. Because if Jake McMillan was agitated before when he was winning, he was going to be downright homicidal now.

She located an available server and directed him to the tray of beverages on the counter. He followed her into the casino and placed the tray on a serving stand just to the side of the poker table. Mallory struggled to hold back the grin she knew was going to break loose when she saw the look of defeat on the disgruntled dealer's face.

But Jake McMillan was smiling.

She blinked for a moment, certain she'd misunderstood. He should be losing. But there it was, a huge grin on his normally blank face.

It wasn't possible. Had her touch failed to make him unlucky? Was Jake McMillan somehow immune to her?

A quick glance at the stack of chips in front of him didn't do anything to alleviate her concerns. Not only was Jake losing, almost a forth of his chips were gone. A check of the rest of the players confirmed the worst— Silas Hebert was the big beneficiary.

What the hell was going on?

Jake had put up his own cash for this tournament just like every other dealer. Did he really want to throw away money that badly? Because at the rate he was going, he would be reduced to nothing by midafternoon. Mallory didn't even want to think of the consequences if Jake lost to Silas on the first day of the tournament. Reginald wouldn't only kill him—he'd follow him to hell and torment him personally for all of eternity.

Not that her own fate was any better. If she didn't gain back control of the table, Reginald would undoubtedly find a place even worse than hell and make sure she was a permanent resident.

Realizing there wasn't a second to spare, she grabbed the drinks and hustled them around the table, careful to make deliberate contact with every player and more than one with Silas. She totally disrupted the game with her ungraceful maneuvering, but that was just too bad. When she was satisfied that she'd done everything she could to reverse the situation, she slid back onto her stool and looked straight at the frowning face of Jake McMillan.

"If you're done with your serving, Ms. Devereaux," he said, "we'd like to continue with our play."

Before she could respond, he focused his attention on the deck and began to deal, his jaw locked tight with obvious aggravation.

It almost seemed like he'd wanted to lose.

The thought ripped across her mind in a flash, but she dismissed it as quickly as it had come. That wouldn't make any sense. Jake may not care anything about Reginald, and she was certain he didn't give two wits about her, but why would he throw away his own money?

She looked once more at the reduced pile of chips in front of Jake and across the table to Silas's larger, more impressive stack. It was her fault. That much she would take responsibility for, but it still didn't explain why Jake had seemed so happy with the situation.

Then in a flash, still shots of the day washed over her—Jake discarding a full house, Jake smiling at Silas Hebert when she returned to the table, Jake's obvious anger at her when she turned the table back the other way.

She stared across the table at him and wondered if Jake McMillan was playing for Reginald or for someone else entirely.

When the afternoon break rolled around, Silas Hebert slid off his stool and headed across the casino toward the lobby. He stepped to the side just in front of the exit doors and let the remainder of the players file past him. He reached into his pocket for a cell phone and turned back toward the tables, studying the dealer and the attendant with watchful eyes.

Something wasn't right about this tournament, of that he was sure.

The fix was on somehow, but so far, he hadn't been able to determine how they were making it happen. He'd played with the best of cheaters and if the dealer was palming cards or cutting the deck somehow, he was better than Siegfried and Roy.

He watched as the attendant, Mallory, reached across the table for the empty glasses and loaded them onto a tray. The dealer shoved the spent cards into a pile, readying them for shuffling before they continued for the afternoon. All the while, he stole glances at the attendant, an aggravated expression on his face.

And that's where Silas got confused.

If the dealer and the attendant were both in on it, they might be able to pull it off. Although he still couldn't figure out how. From her seat at the table, Mallory couldn't see anyone's hand, and the dealer had been careful to avoid placing cards while she was serving. No, everything had been conducted completely aboveboard. Plus, the tension he could sense between those two didn't at all indicate there was any way they were working together.

But he still wasn't winning.

And that just wasn't possible. The dealer was a pretty damned good card player, but not the best Silas had played. And beaten.

The woman stacked the last of the glasses on the tray and without so much as a glance at the dealer, turned and walked across the casino toward the exit on the other side. The dealer barely lifted his head from the cards as she walked away, but Silas could tell he was watching her, studying her with an intensity he didn't understand.

But he was damned well going to.

He flipped his cell phone open and punched in some numbers. As soon as the man on the other end answered, Silas began to bark out orders. "I need you to run a couple of checks for me. Man by the name of Jake McMillan. Might be the guy you were expecting. About six-two, in good shape, brown hair. Claims he's from Atlantic City.

Not sure on that part, but he's definitely a Yankee. Other one's a woman, name of Mallory Devereaux. She's Cajun and most likely lives in the area."

There was a bit of a pause on the other end and Silas could hear the rustle of pen on paper. "The guy sounds right," the other man said finally. "What am I looking for exactly on the woman?"

"Everything you can get," Silas said. "E-mail what you can, overnight the hard copy to my hotel. Once I have the info, I'll give you a call back and let you know how to proceed."

"Got it. How's the tournament going?"

"Not so good at the moment. I think that dealer and the attendant are making something happen, but I haven't been able to place how."

"This is nothing to play around with, Silas. I know you've got your reasons, but you need to consider the risks."

"I don't need you to tell me the risks. Do you think I got this far being foolish? If I can't straighten things out soon, I'll bow out, but not a moment before." He snapped the phone shut and watched as one of the other dealers opened the door next to him and strolled into the kitchen. The man nodded as he passed, and Silas wondered how much he had heard.

No matter. He couldn't have been close enough to overhear more than the last comment and that in itself wouldn't mean much. He glanced once more across the room. Jake McMillan had finished fiddling with the cards and was headed across the casino some distance behind Mallory Devereaux. His expression was a mixture of aggravation and confusion.

Silas didn't know how they were managing it, but

somehow that dealer and the woman were up to something, and there was no way he was letting a Yankee and some two-bit floozy get the best of him. He had serious business to settle with Reginald—the last of his business with the St. Claire family. And by God, he was calling that debt one way or another.

Whatever the dealer and attendant were doing, he was going to find out.

Then he was going to deal with them. His way.

Jake stepped into the lobby, hoping to get away from the rest of the casino crowd, and was relieved to find the area empty. He needed to think and think fast. He'd been dead wrong about Mallory Devereaux. Whatever the hell was wrong with her—and he still didn't want to know—it worked. Now if only she would work her magic for him again.

He paced the length of the lobby and stared out the windowed walls at the Gulf. Convincing Mallory to help him was going to be tricky. After all, she was probably just as shady as her uncle. But he would have to trust her—at least a little—or this bust was never going to happen.

"McMillan."

Jake turned. "Brad," he said, and nodded. "How's it going?" He was somewhat surprised he hadn't heard the other dealer enter the lobby.

"Not bad. I'm up about twenty K and looking for a bit more before the end of day. I've got a real amateur at my table. Me and the others are eating him alive."

"Makes it easier. That's for sure."

Brad smiled. "How about you? Based on what I heard, you must be putting it to them good."

Jake stared at Brad. "I'm doing pretty good I guess. Why? What did you hear?"

"One of your players was on his cell when I left the casino, saying as how he might cut out soon."

Jake felt the panic run through him. "Which player?" He struggled to keep his voice steady.

"That Silas dude." Brad laughed. "That's pretty damned good, man. Silas Hebert is sort of a legend in Louisiana when it comes to card playing. If you're whooping him enough to make him consider leaving the first day then I may need to get some pointers from you."

Jake nodded and tried to control his emotions. "Yeah, sure. Maybe we can talk at lunch tomorrow. Listen, I've got to run. Got a couple of things to take care of before break is over."

"No problem, man. I'll catch you at lunch tomorrow. And hey, there's a fishing rodeo this weekend if you're interested."

God help him. Jake managed to exit the lobby at a normal pace, but as soon as he was out of Brad's viewing range, he quickened his step and hurried toward the kitchen where he'd seen Mallory go when the break started.

He had a plan. It was going to be called into action a little sooner than he had expected. He just hoped like hell it worked.

Mallory hurried to the kitchen as soon as the break started, hoping Scooter knew where her uncle was hiding. She hadn't seen Reginald since lunch. Unfortunately, Scooter wasn't available either, and a dishwasher informed her that Scooter had been in the engine room since right after lunch, assuring the return trip to shore would take place as scheduled.

She considered briefly which worried her more—Jake's

ulterior motive for playing the tournament or Scooter working on the engine, but they were running too close to call.

She glanced at the clock on the wall and wondered if she had enough time left on break to accomplish anything. There were too many inconsistencies in Jake McMillan's behavior to ignore. And even though at the moment, she might not trust Reginald any further than she could throw him, she knew her uncle would crawl up Jake's butt with a microscope if he thought for even a second that the dealer wasn't doing his best to win.

At least Father Thomas hadn't said a word about her cooling ability. Mallory had inwardly cringed every time he'd opened his mouth. But for whatever reason, and Mallory was seriously considering divine intervention, the priest had stuck only to mangled Bible verses and hadn't imparted any personal secrets.

Deciding that some fresh air might help her think more clearly, she left the kitchen and stepped outside a set of sliding doors onto a small balcony. She'd barely closed the door behind her and turned to look out over the Gulf when the door slid open and Jake McMillan stepped through.

"We need to talk," he said, his voice hard, his expression serious.

Mallory studied him for a moment, then glanced inside. They were in full view of the kitchen staff, so surely he wasn't going to attempt anything stupid—like pitching her overboard.

"You're right about that," she said, and immediately made the decision to take this matter into her own hands. She could always fill in Reginald later. "What the hell is wrong with you?"

Apparently, the question was not one Jake had expected because he was taken aback for a moment. Then a hint of anger crossed his face and Mallory knew they were back on common ground. "Don't you think that's what I should be asking you?"

Mallory shook her head. "Don't give me that shit. What I really want to know is how long you've been working for Silas Hebert."

Jake stared at her, the stunned expression on his face so sincere there was no way he was faking it. "I'm not working for Silas Hebert," he finally managed to get out. "What the hell gave you that idea?"

Mallory narrowed her eyes at him. "Nothing special, except the fact that you're throwing hands, and you were all excited when you started losing to Silas, then angry when I reversed the luck."

She studied him for a moment more, then blew out a breath. "Whether you're working for him or not—and the jury is still out on that one—if you lose Reginald's money to Silas Hebert, there's the possibility you won't be around to tell about it. Do you understand what I'm saying?"

Jake stared at her in surprise. "I knew your uncle was kind of shady, but what you're suggesting is a lot more dangerous."

"I'm not saying I know for sure. But there's always been rumors . . . I just don't know what's true and what's bluff."

"But you aren't willing to run the risk."

"Hell, no."

Jake looked out over the open water and ran one hand through his hair. Finally, he turned back to her. "Look, I'm not interested in losing anything, especially to Silas Hebert. I hate the man for a list of reasons I don't have time to explain. But I don't want him to leave this tournament without losing more money. And if he doesn't ever win a hand, that's exactly what he's going to do."

"You see, that's part of my problem. You're not even from here, so how in the world do you even know who Silas Hebert is? It doesn't add up, Jake."

"There's not enough time to explain everything now. I promise, I'll tell you what you need to know as soon as we finish playing today. But you've got to trust me on this. I need Silas to stay in this tournament—at least for a little while longer."

Mallory studied Jake's face, but she couldn't get a read on him. She thought he was telling the truth, at least in part, but a big hunk of important material was missing from his story. Trust him. How in the world did he think she was going to manage that? The list of people Mallory trusted could be counted by a three-year-old.

And now a veritable stranger, who had given her every indication that he was up to no good, had asked her without any explanation to place her future in his hands.

"I'm sorry, Jake," Mallory said finally. "I can't afford to let Silas win, not even short-term. My job here is to shut down the table. Otherwise, Reginald pays me nothing. And I have to have the money. This week. I don't have any other options. I can't trust you."

"Then don't," Jake said, frustrated. "But I'm telling you, I can explain everything. All I ask is that you don't get me removed from the tournament before we have a chance to talk."

Mallory studied him again. "Fine," she finally said, knowing that in the end, she had ultimate control of the table. "I won't talk to Reginald until after I've talked to you. But you better have a pretty compelling reason for wanting Silas Hebert to win money, even if only for a moment."

Jake gave her a grim nod. "The reasons are compelling enough, and you'll get your explanation, but not before I get what I came out here for."

Before she could respond to his cryptic words, Jake grabbed her shoulders and lowered his head to hers. His lips pressed against hers with an energy she'd never felt before—an energy that raced through every square inch of her body.

Her mouth responded as if completely separate from her mind, because certainly this wasn't a good idea, but damned if she could remember a reason why not. His lips parted and hers went right along with him, their tongues mingling in a sensual dance that made her moan. Her silk blouse brushed against her hardened nipples and the heat began to rise, first in her center, then spreading throughout her body.

Jake pulled her closer and she felt his erection brush against her. The contact was slight, but enough to make him tense up and pause.

Suddenly, he dropped his hands and stepped away from her. The desire on his face was plain as day, and Mallory could tell his self-control was as precarious as her own, body warring with mind in the endless battle of whether this was a good idea or a really bad one that felt like a really good one at the moment.

He stared at her for a moment, indecisive, then shoved the sliding door open and slipped inside, never even looking back.

She watched him, the heat from her body still radiating out every pore. Well, that definitely honked up the afternoon play. Nothing short of molesting the other players was going to level the playing field after that kiss. She ought to be angry, but instead she smiled. Jake McMillan had thought he'd grab a quick kiss to ensure a run of bad luck this afternoon. He'd thought he was being sneaky, but he'd gotten far more than he bargained for.

Apparently, Mallory had just come in contact with the only human being in the world who ignored basic attraction as much as she did. That kiss had been an eye-opening experience and the passion of it, while it had shaken her a bit, had obviously confused the hell out of Jake. Which not only gave her the upper hand, it made the rest of the week look far more interesting.

Chapter Seven

Jake barely managed to hold it together for the remainder of the day. Oh, the play went all right. He was smart enough to know not to jump into any high-stakes pots, and quite frankly, he didn't have a hand all afternoon to even warrant the ante. Whatever Mallory Devereaux served with a mere touch, it was strong medicine.

He'd witnessed that whole spaghetti incident at lunch with Walter Royal, but hadn't recalled that shaking hands with Mallory had immediately preceded the entire event until now. Good Lord. A mere handshake had completely destroyed four dinner servings, a metal dining table, and a really bad imitation Italian suit.

And he'd kissed her.

A scary thought when he had no idea how long the effect would last and he still needed to drive safely to the motel after the play ended for the day. God help him, now he was worried about driving a car—something he'd been doing for over eighteen years.

What else was there to consider? The stairs with the

loose handrail at the motel, using his laptop, walking and chewing gum? The list could go on forever. Heck, even a trip to the men's room could turn into a disaster if he wasn't careful.

What in the world had he gotten himself into?

As the players filed out of the room, Jake placed the chips in the racks and slid them on the shelf under the table. He'd hoped to catch Mallory as soon as the players had left, but she'd gone into her table-cleaning routine and had followed the tray carrier into the restaurant. It figured. Just when he needed the woman to stick around, she'd gone off to take care of something as stupid as dirty dishes.

Not even bothering to hold in a sigh, he reached for the spent cards and the shoe. As he lifted the shoe from the table, a piece of paper appeared from beneath. Jake stared at the paper and frowned. Where had that come from?

He lifted the paper from the table, unfolded it and was surprised to find a message from Mallory.

We can't talk at the casino. Too many eyes and ears. I'll meet you at your motel room at 8:00.—M

Jake glanced around the room, relieved to find it empty. No one had seen him read the note. Obviously Mallory Devereaux was smarter than he'd given her credit for and her sleight-of-hand wasn't bad either.

So eight o'clock it was. But this time, no more kisses. Hell, he wasn't even going to stand close to her. It wasn't worth the risk—especially not with a room on the second floor of a sixty-year-old motel.

Jake finished clearing the table and grabbed his car keys. He'd just walked off the boarding ramp and into the parking lot when he saw Mallory get into her truck and back up. The big lettering on the side read:

HARRY BREAUX DEMOLITION
FOREMAN—MALLORY DEVEREAUX

Jake did a double take and read the lettering again as she turned to exit the parking lot. Demolition? Okay, so given her propensity for disaster, maybe it made sense, but foreman? A title like that meant Mallory Devereaux wasn't some full-time two-bit floozy, shaking her boobs and screwing men out of money at her uncle's poker table. She had a legitimate job and probably a pretty good one, based on his limited knowledge of his uncle's construction business.

So why was she moonlighting as a card bimbo?

A good question and one he wanted an answer to before he met with her tonight. Out on the balcony, she'd said she had to have the money this week. But why? Leverage was always a useful thing. It might be considered playing dirty, but at this point Jake really didn't care. If Mallory Devereaux had any reason for playing in this tournament, other than picking up some quick cash to replace dishes or whatever other mishaps she managed on a regular basis, he was going to find out what it was.

And he knew just the place to hear all about it.

J.T.'s Bar wasn't exactly the type of place Jake usually frequented. But then when it came right down to it, the only place Jake frequented that didn't have anything to do with his job was his condo in Jersey. Bars were loud and filled with smoke and women looking for you to pick them up. Shopping centers were full of harried moms and screaming kids. Neither was his cup of tea. Too much noise, too much activity.

Too much neediness.

And ultimately, it was the neediness that kept Jake from mixing with so-called normal society. His job was far from the norm and the last thing he wanted was someone waiting up late for the phone to ring, or staring at the front door waiting on him to walk through it.

He was only a kid when his mom had put him to bed that night, so many years ago. She'd done her best to pretend that everything was normal, but he knew it even then. Something was terribly wrong. He remembered sitting in his bed, covers wrapped around him, waiting for his father to walk through the front door, for his mom to kiss him when he walked into the house, waiting for his father to sneak into Jake's bedroom and ruffle his hair.

He was still waiting.

No way in hell was he going to put someone he loved in that position. So right now, that meant not loving at all. Even friends had gotten more difficult as the years passed. His schedule was never regular—he could be gone months at a time, and since he took discretion about his cases as serious as death, he found he didn't really have much to contribute to general conversation. Maybe if the conversation was about the latest in firearms or high-tech surveillance equipment, he'd have something to say, but how many "regular" guys sat around talking about guns and listening devices?

Although, now that he thought about it, that whole gun conversation would probably go over big in Royal Flush.

He pulled into the parking lot of the bar and stared at the gray metal building with the bright red lettering. His partner Mark had been the only person he'd call more than an acquaintance, and that was because they understood each other—knew intimately what the other did every day for a living. The pressure of the job wasn't just about catching the bad guys but learning how to deal with ones who got away.

And the victims.

The live ones were the worst, he'd decided. It was hard to deal with murder—hard to face the families. But living victims were a walking, talking testimony to the failure of mankind to take care of its own. The failure of law enforcement to protect those weaker and unable to protect themselves.

Granted, there was no way to catch all perpetrators, but sometimes he wondered if what he did made a difference at all. Did his putting those ten or twenty criminals behind bars save lives, or did it just open a job position for the next criminal to step into? It sometimes seemed to Jake that he made a bigger impact with the youth program he volunteered for. He may only be able to measure the difference he made one child at a time, but at least it was there for him to see.

They were questions he'd been asking himself a lot lately, and somehow that bothered him more than anything else. He'd always thought he needed to follow in his father's footsteps—protect the innocent, like his mother, from all the bad that was out there. He'd never considered the preventive maintenance that could be done on the front end. But chasing the likes of Silas Hebert for so many years had made him question the amount of time spent and people used to pursue one man. Granted Silas Hebert was a big gun and ran a huge organization, but the reality was, putting him in jail wouldn't alleviate the problem—it would only alleviate the problem from that one man.

He turned off the ignition and took one final look at

the bar. Mallory Devereaux was probably the type of woman who had friends. And if she worked construction, there was little doubt in his mind that he would find some of those friends in this bar. The question was, would they talk to him?

There was only one way to get an answer.

At first, he was surprised to find so many people in a bar on a Monday night, but then Royal Flush wasn't exactly a cultural mecca, so he supposed the locals took what they could get. What they could get was a metal building with a cement floor, country music playing a little too loud and enough cigarette smoke to get a contact high in a neighboring state. He'd barely stepped inside the door before he was jostled around by a group of men headed for the pool tables.

Realizing he needed to find a seat or be steamrolled by local linebackers, he scanned the bar and spotted an empty stool at the far end. Squinting a bit in the dim light, he studied the guy on the stool next to the empty one. He looked familiar, but it took a minute for Jake to place him. Then he remembered, this guy was on the boat all day, but wasn't a player. In fact, the only thing Jake had noticed he did was drink beer. Granted he'd consumed an admirable amount if the stack of spent bottles in the lobby was any indication—sort of a leaning tower of beer arrangement on a coffee table. Obviously he'd needed more.

Which was fine by Jake. Drunks were usually easier to get information from, and since he'd seen Mallory sitting with the marathon beer drinker and another dealer at lunch, he had to assume this guy knew her. Maybe well enough to cough up some information. Mind made up, he began to thread his way through the clusters of bodies, the mingling of smoke and cheap perfume almost knocking him out.

He was only a couple of steps from his destination when the heel on his dress shoe decided to take a leave of absence. As the shoe, now sans any rubber treading, hit the polished concrete, he promptly slid a good foot farther than he was actually stepping. Jake put one hand down on the table next to him, trying to steady himself, and managed to dip his fingers in a very agitated-looking woman's Bloody Mary.

Apologizing profusely, he took a twenty from his wallet and presented it to the woman. Her companion, a guy resembling a cross between a WWF performer and a Harley biker, grabbed the money and glared at him. Taking the hint, he located his missing heel and stuck it in his pocket, then hobbled like a one-legged man over to the bar. It took him a while to make it, but at least there were no more disasters along the way, and the stool was still empty when he got there.

Taking a good look at the legs of the stool, he pressed down on the back of it before pulling it out and sitting. He took a second to ascertain that no more mishaps were in the works, then nodded to the guy next to him. The guy stared at him for a moment, confused, then smiled.

"Hey," he said, and pointed a finger at Jake. "You're the dealer at Mallory's table. I saw you when everyone was leaving."

Jake nodded and extended his hand to the other man. "My name's Jake."

The other man grabbed his hand and shook it, surprising Jake with his viselike grip. "I'm Scooter. I'm the maintenance man for this tournament." He gave Jake a big grin. "Mostly I'm maintaining a buzz. Lucky nothing's broke yet. Well except the engine, but that was no big deal."

There was an encouraging thought, Jake decided. They were on a pit of a boat, out in the middle of the Gulf of

Mexico, surrounded by criminals, and the drunken idiot in front of him was whom they were depending on to get them back and forth to dock. The same man who thought a broken engine on a boat cruising approximately two hundred miles offshore was no big deal. The labor pool in this town was seriously lacking.

Scooter stopped smiling and studied Jake for a couple of seconds. "You feeling all right now?" he asked, "'cause I ain't got time for a cold or nothing. There's a big fishing rodeo next weekend."

Jake stared at the man, uncertain what to say. He hadn't been sick at all and wondered what had given the other man that idea. At the same time and for some ungodly reason, he found himself really wanting to know what the heck a fishing "rodeo" consisted of, since that was the second time that day he'd heard the expression. But he wasn't about to ask. "I don't understand what you're asking," he said, deciding to stick with the more familiar of the two items. "I'm not sick and haven't been."

Scooter scrunched up his brow in thought. "Damn women never make any sense. You see, at lunch, Amy was saying as how you was hot and Mallory said you was hot but you was kinda an asshole."

He scratched his head, then continued, "So I said if you was hot, I had an extra fan in the engine room that I could put at your table. They just laughed. I thought it was kinda rude and all if you were uncomfortable, but sometimes women are just funny."

Jake stared at Scooter, certain the man was another species. No one could be that stupid. Not even in Royal Flush. Something told Jake he wouldn't get any useful information out of Scooter. "Yeah, women can be a mystery," Jake finally said. "But to answer your question, I feel fine." Fine for an asshole.

Scooter nodded. "Well, you let me know if you get hot again and I'll fetch you that fan. Summer colds are a bitch." With that Scooter jumped off his stool and hurried across the bar to a dartboard, calling out to someone as he went.

Jake stared after Scooter a moment more, then lifted one finger for the bartender. Someone in this town had to have evolved beyond the primates. Maybe he could get the information he was looking for from the bartender.

The bartender shuffled over, eyeing Jake from top to bottom. "You visiting?" he asked.

Jake shook his head. "No. I'm dealing in the poker tournament."

The bartender studied him a moment more, not looking entirely convinced. "You're wanting me to believe Reginald hired a Yankee to deal for him?" He laughed. "C'mon, man. You can do better than that."

Jake stared at the man, trying to hold in his frustration with small towns and small minds. "I've barely said five words to you. What indication could you possibly have that I am a Yankee?"

The bartender smirked. "Well, we could start with the words 'what indication.' Someone from south of the Mason-Dixon would have said, 'Who the hell are you calling a Yankee?' Then we would have fought."

Jake held in a sigh. "I'm not looking for a fight. I just wanted to relax a bit before I head back to my motel. It's been a long day."

The bartender studied him a moment more, then nodded. "I guess that's all right then. But mind you, I serve alcohol and beer here. No club soda with lime, no shaken not stirred, no drinks without alcohol. You sit at my bar, you drink like a man. So what's it gonna be?"

"Jack Daniel's on the rocks."

"Then I guess I'll be letting you stay," the bartender

said, and walked to the back of the bar to fix the drink.

Now Jake did sigh. He hadn't intended to throw any back before his meeting with Mallory. The reality was, Jake rarely drank at all. He never wanted his senses less than 100 percent, because he never knew when the phone might ring. There were no real holidays or days off with the FBI—every day was a potential workday, no matter what the schedule might say.

Now he was sitting in a bar in the middle of Hicksville, slowly dying of lung cancer, and his manhood had been put into question based on the selection of his drink. And he'd fallen for it. But if he'd have thrown out "light beer" like he'd been tempted to do, he was afraid the bartender would have removed him right then or just shot him where he sat.

He was thirty-five years old, with a college education and a good pension some years down the line, and he'd just succumbed to peer pressure from a redneck.

Maybe he did need that drink.

The bartender slid the glass in front of him and stood there staring, probably waiting to make sure he was really going to drink it and not pour it under the bar like a five-year-old. Jake reached for the glass and took a strong swig, careful to keep from wincing at the bitterness of the liquor. He sat the glass back on the counter, but kept his hand wrapped around it, just so the bartender would know he wasn't done.

"Name's J.T.," the bartender said. "You're sitting in my bar."

Jake extended his hand across the counter. "I'm Jake McMillan."

J.T. stared at his hand for a moment, then finally shook it. The bartender's grip was as strong as Scooter's, and Jake fought the urge to shake some blood back into his fingers when the man released his hand. The men in this town had grips that would take the jaws of life to pry them loose and just for a moment, Jake wondered what the heck they did in their spare time.

J.T. twisted the top off two beers and slid them down the counter, then placed his elbows on the bar, leaning toward Jake. "So how did a Yankee hear about a private poker tournament all the way in Royal Flush? The town ain't even on a map. Hell, most of Louisiana don't even know we're here."

Jake shrugged. "I've got a buddy who runs a craps table in New Orleans. I'm visiting him for a bit, so he gave me the tip."

J.T. smiled. "And you thought you'd dash down here and make some quick money off a bunch of hicks, right? How's that working out for you?"

"Not bad. I had some good hands today. Hopefully, I'll come out okay by the end of the week."

"Maybe. Maybe not. Those are no lightweights you're playing against, but then I guess it didn't take you long to figure that one out. Who's your main competition?"

Jake took another swig of his drink, not really wanting to answer the question, but not seeing any way out of it if he wanted to turn the conversation around to Mallory. "There's a man named Silas who seems pretty good."

The bartender shook his head in dismay. "Silas Hebert is playing in the tournament? I should have known Reginald wouldn't leave well enough alone." He paused for a moment, seeming deep in thought, then finally continued. "Well, if you're thinking of winning any money off Silas Hebert, you might want to stick around for a while, order up another drink, and let me give you a reality check."

"Ah, shoot," Scooter broke in as he hopped back on his stool, "he ain't got nothing to worry about. Mallory's cooling his table."

The bartender stared at Scooter for a moment, in obvious disbelief. Then his face flushed red and when he spoke, his tone was barely controlled anger. "God damn it, Scooter. You're telling me Reginald put Mallory on Silas Hebert? That son of a bitch. I knew this whole mess would come to nothing but trouble, but you had to go and tell her about it." He banged a fist on the bar, causing Scooter to jump. "Damn it, Scooter. Sometimes you don't have the sense God gave a goose."

Jake studied the men with interest. J.T. was mad as a hornet, and Scooter had dropped his gaze down to the bar, not looking the other man in the eye, the guilt on his face clear as day. Scooter was going to be picking up his own six-pack for a while after this tournament was over.

"What's wrong with Silas Hebert?" Jake asked. "Is there something I need to know?"

J.T. turned back to Jake and threw his arms up in exasperation. "Hell, yeah, there's something you ought to know. But telling you would take all night." He leaned over the bar toward Jake and lowered his voice. "Let me give you the short run."

Jake nodded and leaned in toward J.T., who looked both ways, apparently making sure he wasn't overheard. "Silas Hebert is a plague on Louisiana. Hell, on humanity is more accurate. What he can't buy, he takes. What he can't earn legitimately, he steals. More than one holdout from a Silas Hebert offer has turned up at the bottom of the bayou and lo and behold, their heirs are always eager to sell."

Jake forced a surprised look on his face, hoping like hell J.T. bought it, because so far, the man hadn't told him anything he didn't already know. "Why isn't he in jail?"

J.T. waved a hand in dismissal. "Man's got half of Louisiana on his payroll. Besides, you think he'd actually get caught with his hands dirty? Silas Hebert has enough money to convince most people to strangle their own mothers in their sleep. Two-bit hoods are a dime a dozen. He's not lacking bad guys to carry out his work."

Jake nodded, only too aware of Silas's two-bit hoods. "Then I'm surprised someone hasn't testified against him for immunity. I understand that it's easy for him to find people to do his dirty work, but they can't be all that smart if they're working for hire so easily."

J.T. looked Jake straight in the eye. "They'd have to actually make it to trial before that could happen, now wouldn't they? Dead men don't tell tales."

Jake took another gulp of his drink and processed what J.T. was saying. Apparently, Silas's reputation was no big secret in Louisiana. And while the evidence—or witnesses—might be lacking, no one seemed to have trouble believing that Silas Hebert was capable of the urban legend that surrounded him. "Why in the world would Reginald St. Claire invite someone like that to play? I mean, I got the impression there was some bad blood between them. If this Silas is such a bad guy, why have him there?"

J.T. shook his head in obvious disgust. "I have no earthly idea, but whatever the reason, it can't be good. Reginald St. Claire and Silas Hebert hate each other more than any two human beings on earth. If Reginald has Silas at his tournament, he's up to no good—*that* I guarantee you.

"And since this idiot here," J.T. continued, waving one hand at Scooter, "went and told Mallory about the tournament, now I have to worry about what the hell she's in the middle of."

"I wondered why she was working there," Jake said. "It said on her truck she's a foreman for a demolition company. Why would someone with a good, legitimate job want to be part of this? I know Reginald is her uncle, he said so himself, but that only means she should know better than to mix up with him."

J.T. nodded. "Mallory knows exactly what her uncle is, and God knows, I tried to talk her out of this tomfoolery, but she had some personal business she needed taken care of, and she saw this as her only way."

What personal business? Jake studied J.T., trying to figure out how to broach the question without looking suspicious. Obviously the man had a close relationship with Mallory—father figure, maybe? Boyfriend seemed a bit odd given the age difference, and J.T. didn't act like a man protecting a lover. He was just about to take a chance and ask outright, when Scooter decided to join the conversation again.

"C'mon, J.T.," Scooter said. "You need to cut Mallory a break. If she doesn't get that money for the IRS by next week, Harry's going to lose the business to Walter Royal, and Royal came right out at lunch today and told her to start looking for another job."

Jake stared at J.T., suddenly understanding the reason behind the spaghetti incident. No wonder she'd put the whammy on him. Of course, it sounded like the jackass had it coming, but despite all that, Jake made a mental note not to get on Mallory's bad side.

J.T. cut his eyes at Scooter. "There are worse things to be than unemployed. And keep your discussing of people's personal business to yourself. It's bad enough Father Thomas can't keep his lips zipped. This town doesn't need two drunken fools."

Scooter stared down at the bar again, looking like a chastised child, but he didn't say another word.

J.T. turned back to Jake and studied him for a moment.

"I know you don't know me from Adam, but I'm gonna ask something of you anyway." He reached into his pocket, pulled out a business card and handed it to Jake. "That's my home, business and cell phone numbers. If there's any trouble, any trouble at all, you call me."

Jake took the card and nodded. He was just about to put it in his shirt pocket when J.T. grabbed his arm, preventing him from moving. The bartender looked Jake straight in the eye, his expression serious and deadly. "Mallory is like a daughter to me," he said. "I'll do anything to protect her. Anything. No matter who I have to roll over. Do you understand?"

Jake studied the man in front of him, no doubt in his mind that the last words he'd uttered were the absolute truth. If something happened to Mallory Devereaux, somebody would undoubtedly be posting bail for J.T.

Mallory was obviously a woman who'd earned love and respect from people she wasn't even related to. People she wasn't sleeping with. That said a lot about someone, he thought. It also made using her a little more difficult but certainly not impossible.

After a quick change into her usual jeans and T-shirt, it took nothing more than a phone call to J.T.'s and a quick conversation with Raelynn to find out where Jake was staying. Mallory had left the note under the card shoe because she hadn't wanted to risk talking to him at any length at the casino, and she figured the local gossip had already run the gamut on the new good-looking guy in town and where he was holed up.

Raelynn informed Mallory that Jake had taken a room at the Royal Flush Motel for ten days starting last Thursday and had paid up front in cash. He drank a ton of Dr Pepper, but apparently no liquor—at least not at the motel—and he didn't smoke or order porn on the motel television. His shirts were all recently ironed and hung in the closet according to color.

So far women had hit on him at both Cindy's Café and Lucy's Catfish Kitchen, covering everything from breakfast to dinner, but he hadn't bitten so far. In fact, his incredible disinterest had offended several of the women of Royal Flush who were more accustomed to getting their way with men. They'd finally decided that perhaps Jake McMillan didn't prefer women. Based on the kiss they'd shared at the casino, and Jake's subsequent reaction, Mallory knew different but she wasn't about to point out to Raelynn that the other women's grumblings were nothing more than sour grapes.

It was just before 8:00 P.M. when Mallory pulled into the motel parking lot. Jake's rental car was parked in front of the building at the far end. It had been easy to spot because it was the only one on that side of the lot. Unless bass were running hot or it was duck-hunting season, the motel never did a booming business. But apparently Jake McMillan had still gone out of his way to get a room at the very end of the motel and away from any of the few other patrons.

She scanned the cars on the other side of the lot and let out a breath of relief. Definitely none of the banged-up pickups belonged to any of the players. Not that she'd figured any of those men would stay at the Royal Flush Motel. She'd already heard several of them mention getting together for drinks later at a luxury hotel between Royal Flush and New Orleans and figured that was where the vast majority of the out-of-towners had congregated. After all, it put them closer to their creature comforts— easy hustling and even easier women.

She turned to the left and parked her car a couple of

spots down from Jake's, next to a pole with a burned-out light. If anyone got close enough, they'd still know it was her truck—the HARRY BREAUX DEMOLITION sign on the side sort of gave that one away. But from a distance, perhaps no one would pay attention.

Once more, she scanned the parking lot, making extra sure it was uninhabited, then pushed open her truck door and stepped outside. She'd no sooner slammed the door shut on her truck than the parking lot light above her flickered on, illuminating a forty-square-foot area and putting her truck directly under a spotlight.

Cussing under her breath, she hopped back in the truck and backed out of the spotlight to the edge of light mingling with the cast from the next lamp post. As she switched off the ignition, the first light went out again. It figured.

Just in case the light was planning on coming to life again, she jumped out of the truck and hurried across the lot and up the rickety stairs to the door in the far corner of the building. So far, no one had seen her arrival, and that's the way she wanted to keep it.

Her mind was racing with the possibilities of Jake's revelation and what it might be, and she was somewhat surprised at just how nervous she was about facing him again.

This is going to be fine. He's just going to tell you what he's up to and you can decide what you want to do about it. He's probably not a serial killer.

At that thought, she stopped short. Stupid, stupid, stupid. What the hell did she really know about Jake McMillan? And here she was at a secluded motel, meeting a man who obviously wanted her out of the way. It was worse than a cheap horror movie. And she was the one who insisted that they meet here. She was also the one who thought it was a good idea to keep their meeting a secret—at least until she found out what Jake had to say.

So the reality was no one knew she was coming here. And if she disappeared, no one would know why.

Apparently that kiss had made her completely lose her sensibilities—and survival instinct. She looked at the door, a mere five feet away, and blew out a breath. Stay or go. It should have been an easy choice. She should spin so fast she broke an ankle, then hobble as fast as possible back to her truck and drive far, far away from Jake McMillan.

But then everyone had always said she was hardheaded.

Her instincts were rarely wrong and her impression of Jake was that she annoyed him, confused him, but in no way had she ever felt threatened by him. Determined not to change her mind, she made the five steps to the door and raised her hand to knock. Before her knuckles made contact, the door was yanked open and she stared directly into the angry face of Jake McMillan.

Chapter Eight

"Are you going to stand out there all night?" he asked. "You're drawing attention."

Mallory glanced over her shoulder at the parking lot. Empty. "Who exactly am I drawing attention from—the mosquitoes?"

"Just get inside," he ordered, and stepped back from the doorway so she could enter.

She'd taken one step inside the door when she saw the gun peeking out of the band of his jeans. Before she could retreat, Jake grabbed her arm, yanked her into the room and slammed the door behind her, positioning himself between her and the only exit.

"What the hell is wrong with you?" he asked.

This is it. I'm going to die and I'm not wearing underwear— or a bra. Jesus, she'd be talked about for the next hundred years.

"Hel-lo!" Jake's voice boomed. "I asked what the hell is wrong with you?"

It was too late for caution. Might as well try the truth.

"You have a gun," Mallory said, and pointed to his waist-band.

Jake threw his hands up in the air in obvious exaspera-tion. "Of course I have a gun. Don't tell me you don't own a gun." He paused for a moment and frowned. "Okay, maybe given your *situation* you don't own a gun, but a lot of people do."

"I have a gun," Mallory said, irritated that her tone was a bit defensive. "But I don't wear it on me."

"That's because with the clothes you wear, there's no place to put it." Jake reached into his pocket, pulled out his wallet, then flipped it over and showed her the identi-fication inside. "I'm FBI. I have a license to carry, and short of your uncle's casino and showering, this gun is al-ways on my body."

The unbidden picture of Jake in the shower flashed across Mallory's mind. There was definitely a weapon in-volved in the visual, but it wasn't the gun in his waist-band. Shaking away the thought, she tried to concentrate on what he'd just said because it was the last thing she'd expected to hear.

"FBI? What in the world does the FBI want with my uncle?"

Jake raised one hand in protest. "We don't want any-thing from your uncle, although given his list of friends, I'm sure there would be plenty to find."

"Reginald's no saint, but he's relatively small-time as far as I know. His crimes don't extend beyond Royal Flush, well, and probably New Orleans, but the FBI would hardly be interested in my uncle's taste for women of the night."

Jake grimaced. "I don't even want to think about it."

"Then who are you after, and does Reginald know who you are?"

Jake shook his head. "No. Reginald doesn't know and he can't find out. Regardless of your relationship with your uncle, he can't be trusted and I can't afford a leak."

"But you think I can be trusted? Aren't you taking a big chance, Agent McMillan—if that's even your real name?"

His expression shifted ever so slightly at her last statement, and Mallory knew she'd hit on the truth. She didn't know a single thing about the man in front of her, except that he claimed to be FBI and he was using an assumed name.

Jake stared at her for a moment, then sighed. "I'm taking a huge chance. One that could cost me my job and other things far more important, but I'm out of choices. I have to bust Silas Hebert. We both want the same thing—in a manner of speaking—it's just that my way is going to take a little longer. I need your help if this is going to work. And you need me to win if you're going to get the money you need for the tax note."

Mallory blinked in surprise. "How did you know about the tax note?"

"I heard it at J.T.'s Bar this evening. I figured nothing in this town was a secret for very long and if you were working the tournament, someone at the bar would know why. I had to know where you stood on all this before I could confide in you."

Mallory sighed. "The joys of living in a small town." She shook her head, then focused back on Jake. "What does the FBI want with Silas Hebert? Not that I care, mind you. I'd love to see him arrested for anything, but why now? Why this tournament?"

Jake's expression hardened and his mouth set in a thin line. "I can't tell you everything. Hell, I'm not supposed to tell you anything at all, but I will say this—the FBI wants to bust Silas for money laundering and counterfeiting. We have reason to believe he's been laundering counterfeit cash through casinos for years. Dealing is the only way I have a chance of getting my hands on cash directly from Silas. Once it's put into a casino system, we have no way of proving the funny money came from him."

Mallory felt as if she'd been hit by a truck. Money laundering? Counterfeiting? Surely it wasn't possible, but if what Jake said were true, it all made sense. And meant that the last time her father had gone to prison, he might have been telling the truth when he said he hadn't done the crime. A flood of emotions ran through her, and she struggled to maintain a normal expression. The last person she felt like discussing her embarrassing family with was Jake.

She cleared her throat and tried to make her voice as controlled as possible. "So that's why you need Silas to win some of the hands. If he leaves too soon, you won't be able to collect more buy-in money. But if he still thinks he has a chance to win it back—"

"—he'll continue to play. Another dealer, Brad, overheard Silas this afternoon saying he might leave early. If he does, everything is over for me." Jake paced a couple of steps across the room, then back again. "We both want the same thing. My way is just more subtle. That's why I need you to turn down the volume, or whatever it takes to bring me to a more normal playing level."

Despite her shock at Jake's earlier revelation, Mallory couldn't hold back the smile that crept across her lips, "So you're finally willing to admit that I *do* have the ability to cool cards?"

Jake ran one hand through his hair and stared past her at the wall. "Yeah, all right, I'll definitely give you that something weird happens if you touch people. I don't know how, and quite frankly, I don't want to. I just need you to control it so I can do my job."

Mallory frowned and sank down on the edge of the bed. "Do you think it's that easy? Jesus Christ, Jake, if I could just turn it on and off like a faucet, my life wouldn't be the miserable wreck it usually is."

Jake blinked and stared at her. "You don't have any control? You mean to tell me you've made it to adulthood walking around as a ticking time bomb?"

"Basically, and I'd really appreciate it if you could skip the reminders. I don't need them. I live it. I know how it is."

Jake plopped down on an ottoman near the dresser. "Wow. That wasn't what I expected to hear at all. I thought you worked up the whammy, touched someone, and then it was all over but the crying."

"I wish. If it were so easy to direct, I would keep it from coming back on me." She let out a big sigh and shook her head. "Did they tell you at the bar that I have a master's degree in civil engineering?"

Jake stared at her in obvious surprise. "Then why in the world . . ."

"Don't I work for some big construction company in New Orleans constructing office buildings and churches?" She let out a single laugh. "Yeah, that would have been great. And don't think I didn't try, but when the insurance company refuses to underwrite a site as long as you're an employee, it cuts down a bit on job opportunities."

Jake stared at her a moment. "Oh, man, that sucks."

"And that is why I do demolition. It seems my natural ability lies in destroying things, not creating them."

Jake shook his head. "I don't even know what to say. I never thought about this being beyond your control. Hell, the truth is, I don't really want to think about it at all. It crosses into a territory I don't know anything about and have never believed in. It's a lot to take in at one time." He rubbed one hand across his jaw. "I guess I just

118

went for the simpler reason for the demolition job. I figured since you were friends with the owner, you worked for him. At least, that's what it sounded like at the bar."

"Harry's more than a friend. My mother took off when I was thirteen. Dad was in prison again, one of his many visits. Reginald talked to Harry and his wife and they took me in and raised me as their own. No questions, no government handouts, nothing. Just like that, I had the home I could never have gotten from my own parents."

Jake gave her a curious look. "Why didn't Reginald keep you himself?"

"It's a difficult situation all the way around, but the truth of the matter was, Reginald didn't want me raised around his business. I guess he figured the only way I had a chance to break the criminal cycle was to go to a home where people made their money legitimately." She shrugged. "He's helped me along, you know, but he's always maintained somewhat of a distance from me. I think he worried that I would follow in my parents' footsteps."

"And all of that is why getting the money for the tax note is so important to you."

"My whole life depends on getting this money. Without Harry's business, I have no future."

"And without getting an exchange of cash, I can't bust Silas. Somehow we have to find a way to make them both work."

Mallory shook her head, wanting to help Jake bust Silas, now more than ever, but too afraid to gamble what was at stake. "It's too risky. Even if I tried to swing the table, Silas is too good. He'll capitalize at the right time and never go in for more than he can afford to lose on the downswing."

"I'm way better than an average player," Jake protested, "and I've been preparing for this a long time."

"Look, I'm not trying to insult you, but the reality is, you're out of your league. Silas has been hustling people for years. Maybe you just need to wait for the next opportunity and try again. I'd be willing to help if you could arrange it. Anytime—you just let me know where to be."

Jake jumped off the ottoman and started pacing again, his face filled with frustration and indecision. "Look, our source indicated that Silas will be leaving the country after this tournament—for good. If we want any chance of taking him down, it has to be now."

Mallory heard the strain in his voice and knew this wasn't just a ploy from Jake to get her to help. "Maybe your source was mistaken. Can you check again?" His source had to be wrong. Everything couldn't come down to the next four days. It just couldn't.

Jake shook his head, the look on his face pure misery. "The source was my partner, Mark. He was undercover in Silas's organization and went missing about a month ago. If we don't bust Silas now, I may never know what happened to him. His wife and kid may never know what happened to him."

Mallory sucked in a breath. She couldn't imagine the thought of Scooter or Amy disappearing and her never knowing what had happened. Never being allowed to fully grieve. And as much as she loved them, neither of them was her spouse or a parent.

Her mind immediately flashed to Harry. He may not be her biological father, but he'd filled all the other requirements and those were the important ones. How would she feel if Harry was to disappear and she never knew why? If she and Thelma lived the rest of their lives not knowing?

"Are there other agents looking for your partner?"

Jake nodded. "Yeah, we've traced the location of every call he made to the agency and canvassed those areas, but we've come up with nothing. We have agents placed at both of Silas's homes with listening devices, infrared cameras, the works. It's like he disappeared into thin air. I was hoping to find some leads during the tournament, you know, someplace to look that the FBI couldn't trace back to Silas, but he's barely talked at all and when he has, it's only been about cards."

"I'll help you," Mallory said, before she could change her mind, "but it has to be on my terms."

The relief on Jake's face was apparent. "All right. How do you want to do it?"

Mallory thought for a moment. "We can't really risk being caught together at the tournament. That kissing stunt you pulled today could easily have been seen by Reginald, and he would have thrown you out on your ear."

"Maybe," Jake agreed, and Mallory gave him a hard stare. "Okay," he said, "more like certainly, but we still have to find a way to shift things. I can't keep throwing hands or Reginald's likely to notice the same as you."

"Okay. How long did the kiss take to wear off?"

"How would I know?"

"When bad things stopped happening. What's the last bit of bad luck you can remember?"

Jake considered this for a second. "My watch stopped at the casino, the heel came completely off my shoe at the bar, I got a flat tire on the way to the motel, and I cut myself shaving about thirty minutes ago—but I always do." He shrugged. "How do I know what's you versus regular life?"

Mallory smiled. "I'm hell on watches. That's why I don't wear one. The shoe is odd enough that I'll take

121

credit for that one too, and probably the tire. If you always cut yourself shaving, that one was probably you. But you might want to rethink using a regular razor until after the tournament is over—just in case."

"What in hell have I gotten myself into?" Jake shook his head. "Lunch tomorrow is T-bones. Like I have any business around a steak knife."

"Maybe you should consider soup and salad." She did a quick mental calculation and thought about the options. "Okay, that's about four and a half hours, give or take."

Jake nodded in agreement.

"If we could arrange to meet tomorrow before the tournament starts—somewhere where we won't be seen—I can probably manage enough bad luck to last until lunch. After that it will appear that the table has shifted to you. Would that work?"

"It's going to have to," Jake said simply. He studied her for a moment, then finally spoke. "What exactly are you going to do to me?"

Mallory smiled. "I'm an engineer. We usually go with proven methods, so it looks like another kiss is in order. Think you can handle that?"

"That's fine," he said, the relief on his face so apparent that Mallory had to laugh.

"What in God's name did you think I was going to do to you?"

Jake shrugged and had the decency to look a bit embarrassed. "I don't know. Hell, you people are far from what I consider normal. I have no idea what you do around here for fun."

"Mostly we kill stuff and mount it on our walls, but I don't think we'll have to take this that far."

* * *

Even though it had seemed like their conversation had taken forever, the night was just getting started when Mallory pulled away from Jake's motel. She should head home and do some thinking—God knows she had a lot to think about, a lot to work out in her mind, but for whatever reason, she felt like hanging out with a crowd of people.

And Mallory Devereaux didn't often crave the company of others.

She automatically turned her truck toward J.T.'s. It was the one place she could go where she felt almost normal, even if only for a couple of hours, and tonight the need to feel normal was almost overwhelming. A bunch of locals drinking beer and hustling out-of-towners over pool was just the fix she needed. Country music pumping over the sound system and women wearing too much makeup and not enough clothes. You had to love it. Plus, J.T. always had a stock of her brand of beer in plastic and no one made any moves to duck or avoid her as she walked through the bar, the way some people did when she was in town doing her weekly domestics—grocery shopping, post office.

As she stepped inside the bar, Mallory saw Amy sitting with her butthole boyfriend, Patrick, at a table in the corner. Amy motioned for Mallory to join them, so she waved her hand at them and hoped she could get through the most basic of conversations without throttling Patrick.

The long-standing feud between the two of them was a result of the very first night they'd met a little over six months ago—when Mallory had caught Patrick propositioning a hooker at a bar in New Orleans and had gone straight to Amy with that information. Of course, the asshole had played it off as a joke to her naive friend, but ever since then, the line was drawn. Patrick was a loser and a cad, and any time Amy had her back turned, Mallory inflicted her wrath on him.

If they hadn't been in the same master's program at the university, Mallory doubted seriously that Patrick would ever have gotten on Amy's radar. But no matter her efforts to separate her friend from the louse, Patrick had remained a fixture. For whatever reason, Amy refused to acknowledge the truth concerning her boyfriend, and until Amy was ready to face the facts, there wasn't a darn thing Mallory could do. In this one way, her friend reminded her entirely too much of herself.

Plastering a smile on her face, she took the final steps to Amy's table.

"Hi, Mallory." Amy greeted her with a huge smile as she approached. "Have a seat."

Mallory slid into a seat across the table from Patrick. He looked disgruntled but then what else was new? Patrick lived disgruntled. Until the entire world bowed down to Patrick's greatness, the man would remain a miserable bastard.

Which meant Mallory would pretend politeness while at the same time, ribbing the hell out of the loser whenever an opportunity presented itself. "Hi, Patrick," she said, knowing that merely her greeting the man would irritate him. "Haven't seen you in a while." *Thank the heavens*.

Patrick barely glanced at her. "This place isn't exactly up to my standards, but it seems to fit yours perfectly."

"It used to."

Patrick sputtered, but nothing seemed to be forthcoming any time soon. Not wanting to watch the painful motions of the idiot trying to come up with a witty retort sometime in this century, Mallory ignored him and turned to Amy. "How was the rest of your day?"

Amy, who had been frowning at her boyfriend, turned to her with a smile. "I got rid of the guy with the ball cap by midafternoon. The one I told you about at lunch?"

Mallory nodded. "Thought all women were stupid. Yeah, I remember."

"He's from Louisiana," Patrick interjected. "He doesn't have a lot to go on."

Mallory looked at him and smiled. "Oh you mean like the women sitting at this table, for example? By the way, how's that master's calculus class going this time around?" She turned back to Amy. "Anyway, you were saying?"

Amy lowered her eyes for a moment, a flush creeping over her face, then finally looked back at Mallory and took a breath. "He went all-in on three of a kind, when he knew I'd only taken one card and hadn't folded."

"Moron. Good thing he has a lot of money and a good attorney. He'd never be able to defend himself."

"What does he need an attorney for?" Patrick asked. "I thought this was a private poker tournament."

"Oh, Amy didn't tell you? This poker tournament is special. It's a festival of criminals. The guy Amy shut down this afternoon was the prime suspect in three murder investigations in the past five years—all were female—two were his wives." Okay, so she might have made that part up, but it was all in good fun.

Patrick looked at Mallory, then back at Amy, obviously waiting for Amy to laugh or otherwise indicate that Mallory was jerking him around but that signal was not going to come. "Amy? Is this true? You're dealing poker to a bunch of criminals?"

Amy stared down at the table. "Seem to be, yeah."

Patrick jumped up from the table and glared down at her. "What the hell are you thinking? Getting involved with men like that—beating them at poker? Are you trying to get yourself killed? And what about me? I don't have anything at all to do with this classless adventure of yours, and just being with you, I could be at risk."

"Not likely," Mallory interjected. "He only kills girls." She looked up at the red-faced Patrick and tilted her head to one side, studying him for a moment. "Well, maybe you should worry a little."

Patrick glared at Mallory. "I'm going to the bathroom," he said to Amy. "If it's even usable. Then we're blowing this hellhole." He spun around and headed across the bar, knocking shoulders as he went.

Mallory shook her head as she watched him stalk away. "He'll be lucky if he makes it to the men's room without getting in a fight with the way he's walking." She turned back to Amy. "I'm sorry, Amy. I could have been nicer, I suppose, but he just rubs me the wrong way. I shouldn't have said anything about the tournament, though. It was wrong of me to put you in that position."

"He would have found out anyway. There was a reporter at the docks when I got off the boat this evening. Reginald's little showdown is going to be all over the newspapers tomorrow."

"Really? Wow, I never expected to see my uncle's picture in the paper unless it was directly above a 'Wanted' declaration. Reginald must be fit to be tied with the news broadcasting how stupid he was to host such a fiasco."

Amy nodded. "He had a couple of the dishwashers make them leave the parking lot, but some of the attendants had already talked to them."

"Not smart if they want to keep their jobs."

"No," Amy agreed, then was silent. After several seconds, she let out a sigh. "I'm sorry about Patrick. It's not you, Mallory, and I know that. I think he just has so much society raising that he lacks social skills outside of his class."

"Oh yeah, what class is that? Pompous ass?"

"He really is different when we're alone, I swear."

"Great, then as long as you two marry and move to Iceland, the whole relationship should be a raging success." She looked across the table at her clearly miserable friend. "C'mon, Amy. You know you can do better."

Amy placed a crumpled napkin on the table and rose from her chair. "Actually, I can't. I guess I better go to the restroom before I leave."

Mallory frowned but knew better than to waste her time arguing. "Did you ride in with him? I can give you a lift if you want to stay."

Amy shook her head. "We met here, so I've got my own car, but I'm really tired and I need to get some rest before tomorrow." She turned from the table and began to thread her way through the crowded bar.

Mallory slumped back in her chair, wanting so desperately to help her friend but not having any idea what to do.

"You have a run-in with Mr. Personality again?" Scooter asked as he slid into an empty chair next to her.

"Oh, yeah. Did you expect any less?"

"No, but I don't get it—why does Amy keep dating that guy?"

"That is an even bigger mystery than my unluckiness."

"Hell, you're her friend, ain't you gonna do something about it?"

Mallory looked at Scooter for a moment, then smiled. "Yes, I am. Pass me his wallet and keys out of his jacket before he gets back. The least I can do is give him a broken car and a bunch of demagnetized credit cards so he can't pay for a tow."

"Now you're talking." Scooter grinned and tossed the items from Patrick's jacket onto the table.

Mallory ran her hand up and down the car key, then picked each credit card out of his wallet, making sure her fingers covered the full length of the magnetic strip, back and forth. "That's enough," she said, and pushed the items back across the table to Scooter. "Get them back in his coat before he gets back.

Scooter retrieved the items wearing a napkin as a glove and Mallory smiled. Her friend wasn't near as stupid as some might think. Even secondary contact with Mallory was sometimes a problem.

Scooter had just placed the jacket across the chair when Patrick and Amy returned. Patrick grabbed his jacket and glared at Amy. "Why don't you leave before me? With this all this white-trash mess you're involved in, I don't want anyone thinking we're together. I'll call you when I get home."

Amy looked as though she'd been struck, and Mallory prayed desperately that her friend would fight back, but she only nodded meekly. She said a nearly inaudible good-bye to Mallory and left the table, threading her way across the bar.

Patrick watched her retreat, a smug look on his face. As he started to follow, Mallory reached out and grabbed his arm. "You should be nicer to my friend."

"Or what? If you could get rid of me, you already would have." He yanked his arm from her grasp and stalked across the bar.

"Doesn't stop me from trying," Mallory grumbled as she watched him exit. "C'mon, Scooter. Let's hurry and see the show."

Scooter grinned and followed her across the bar and outside into the parking lot.

Patrick had parked right in front of the bar in what Mallory had thought was a handicapped parking space, but a glance at the front of the space revealed an empty pole. He was pressing his key fob and glaring at the door, but it was no use. Finally deciding it wasn't going to work, he jammed his key in the door lock and opened it. With a final dirty look at Mallory, he started his car, revving the engine like an idiot, and threw it in reverse.

The car sputtered once, moved about two inches back, then died.

Mallory could see Patrick cursing as he turned the key over and over with no results. Finally, he jumped out of the car, slammed the door and started yelling at Mallory. "You did something to my car, you bitch. I just know it."

Before Mallory could respond, the door to the bar opened and J.T. and a few of the customers stepped out. "What's all the racket out here?" J.T. asked.

"The only 'racket' here," Patrick said, "is charging three dollars for watered-down beer. Unless you've got a tow truck behind the bar, there's nothing you can do to help."

J.T. stared at Patrick for a moment, then shook his head. "You got some set of balls on you boy." He looked over at the immobile car, then back at Patrick. "Tell you what I can do. Dave, here"—he pointed at a burly guy standing next to him—"happens to drive a tow truck. And I'd be happy to have you towed—straight to the impound."

Patrick stared. "For what? I haven't done anything wrong."

"You're parked in a handicapped spot. As the owner of the building, I have the right to have your car towed to impound."

Patrick whirled around and looked at the parking space. "There's no sign. Without a sign, there's no law."

J.T. smirked and walked over to the pole in front of Patrick's car. By this time, more people were outside of the bar watching the show than inside, and a low murmur ran through the crowd as everyone wondered what J.T. was about to do.

J.T. kicked one foot in the dirt, then reached down and lifted up a battered sign. He shook the worst of the dust off it and placed it up on the pole, shoving his pen through the screw hole to hold it in place. "Looks like there's a sign to me."

A couple of people chuckled, and Mallory covered her mouth with one hand, trying to hold it in.

Patrick stared at J.T., a dumbfounded look on his face. "You can't do that."

"I just did." J.T. waved one hand at Dave. "I do believe this car is parked illegally. Would you mind removing it from my lot?"

Dave grinned and pulled his keys from his pocket. "Give me ten minutes and she'll be gone." The big man headed across the parking lot toward a tow truck parked off to one side.

Finally realizing that J.T. had every intention of towing his car, Patrick turned from bewildered to angry, but for once was smart enough to keep his mouth closed. He glared at Mallory, then spun around, walked back over to his car, and climbed inside. He was still sitting in the driver's seat, fuming, when Dave lifted the car from its spot and began to pull it away.

Mallory looked over at J.T., smiling. "That was fantastic."

J.T. nodded. "Never could stand that son of a bitch."

"That makes two of us."

J.T. motioned Mallory to step close and she edged her way along the parking lot, careful to avoid touching any of the regulars, until she was standing just inches from the bar owner.

"I was trying to catch you before you left," J.T. said. "That's why I came outside in the first place, although I'm glad to help with the disaster part of the night."

"What's up?"

"Just wanted to let you know that Harry dropped by this afternoon. Said that Walter Royal sent two of his flunkies over to measure the construction trailer. Said they needed to recarpet for the 'new management.'"

Mallory felt her face flush with anger. "Asshole."

J.T. nodded. "Got that right. I know I didn't want you playing in this tournament, Mallory, and that's still the case. But I hope to God you make the money to buy Harry's business before Walter Royal can. That bastard has just about ruined everything in this town."

"I'm going to get the money."

J.T. nodded. "You need anything, you let me know."

"Just keep your ear to the ground. Let me know what you hear about Reginald or Silas or hell, anything that might be useful."

"Things like Silas canceling his lease on a row of warehouses just outside of town and the owner scheduling Harry to demolish them week after next?"

Leased warehouses? Mallory's mind whirled with the possibilities.

Jake had said the FBI had checked everything that Silas owned, but they'd have no way of knowing what he'd leased. She thanked J.T. and headed across the parking lot to her truck. She needed to make a phone call to Harry to get the exact address of those warehouses; then she needed to let Jake know where to start looking for his partner.

Chapter Nine

Jake cursed as his rental car dipped into another pothole the size of Rhode Island and flung him up off the seat and into the roof. Where the hell did Mallory have them meeting? His alarm clock had gone off thirty minutes late and he'd been rushing ever since. He and Mallory both thought it best to wait as late as possible to enact their plan, so at least it was daylight when Jake left the motel that morning. But you would never have known it was daylight now. Huge, thick trees lined the sides of the dirt road that was barely more than a path, blocking out any light from the narrow strip he drove on. Without his headlights on, he'd probably already have fallen in and disappeared forever in one of those potholes. For all he knew, that might be the locals' plan to keep foreigners out.

The road made a quick left turn and came to a dead end right up against the bayou. Jake slammed on the brakes, the car sliding a couple of inches in the mixture of dirt and gravel that was serving as a parking lot. Mallory was parked over to the side, her truck tucked in between two massive cypress trees.

She was leaning against the bumper of her truck, her tight-fitting, faded jeans and white tank top reminding him that Mallory Devereaux's body was as near to perfect as any he'd ever seen before in his life. Hollywood could have learned a thing or two by looking at this woman— tanned and toned on every square inch of her body.

Or at least he assumed the tanned part, since he didn't exactly know, but it was such a glorious visual, he was just going to leave it that way.

He shook his head and took a deep breath to gather his thoughts. Mallory's tan lines, or lack thereof, were not part of the plan. Not the plan to bust Silas and definitely not the plan for his life. Women like Mallory, interesting women, attractive, intelligent, were the type he never spent time with.

That might lead to having feelings. Having feelings led to thinking about commitment and any number of other completely normal activities that had no place in an FBI agent's life. So he'd avoided these women like the plague.

Not to say he was a priest or anything. That simply wasn't the case. It's just that he'd always been smart about his choices—mostly good-looking but brainless bimbos. They were safe because he knew he could never form any kind of attachment, regardless of whether he spent time with them or not. And the reality was he never had to spend much time with any one of them because there were so many to choose from.

Women like Mallory were a rare breed. Thank God.

He shut off the car, pulled the keys from the ignition, then shoved open the door and stepped outside. He had to stop thinking. Stop thinking about anything but busting Silas Hebert. Concentrate on the cards and nothing else.

"Quite a stop you made there," Mallory said, and grinned.

Jake shook his head. "How the hell was I to know the road was going to turn into a bayou?" He glanced around the tiny clearing, with an even tinier path leading straight into the water. "What is this place, anyway?"

"Used to be a house here when I was a kid. Well, more like a shack, really. The local voodoo woman lived here. Even though my mom forbade it, I'd sneak over here sometimes, trying to see her doing some magic."

Jake stared at Mallory, trying to decide whether she was pulling his leg or not. Her expression never wavered. "Don't tell me you believe in that crap, too."

Mallory shrugged. "I don't know. I guess I've never thought about it really. I mean, there are obviously some things in the universe that go against the norm and with no explanation that we can see, or I wouldn't exist the way I do. I can't say that I've ever seen any voodoo first-hand. I really don't know anything about it."

Jake nodded and looked around the clearing again. "So where is the woman now?"

"Dead maybe? Moved? Who knows? Hell, she looked old when I was a kid. That would make her ancient now."

"But someone still comes back here," he said, and pointed to the path.

Mallory grinned. "That would be me and Scooter. Best speckled trout you'd ever wanted to eat are about a hundred yards off that edge of the bayou." She pointed to the tiny trail leading into the water. "We keep it a secret, though. Don't want everyone in Royal Flush thinning out our fish."

Jake nodded like he was interested in the reply, like he was even thinking about speckled whatever and not the fullness of Mallory's lips. He needed to get a grip on himself.

He glanced down at his watch, then back at Mallory. "We've got about thirty minutes to get to the casino. I guess we'd better get this over with."

Mallory studied him for a moment, then smiled. "Are you nervous, Agent McMillan? Because if I didn't know any better, I'd say that kissing me worries you more than the possibility of shooting someone."

Jake felt his blood race at her teasing, but far from making him angry, it excited him.

And scared the shit out of him.

"The only thing I'm worried about is Silas getting away," he said. "And if it means kissing one of those speckled things you catch to bust him, I'd do that too." To back up his point, he made the three steps over to her and before she could even respond, he'd grabbed the back of her head and lowered his lips to hers in a crushing blow.

Apparently surprised by his speed, she stiffened momentarily, but as his lips parted hers, he felt her slacken against him as her hands came up his back and twined into his hair. Her lips were as soft and hot as he'd remembered from the day before. He felt her tongue on his in a slow erotic dance. Involuntarily, he moved closer to her so that his body pressed against hers, inch by inch. He trailed one hand from her neck down the thin cotton fabric of her shirt, stopping over one of the perfect breasts to stroke the nipple beneath.

She groaned, and he felt himself stiffen in response.

In an instant, he tore away from her and took a step back, his breath still ragged. She stood staring at him, her expression unreadable, but for the first time since he'd met her, Mallory Devereaux didn't have a thing to say.

"I guess that will do?" he asked, trying to clear his head of the moment, of Mallory.

Mallory stared at him a moment more, then nodded. "That should take you to lunch at least." She glanced up at the sun above the as if she were checking the time. "Guess we better get going or we'll be late. I'll take off first. It wouldn't do for Reginald to see us arrive at the same time." She gave him a small smile. "See you in a few."

And with that, she spun around and hurried to her truck. It gave him a little satisfaction to notice that she never looked back. Too taken by the moment to risk looking at him any longer, was what he figured. Which was only fair when he had barely maintained control himself.

So the hard exterior that Mallory wore was just housing the woman inside. All woman. All natural woman.

And damned if she hadn't been telling the truth—she didn't wear a bra.

Mallory drove to the casino on autopilot, still shaken by the kiss. If the first kiss had been an awakening, this one had come in for the kill. Never in her life had she wanted a man with every single square inch of her skin, every hair follicle. Her body had betrayed her and sold itself out 150 percent to Jake McMillan.

And that was a problem for so many reasons she couldn't even count them all. Being involved with Jake, or any other man for that matter, wasn't an option. She knew that, believed it with all her heart.

But she still wanted him like she'd wanted no other.

Desperately wanted a man whose real name she didn't even know.

She pulled into the casino parking lot and took the spot nearest to the ramp. She grabbed her bag of clothes and jumped from the truck, eager to get inside and get focused on the tournament—focused on the rest of her life.

She needed to keep her mind clear. No distractions. That was today's rule.

Until she found Amy crying in the ladies' room.

Dropping her bag just inside the door, Mallory rushed over to her friend, who was huddled on a couch in the far corner. Mallory sank onto the table across from her. "Amy, what's wrong?"

Amy lowered her head so that Mallory couldn't see her face, but she saw her shoulders shaking and knew the tears were still rolling. For the millionth time in her existence, Mallory cursed her inability to touch someone—comfort someone that she loved. "Did someone hurt you? Do I need to talk to Reginald? Oh, hell, was it Reginald who upset you?"

Amy sniffed a bit and wiped at her eyes with the back of her hand. It was several seconds more before she lifted her head to face Mallory. "It's Patrick."

"What's happened with Patrick?" Mallory asked. *Do not hope for death. That's wrong. Maybe an accident involving his penis.*

"He broke up with me," Amy said, and sniffed again. "Just like that. Six months, two days and five hours together, and he said we didn't have anything in common anymore. How can he say that? We're the same as we were when we met." She turned her wounded, puppy-dog expression on Mallory, looking for an explanation—some reason to make sense of her current disaster.

Mallory felt instantly guilty. Even though she knew the problems she'd bestowed on Patrick at J.T.'s hadn't been the ultimate reason he'd dumped her friend, they had probably sped up the process. "I'm really sorry, Amy. You know how I felt about him, but I never wanted to see you hurt."

Amy sniffed and nodded. "I know. None of this is your fault, so don't start thinking it is. Patrick was rude to you

137

from the start, and honestly, I think I'm more embarrassed than hurt."

"Really?"

"Yeah. I mean, I've known this day has been coming for months now, and I continued to inflict Patrick on all of you anyway."

Mallory stared at Amy in surprise. "You knew this was coming?"

Amy shrugged. "Patrick hasn't been the same since my PhD application was accepted and his wasn't. I kept thinking he would eventually let it go, but my doing better than him always bothered him. I just never wanted to admit it."

Mallory twined her fingers together to keep them from reaching up and touching her friend. "It's his loss, believe me on that one. You could do so much better."

Amy stared at her, her expression doubtful. "Can I really? Because I don't think so. Most men don't take me seriously at all based on the way I look. Then when they find out what's inside this head of mine, they usually shy away." The look she gave Mallory was sheer misery. "I scare them. I scare men. It feels awful, Mallory. And I worry all the time about being alone the rest of my life."

Mallory nodded, trying to block out the thoughts of Jake that came unbidden to the forefront of her mind. "I understand. You know I understand."

Amy nodded and gave Mallory a small smile. "I know you do. It's just not right, Mallory. Two good-looking, successful women and not a man between us. This sucks."

"It does suck. But you're going to be fine. You'll move on from Patrick and find someone who isn't threatened by your brain." Of course, Einstein was dead, but she'd work on the man angle a little later. "C'mon, Amy, you couldn't have liked him that much anyway. He wears his pants too short. Looked like he was ready for high waters."

"He's tall. He has trouble finding pants the right length."

"So you're telling me the man is a math whiz, but can't manage an inseam measurement?" She shook her head. "I'm not buying it. And you need to remember your dating rules."

"My rules are dumb."

"That's not the point. They're your rules and I think you've broken Number Two. What does Number Two say, exactly?"

Amy sighed. "When assessing a man as husband material, you have to ask yourself: If I were to die a tragic death, would he dress my children stupid?"

"Now see? Based on Amy's Rules for Dating Number Two, you should never have gotten past an introduction to Patrick. Not with his ankles looking all girly in a pair of slacks."

Amy giggled. "Okay, maybe you're right. Maybe I just saw being with Patrick as better than being alone. It's hard, Mallory, and it's scary to wonder if that perfect man for me is out there."

An image of Jake flashed across Mallory's mind. "There is no such thing as the perfect man. There's only the temporary fantasy."

Jake took his place at the table and tried to keep himself from looking at Mallory as she walked into the casino. His restraint lasted about a second and a half. Maybe less. She was wearing the black miniskirt again today, this time with a gold top in some shiny fabric that crisscrossed in the front, diving down between her incredible cleav-

139

age. Her legs that were bare yesterday were encased in black fishnet hose, and he found himself desperately wanting to see that line up the back.

He heard a wolf whistle off to his left and glanced over to find Brad grinning. God help him. Shaking himself into some semblance of normal, he focused on shuffling the cards. Unfortunately, a motion that he'd done thousands of times gave his mind plenty of wandering time, and it was all he could do to keep from wondering whether Mallory skimped on her underwear as she did on her bras.

"Good morning, gentleman," he said, forcing himself to focus on the players—on the job. "I don't suppose any of you are ready to play some cards?"

He received a couple of chuckles and a "Praise God" from Father Thomas. Only Silas Hebert remained silent as he studied Jake with an intensity that was a bit unnerving. Yesterday, Silas had been watching for the fix, studying Jake's hands, the motions he made concerning the cards, but he'd never focused on Jake himself. It couldn't be good if he were doing it now.

Was there some way his carefully constructed cover could be blown?

Surely not. If Silas thought for a moment that Jake was FBI, wouldn't he have merely left the tournament and not returned? Fifty thousand was a drop in the bucket to a man like Silas. It was hardly enough of a reason to risk arrest, especially on the eve of his "retirement."

Jake shuffled the last section of the cards and placed them into the shoe. Giving the men a nod, he began to deal, all the while aware that Silas's eyes were on him.

An hour and a half later, Jake was more worried than ever before. Sure the play had gone as expected—given his very thorough and incredibly satisfying kissing of

Mallory that morning, he hadn't won a single hand and hadn't even had a hand worth trying on. The rest of the players, running short on a touch from Mallory, had leveled out a bit in playing ability, but Silas was the superior player in the group.

Silas's wins weren't the cause of Jake's worry. Despite his concentration on play, Silas spent a good portion of the morning studying Jake. But then Silas had shifted his attention to Mallory, which made Jake even more anxious for the midmorning break and an opportunity to check in with his captain. If Silas were already checking his cover, Jake wanted to make doubly sure his story would hold.

Jake collected the cards as the men filed away from the table, Mallory trailing behind them. As soon as they exited the casino, he stepped out on the balcony directly behind his table and pressed the captain's number into his cell phone. The phone had barely begun to ring before his captain answered.

"Randoll. What the hell are you doing calling in the middle of the morning? Is something wrong?"

"I'm not sure."

"What do you mean, you're not sure? Either something's wrong or it's not."

"Fine, then I think something's wrong and I need you to verify it for me. I got this weird feeling off Silas this morning like he was studying me. It made me wonder if he's doing a check. I need you to see if someone's calling my covers."

"It's a little early for him to already be suspicious, isn't it?"

"For most people, I'd say you're right, but Silas seems to take paranoia to a whole new level. Then again, I guess that's why he's still in business."

"You're probably right. Our team finished the sweep of

those warehouses early this morning. They're clean as a whistle—too clean, if you get my meaning."

"Damn. We're always two steps behind."

"Yeah, well, I'm hoping you're going to change all of that. I'll check your cover stories, see who's gotten a feeler. Check in on your lunch break. I should know something by then."

"Will do," Jake replied, and flipped his phone shut, wondering if his cover had held and figuring if it hadn't, he wouldn't even need to check in with his captain. He'd probably know it if his table was one player short after break, but as he entered the casino and looked across the room, one part of his fears was put to rest. Silas Hebert was already back from break and sitting at the table, waiting for the play to begin and seeming not to have a care in the world.

And maybe he didn't.

The lunch break couldn't have come a moment too soon for Mallory. The play had seemed to drag, every single second. On the plus side, the kiss had apparently worked and Jake hadn't drawn a winning hand all morning. He was playing ultraconservatively, so he hadn't really lost much more than the ante on each round, and the other players, devoid of her touch for the morning, had each managed a hand or two off Silas, who'd easily won all the rest. She guessed, in the big scheme of things, their plan had been a success, even though it looked like the beginnings of a disaster.

She placed the used glasses on the tray for pickup and headed across the casino toward the restaurant. Jake had rushed from the table with the players without so much as a backward glance at her, and for a moment she had been disappointed. Then that moment had passed when she remembered Jake couldn't do anything to draw attention to them.

She was just about to push open the door to the restaurant when her cell vibrated. She pulled it from the clip on her skirt and checked the number. It wasn't one she recognized. Figuring it was probably an accident and the caller would realize it when the message played, she stuck the phone back in the holder and reached for the handle on the door.

Her phone began to vibrate again.

She frowned and pulled the phone from the holder again, checking the number only to find it was the same one as before. Deciding two in a row merited an answer, she flipped open the phone and pressed the "talk" button. "Hello."

"Mallory?" A familiar voice sounded in the phone but she couldn't quite place it.

"Yes?"

"Mallory, it's Jake."

She hurried away from the door, not wanting to risk being overheard. "Why are you calling me? Is something wrong?"

"Maybe. Did you notice anything strange about Silas this morning?"

Mallory thought back, trying to remember anything at all about Silas that stood out. "Not really. Why?"

"He suspects something is up. He was studying me this morning, me personally, not the way I was dealing or playing. Then he shifted after an hour or so and studied you."

Mallory felt her heart beat a bit faster. "I didn't even notice. How could I not notice?"

"He wasn't obvious. Successful criminals have perfected the art of subtlety. Probably no one but law enforcement would have noticed—and they would have to have been looking for it."

Mallory nodded, even though she knew he couldn't see, trying to reassure herself more than anything else. "Okay. So what do you think he's up to?"

"I made a call to my office on the morning break and asked them to do some checking for me. I just got off the phone with them. Silas is having an intense background check performed on me. One of his men has called all my plants to confirm my background. So far, my cover isn't broken, but we aren't sure how much longer it will hold."

"Holy shit!" Mallory sank into a chair and considered the seriousness of Jake's words. "What if he finds out? He'll leave and you won't get to bust him. Is he checking on me? I'm a local, and everyone knows I'm not a cop."

"I don't think Silas is thinking along the lines of law enforcement—at least not yet. I think he suspects me of fixing the tournament and he's wondering if you're in on it with me. He's probably trying to find the link between us. As to whether or not he's checking on you—I'd say probably. But since you don't have an FBI cover in place, we'll have no way of knowing if he is or what information he gains."

Mallory blew out a breath. "Okay. So he won't find anything that connects the two of us because there wasn't anything until now. But if he keeps digging, he might find out about you, or about me being a cooler. So what do we do?"

"We're going to have to move up the plan a bit. I know I wanted to extend play for as long as possible to make Silas comfortable, but the longer we play, the longer we run the risk of my cover being blown. My bad luck should be worn off by the time afternoon play starts. I need you to make sure Silas loses."

"And if he loses too fast and quits?"

"It's a risk I have to take. There are no other options."

"Then I'll get on it after lunch."

"Great. Thanks."

She heard a click when Jake disconnected and flipped her cell phone shut to check the display. Sure enough, it started blinking, then blacked out altogether. "It never fails," she mumbled, and stuck the phone back in her holder. She had an extra battery in her gym bag. Heck, she had five extra batteries in her gym bag and more in her truck. Watches weren't the only electronic device Mallory was hell on.

She scanned the casino and realized she was all alone. Sinking into a chair, she tried to decide what move to make next. After Jake's revelation last night on Silas and the money laundering, she'd wanted to run straight to her uncle and start asking questions about her father. But if she did that, Reginald would definitely wonder why.

The last thing Mallory wanted to do was to blow Jake's cover, and unfortunately she had to agree with him on her uncle's lack of trustworthiness. Besides, there wasn't a damned thing she could do about the situation, even if her suspicions were correct. And ultimately, the truth couldn't make a difference to anyone but her. Which meant that dragging the truth out of Reginald would just have to wait until the tournament was over.

She rose from the chair and headed toward the dining area. Might as well have some lunch. She wanted to check on Amy, see how she was holding up post-Patrick, and maybe a miracle had happened and Scooter had actually gotten some information on Reginald.

Her friends were at the same table they had occupied the day before, and Mallory was pleased to note the vacant tables surrounding them. She headed across the room toward her friends with a smile. "I see we've got the best table in the house again," she said as she took a seat.

"Yeah," Amy agreed. "I think everyone crowds around the kitchen hoping for faster service. The last thing I want is anyone rushing around you with dishes." She grinned, and although Mallory could tell her friend was still not back to normal, the edge was fast wearing off Patrick. Give her another day or two and Amy would probably adopt a cat and swear off men—at least until one with a high IQ and long pants came along.

"How's the tournament going?"

Amy gave her an enthusiastic nod. "Great. Since I blew the idiot out yesterday, the level of play has gotten better and more intense. It's just the challenge I was looking for to document my theory because the players are all well above average and my theory is still holding against them. I'm winning eighty percent of the hands played."

"Impressive. But then I'm not the least bit surprised. You sure you want to be Alan Greenspan, Jr.? We could arrange a helluva career for you as a hustler. Well, as soon as we worked out a disguise that made you look old enough to actually be *in* a casino."

Amy laughed. "While I have to admit the challenge is a lot of fun—and I'd probably make a bunch more money—I kind of envisioned my future wearing a lot more clothes and inhaling a lot less cigarette smoke."

Mallory laughed and turned to Scooter. "What about you, Scooter? You find out anything interesting on Reginald? I haven't seen the old dog all day. He must be up to something."

"'The game is afoot,'" Scooter said in his version of a British accent. "He's been a weird one today. First he had me reposition a camera on table three where he could watch all the players from behind the dealer, you know, kinda looking over his shoulder.

"So I'm rewiring the rest of the monitors to make room for the new camera angle and all of a sudden Reginald starts cussing and picks up the phone, demanding to speak to the dealer on table three. Then a couple minutes go by and Reginald starts yelling in the phone about twitches and blinks and coughing. I thought maybe someone was sick, but when I checked the cameras, everything seemed normal."

Mallory looked over at Amy and knew her friend had caught on to what Reginald was doing. "No one was sick, Scooter. A player at table three must be giving away his hand by those actions—you know, coughing every time he has a bad hand, blinking if he has a good one—something like that. Apparently, the dealer's not catching it and using it to his advantage."

Scooter scrunched up his brow. "But isn't Reginald telling the dealer stuff sorta like cheating?"

Mallory shrugged. "At this point, I don't really care if Reginald's got a camera in the player's front pocket and is watching his hand live. Was there anything else?"

"Yeah, before lunch. Reginald came down to the restaurant as one of the attendants was bringing drinks out to table five. He sent the attendant back into the kitchen for something and I swear as soon as the girl turned around, Reginald poured something in a couple of the drinks."

Mallory stared at Scooter, feeling somewhat alarmed. "You're positive about that?"

"I saw him clear as day."

Amy looked across the table at Mallory, her eyes wide. "You don't think Reginald would poison anyone, do you?"

Mallory paused for a second before answering because, well, she couldn't really say "no" with conviction.

"Oh man, if all this wasn't so weird I'd say no outright, but now . . . I just don't know. I mean, I don't think he'd kill anyone, but I guess he's not above making them pretty sick."

Amy narrowed her eyes and nodded. "You mean, like making them sick enough to affect their concentration."

"Or leave the tournament altogether." Mallory put her hands up in the air. "It's the only thing that would make sense." She looked back at Scooter, who she could tell was trying to follow the conversation but had probably been left off about three sentences before. "Anything else?"

Scooter shrugged. "Not unless you want to know about the box of guns he's got hidden in the storeroom."

Mallory served the afternoon drinks carefully, spending extra time and care with each of the players. She didn't want to single Silas out for attention. That would be far too obvious, but if she appeared to be in a feel-good, touchy mood with everyone, maybe it would pass for that perky-girl attitude that every woman but her seemed to be able to pull off.

The other men barely noticed her extra attentions, except Father Thomas, who bestowed a blessing on her right there at the table, but she felt Silas's eyes on her as she served his drink, ensuring she rubbed against his body with her arm. His gaze unnerved her to the point of a little spot of fear that began to form in her belly. Like she needed any more reason to worry after Scooter's gun revelation.

She hopped on her stool and waited for Jake to begin the deal, ready for this day to be over with. Ready for the whole tournament to be over with. As Jake began to spin the cards across the table, she leaned over to the side and adjusted the strap on her shoes, making sure she brushed against Silas with her shoulder. It probably wasn't necessary, but she wasn't going to take any risks.

When she straightened up, her eyes locked with Silas's, who had turned to stare at her, an amused look on his face. She yanked herself around on her stool and tried not to panic. That look on his face—it was almost like he knew exactly what she was doing.

She sucked in a breath and tried to remain calm. Jake may have an FBI-invented persona, but Mallory was exactly who she said she was. Granted, Silas wouldn't have found a connection between her and Jake, but it wouldn't have been difficult to find one between her and Reginald. In itself, that wasn't cause for concern, unless Silas kept pushing and checked with locals in Royal Flush. If he knew she was Reginald's niece *and* a cooler, he might assume the previous day's misdirection in cards was all her.

Which was true, but where did that leave her? It probably took the spotlight off Jake, which was a good thing, but what if Silas decided he wanted to pay Reginald back for setting him up by removing Mallory from the game— permanently? All the tales she'd heard about Silas Hebert while growing up came rushing into her mind, making her pulse race. Even though most of them had come from her parents, she figured at least half had some truth in them.

Enough to scare the daylights out of her.

She blinked once and took a huge swallow of the cold water she'd brought for herself. *Focus on the game.* With any luck—mostly the bad kind—this whole fiasco would be over by this afternoon. At least the Silas Hebert part.

She checked the cards on the table and wasn't surprised to see Jake and Silas the only two remaining in this hand. But then Silas saw Jake's bet and raised him double that. Of course, Silas might have thought the table was still in his favor and Jake was bluffing. In that case, a bet that large would make sense.

Jake considered the raise for a second, then pushed over a stack of chips. "Call," he said, and flipped his cards over—an inside straight, seven through jack.

"Not bad," Silas said, and gave him a smile, "but not enough to beat a full house." He flipped his cards over and revealed the pair of fives and three tens.

Jake hesitated for just a moment, but managed to contain his surprise. Mallory was glad Silas was looking directly at him, because she was certain she'd done a horrible job in concealing her own.

What the hell had happened?

Surely it was a fluke, a mischance. The next hand would go the way she'd set it up to. But as Jake lifted his hand for the next round, she could see his mouth tighten ever so slightly. She wondered for a moment what that might mean but got her answer just seconds later as he folded his hand and bowed out of the round.

Okay, she could pass off one hand lost as a fluke, but two? Two was something more than a fluke but not yet a disaster.

Mallory stared at Jake, but he didn't even glance up. She knew he was maintaining his distance to avoid risk, but part of her wished he'd turn his gaze on her, if only for a moment, so that maybe she could see what was going on in his head.

What was he thinking? Was he worried?

Because if he hadn't been before, now might be a good time to start.

Jake studied his cards in confusion. The hand just wasn't there. The best he could hope to make of the mess was a pair, maybe a three of a kind as a long shot. Which wouldn't have bothered him at all if things were going the way they were planned. According to the rules of poker, Jake should fold this hand and hope for better on the next round. According to the laws of Mallory, this hand should still yield something better than what the rest of the players held.

But Jake hadn't pulled a winning hand all afternoon.

He'd watched Mallory serve the drinks and touch all the players as she went. She'd even given Silas the extra whammy, but the man had continued to play good poker, belying Mallory's touch. The rest of the players were back in a slump. It wasn't that Jake's hands had been bad—just not good enough to edge Silas out on anything.

It was almost as if he and Silas were playing straight up—no Mallory involved.

Jake folded when his turn came and tried to control his frustration. He needed to get a grip. Yesterday, he would have cheerfully sent Mallory to Antarctica if it meant removing her from his table. Now, he not only wanted her at the table, he needed that supernatural bullshit of hers to start working.

Jake was way better than the average poker player, but he'd seen enough of Silas's ability to know he wasn't going to beat him in a straight-up match.

And that left him with nothing.

Chapter Ten

Mallory paced back and forth across her tiny living room, watching the road for Jake's white rental car. Where was he? She looked at the clock again. Two minutes after six. *Calm down. He's only two minutes late.*

She sat for a moment on the edge of the couch, but sitting made her jumpier than the pacing. Hopping back up, she grabbed her work gloves and was just about to go outside to Scooter's shop and cut something in two when Jake's car rounded the corner and pulled into her driveway.

She glanced out her kitchen window at the pier she and Scooter shared, but his boat wasn't at the dock. Obviously the trout were biting. With any luck, she and Jake would come up with a new plan and he'd be gone before Scooter had a chance to get in the middle of it. Of course, that meant Jake needed to have come up with a plan on his own, because Mallory had drawn a huge zero on that end. Unless one wanted to sink to the Reginald St. Claire method of dealing with those who had a winning streak that ran a bit too long.

The players had no sooner settled into the afternoon

game when two of them rushed from the room, clutching their stomachs as they exited the casino. According to her uncle's "rules of play," each player was limited to a maximum of twenty minutes away from the table at any time other than breaks. If at any given time a player ran over the twenty-minute mark, half their chips were automatically forfeited to the dealer.

Which put Reginald up about forty thousand for the moment and made Mallory wonder what the hell he'd dropped into those drinks.

Jake brought the car to a stop in front of her garage and hopped out, giving her a nod as he crossed the lawn to the porch where she stood. "Scooter's gone?" he asked, and looked over at the cabin about thirty yards from Mallory's.

"Yeah, for now. But he'll only be out as long as the fish are biting or until he runs out of beer. All he took was a six-pack, so we don't have that long."

Jake shook his head, and Mallory could see a look of begrudging admiration on his face. "I've never in my life seen a human being drink that much and still function like normal."

Mallory laughed. "Well, Scooter's normal is not as far a stretch to cover as the rest of ours, but yeah, his drinking ability is definitely at a professional level. I'm pretty sure he was single-handedly responsible for last quarter's profit increase at Coors." She waved one hand at the door. As Jake stepped onto the front porch, T.W. rose from his sleeping spot in the corner and angled off toward them.

Jake stared, his expression a mixture of confusion and surprise. "What the heck is that?"

"T.W.'s a basset hound."

"I didn't think they could live to be a hundred, and why does he keep twisting his head that way?"

"He's deaf as a doornail, but refuses to believe it, so he keeps twisting his head, thinking he'll be able to hear better out of the other ear."

T.W. came to a staggering stop in front of Jake, sniffed his pants legs, then lay down on the porch in front of his feet, obviously exhausted from all that strenuous activity. Jake stared at the dog for a moment then looked up at Mallory. "Did you do that to him?"

It took a minute for Mallory to understand what he was asking, then she broke out in laughter. "God, no. He was like that when I adopted him from the animal shelter. On his last leg in more ways than one, you could say. But he's perfectly safe. My bad luck doesn't seem to apply to animals."

Jake looked down once more at the dog and nodded. "What's T.W. stand for?"

"Train Wreck." Mallory grinned, and stepped inside the cabin, motioning for Jake to follow. As soon he stepped inside behind her, the entire cabin seemed to grow smaller, as if his mere presence had filled the room.

There were a million things in the world she had to worry about at that moment, not the least of which was Silas Hebert, Jake's bust and her money, but for some reason Mallory couldn't focus on any of them. Having Jake in her house made her feel strange, an uneasy nervous kind of anxiety, and it took her a minute to realize that he was the first man besides Scooter, Harry, or J.T. who had ever crossed the doorstep.

Of course there was also the fact that the cabin was all of three rooms. And since her couch doubled as her bed and she hadn't bothered to roll it back in, Jake quite literally was standing in the middle of her bedroom, looking around with undisguised interest.

"I like your place," he said finally, and Mallory stared at him in surprise.

"You're kidding, right?"

"Not at all. I'm into simple and functional. This is perfect for one person, and since you've combined bedroom and living, you only need to buy one television."

Mallory scanned his face, waiting for the punch line, but Jake just stood there, in the middle of her tiny cabin, wearing a look of genuine approval.

Which made him even sexier than before.

"You want something to drink?" she asked as she took the three steps into the kitchen and opened the refrigerator.

"No thanks."

She bent down and stuck her head inside the refrigerator, willing the cool air to chill the flush that had started to climb up her body, creeping up her toes toward places better left chilled. She grabbed a Coke can and rubbed it across her forehead, wondering if rubbing it anywhere else would help the problem or cause more trouble.

Deciding she probably didn't want the FBI to know she'd felt up a Coke can, she pulled herself away from the cool air and walked back into the living room, plopping down on her recliner. "Sit anywhere," she said, and waved a hand at Jake.

Jake considered his options for a moment, apparently as uneasy about the bed situation as she was, then finally selected an antique rocking chair in the corner.

"Do you have any idea—?"

"I have no idea—"

They both started speaking at the same time, then stopped and Jake motioned for Mallory to continue.

"I wondered if you had any ideas on how to work

around this?" Mallory asked. "I've been racking my brain all day and I can't come up with anything."

Jake blew out a breath. "I was hoping you'd figure out how Silas is beating your bad-luck touch and we could go back to the original plan."

Mallory slowly shook her head. "I just don't know. It's almost like I never touched him. But it worked on all the others, so I don't know how he managed to get out of it. This has never happened before."

She started to continue when her cell phone rang. Glancing at the display, she saw the number for J.T.'s Bar. What now? "I should probably take this," she said, and flipped the phone open to answer. "J.T.?"

"Mallory, I've got something to tell you," the bar owner said. "And it don't look good."

"What's up? Is Father Thomas in some kind of trouble?"

"If only it were that simple. No, I'm afraid *you* might be in some kind of trouble."

She sucked in a breath. "Why? What's happened?"

"Stanley's been steaming open mail again. And this time he steamed open an overnight envelope for none other than Silas Hebert."

Mallory felt her back tighten. "What did he find?"

"He found a bunch of information about you—personal information—pages and pages of it. What the hell is going on, Mallory?"

"I don't know exactly," she said, deciding that her words weren't exactly lying. "But I'm going to find out."

"Now, don't you go doing anything foolish."

Mallory sighed. "According to you, I already have. Do me a favor and don't tell Harry about this. He'll only worry, and he's got enough to worry over without me adding to it." She flipped the phone shut and stared at Jake.

"Silas Hebert received an envelope of information on me today."

Jake stared at her for a moment. "How do you know?"

Mallory waved one hand in dismissal. "We have a local postmaster who doesn't exactly have an appreciation for federal law. Don't even ask."

Jake gave her a pained look. "I won't."

"So we know for sure that Silas is checking on me. But why the personal history file? What possible difference could it make?"

"I don't know, but I think it's time we found out."

"What do you mean?"

"I mean I'm tired of standing around and waiting for Silas to make the next move. If tomorrow's play goes along the same lines as today, I could be out of the tournament long before Friday. Which means neither of us gets what we need. At this point, I don't have anything to lose by taking chances."

Jake rose from his chair. "I'm going to try to break into his hotel room. Maybe get an idea of what angle he's taking. Maybe figure out how he's managed to turn you off. He's got to be cheating somehow, but damned if I can pick it."

"Cheating," Mallory repeated. "You're right—that has to be the answer." She looked up at Jake and nodded. "Do you think he'll have anything in his room that will indicate how he's doing it?"

"That's what I'm hoping."

Mallory jumped up from her chair. "Then what are we waiting for?"

"Whoa," Jake said, and raised his hands up to stop her. "I said *I* was going to break into Silas's room. You're not going anywhere near the man. It's too risky."

"Really? And how do you propose to break in? According to the local buzz, most of the players, Silas included, are staying at the St. Claire Hotel just outside of New Orleans. I happen to know for certain that there are no ground-level rooms and the hotel has one of those fancy digital door entry systems. You're not going to be able to pick a lock there."

"But you can?"

"Not exactly. But you said you had nothing left to lose, right?"

"At this point, not really."

Mallory grinned. "Then I know just the right people for the job."

Jake wasn't sure how she'd convinced him to go along with her plan. It was crazy—suicide—professionally and perhaps personally. If his boss ever found out he'd used a civilian to break the law, much less three of them, he'd never work in law enforcement again.

But desperation did strange things to people, and Jake had pretty much crossed that line by the end of the day. Which is why an hour later, he found himself wedged into the back cab of Scooter's Dodge pickup, bouncing along a "shortcut" to the hotel while Mallory alternated between discussing the plan with Scooter and checking in with someone named Amy, who had been stationed at the hotel and was feeding them information on Silas's location.

"Silas just came downstairs for dinner," Mallory said, and flipped her phone shut. "He's eating at the nicer of the two restaurants, so we'll probably have an hour and a half or so to get in and out."

Mallory began discussing the night's event with Scooter, making plans for a quiet entrance, which mostly consisted of Mallory explaining to Scooter what a quiet entrance was. Jake hoped he'd been off the beer long enough to decipher it because his driving hadn't exactly been an indication of sobriety. He was just about to suggest that maybe talking *and* driving wasn't a good idea for Scooter when they pulled into the back parking lot of the ten-story hotel.

Jake scanned the parking lot as they pulled to a stop near the rear entrance of the hotel and was relieved to see there were no other people or cars around. They'd no sooner exited the truck when the pretty little blonde who had been dealing at the tournament hurried over to them.

"He's ordered the works—salad, appetizer, wine, everything," the blonde said. "You've got plenty of time."

Jake stared at the girl in surprise. "You're Amy?" He looked over at Mallory, trying to control his aggravation. "It's one thing if your uncle wants to hire children to deal, although I have a huge problem with it, but I'm not going to involve them in this mess. It's bad enough I'm involving you."

Mallory laughed.

Amy glared at him. "I happen to be twenty-three, and I'm not showing you my ID, so don't even ask." She turned to face Mallory and grumbled something he couldn't quite make out and probably didn't want to.

"Don't sweat it, Amy," Mallory said. "You can take care of him with your long-term plan."

Amy glanced back at him, giving him a quick up and down. "I guess so," she said. "But it's a shame you were right in your assessment."

Another woman calling him an asshole. He was really collecting notches in his belt, and not in a good way. "Can someone please tell me the plan for this three-ring circus?"

Scooter looked up from the bed of his truck and pulled out a drill. "This baby is ready to go," he said.

Mallory nodded and started walking toward the back door of the hotel, Scooter and Amy trailing along. Jake sighed, then fell in step behind them. This was going to turn out bad. He just knew it.

When they reached the door, Scooter crouched down and studied the lock for a moment, then changed the tip on the drill to something thinner. He poked the drill bit inside the lock and started to drill.

Jake stared at Mallory, certain she'd lost her mind. "This is your plan? It's one thing to break into Silas's room, but the hotel? He's ruining the lock. Someone will know there was a break-in."

Amy rolled her eyes and turned her back to him, pretending an intense interest in Scooter's destruction of the lock. Mallory looked over at him and smiled. "You have to trust me. Scooter is the absolute best at these things. By the time he's done, we'll be in the building and the only thing management will ever know about this door is that the locking mechanism stopped rotating and their keys won't work. There will be no sign of tampering—at least not from the outside."

"And when they remove the lock and see the inside?"

"They won't remove the lock. They'll call Scooter to fix or replace it. Scooter built a good portion of this hotel and installed all the hardware. They call him about most everything except changing lightbulbs."

Jake stared at Mallory in surprise. He took another glance at the hotel, a beautiful structure with complicated angles and balconies jutting out all over the face. Scooter had built this? He hadn't seen the man without a beer since he'd met him. Hell, he'd drunk two before they left Mallory's cabin. How in the world had he put down his brewski long enough to build a hotel?

He heard a loud click and Scooter looked up with a grin. "That's it." He rose and twisted the knob. It turned easily and he opened the door a crack, peering inside. "The manager's office is the first one on the left, but remember, as soon as I close this door behind you, it's locked permanently. You'll have to come out a different way."

Mallory nodded. "That's not a problem. Scooter, I want you to take your truck and head around front. Once Amy gets me the room key, you two grab some seats at the bar and keep an eye on Silas. Do *not* let him see you. If you haven't heard from me by the time they bring Silas the check, call me on my cell so we can clear out. Then make sure Silas takes the elevator, and we'll head down the stairs."

"Sounds good to me," Scooter said. "All this work has made me thirsty."

Mallory peeked into the hotel and gave the others a nod. "Let's do it," she said, and eased through the doorway, Amy trailing behind her. Jake took one final look around the parking lot, said a silent prayer, and stepped after them.

The master key Scooter had provided for the interior locks worked like a charm on the manager's office, and the three of them slipped inside. Amy hurried behind the desk, booted up the computer, and started hacking into the hotel network. Jake stood anxiously near the door, watching through a tiny crack to make sure no one was coming. He tried not to think about exactly how many laws they were breaking.

He heard Amy give a small cry of triumph and looked over to find her grinning at Mallory. "I told you," Amy said. "Piece of cake."

Mallory just nodded. "Well, you can eat cake later. Get the card so we can get the hell out of here."

Amy pulled open the drawers on the manager's desk and scanned through them. "There aren't any room cards here."

Mallory gave her a look of mild panic. "There has to be room cards. Don't tell me every card in this hotel is at the front desk."

Amy shrugged. "It's no big deal." She reached into her pocket, pulled out a tiny pink wallet and removed a Visa card from it. Then she typed some more into the computer and slid the Visa through the magnetic card reader. The light at the end of the reader turned green, and Amy handed the card to Jake. "I'd better give this to you—just in case Mallory's in a demagnetizing mode."

Jake slipped the card into his jeans pocket.

"Okay," Mallory said to Amy, "You get to the bar with Scooter and keep an eye on Silas."

Amy nodded. "Silas is in Room 514. Be careful. And good luck." She stepped past Mallory, completely ignoring Jake, before slipping out the door.

"You ready?" Mallory asked.

Jake nodded. "Let's get this over with."

They left the manager's office, ensuring the door was locked behind them, and headed toward the back stairwell. Jake unlocked the door, and they slipped inside, hurrying up the stairwell as quietly as possible. It seemed to Jake that it should have taken longer to climb five flights of stairs, but before he knew it, they were staring at an entry door for the fifth floor.

"This is it," Jake said. "Are you sure you want to do this? I really appreciate you and your friends getting me this far, but I don't need your help searching the room. There's no sense in both of us taking the risk."

Mallory shook her head. "Silas had all that information on me, and that makes it personal. Besides, both of us looking will get it done faster so we can get the hell out of here."

He still didn't like it but couldn't exactly argue. Having her involved saved him the time of sorting through things he might not immediately understand. "All right," he said as he pushed the door open and stepped into the hallway.

They tried to appear nonchalant as they walked down the hall, just in case anyone stepped out of a room or off the elevator. The easiest way to be overlooked was to give the appearance of a young couple staying at the hotel, minus the hand-holding part, of course. Hand-holding with Mallory would most likely come with repercussions they didn't need at the moment.

They were almost to the end of the hallway when a door to one of the rooms opened and Brad, the dealer at the table next to Jake, stepped into the hall. Jake inwardly cursed his bad luck and prepared to play the role of the cad who'd decided to hook up with the attendant, but he didn't even get the chance to move into action.

Brad's usual simple, jovial expression was hard, his eyes narrowed at the two of them and flashing with anger. He reached into his pocket and pulled out a badge with the initials ATF on it, then motioned for the two of them to enter his room. Surprised, Jake stepped into the room, Mallory close behind.

Brad shut the door and turned to face them. "What the hell do you think you're doing? And don't even try and pass off some stupid story about a rendezvous." He pointed toward the door. "There's only one room left past mine and it belongs to Silas Hebert."

Brad pointed a finger at Jake. "You have stuck out like a sore thumb since you arrived at the casino. It only took me two minutes to peg you as a Fed and another five minutes to find out exactly why you were here. Why in God's name didn't they get someone Southern for this job? Someone who could blend?" He waved one hand in dismissal. "Never mind. I don't even care. I just want you out of here and lying low."

"I've got my own business to take care of," Jake said. "And it doesn't involve the ATF."

"The hell it doesn't! This tournament is all about the ATF. We've been building a case for over three years, and I'm not about to let a money-laundering bust by the FBI interfere with taking down one of the largest arms deals of the decade."

Mallory gasped and stared at Brad in horror. "Oh, my God! Is that what my uncle's involved in? Arms dealing?"

Brad gave her a derisive look. "Please. Reginald St. Claire isn't a big enough player to do this kind of business. He doesn't have the smarts—or the balls if all his protesting is any indication of his backbone."

Mallory's face cleared in understanding and she narrowed her eyes at Brad. "But he has the connections, right? You were the one who put together this tournament. You made up the list of players hoping to get enough evidence to bust them when they were all together. Exactly what do you have on my uncle?"

"Enough to make him play. Insurance fraud and some creative accounting that the IRS might be interested in, among other things."

Mallory stared at him, disgusted. "And what about all the people you've put in the middle of your crap—the attendants, the dealers, the kitchen staff? You're risking their safety, and you don't even care."

Brad shrugged. "We took the necessary precautions. That was the purpose of the metal detectors. Besides, all the employees had a choice when they took this job. If they didn't know about the players' list beforehand, anyone had an opportunity to step off the boat that first day."

"Without pay," Mallory argued. "They could step off the boat and have no pay coming by Friday."

"Not my problem. And neither is some piddly crap the FBI wants to hang on Silas Hebert. The two of you are not going to fuck up my takedown. If Silas catches either of you spying on him, he'll leave immediately and tell the others that the Feds are here. It won't take five minutes to make this entire tournament a ghost town."

"So Silas Hebert isn't part of your ATF bust?" Mallory asked. "Then why was he invited?"

"We were watching him," Brad admitted, "but so far there is no indication that he's involved with any of the people we're looking to take down." He pointed at them. "The two of you are going to leave here and forget any thoughts you may have had about breaking into Silas's room."

"And if we don't?" Jake asked, trying to control the anger in his voice.

"Then I'll arrest you both and stick you in a cell long enough to make you rethink your actions." He nodded at Jake. "And I'll have your job, unless of course, you want to try and convince me that breaking and entering is now sanctioned by the FBI."

Jake felt his hand involuntarily clench into a fist. He'd never wanted to hit anyone so much in his life, but he had to maintain control. Otherwise, Brad would have every reason in the world to lock him up until the tournament was over. "I guess this means we're not going fishing together this weekend?"

"Ha. That's funny, McMillan. I'll say this—you've got some balls."

"Someone in this room ought to have balls," Mallory

shot back. "If you're quite done lording over people and ruining lives, I think we'll leave. Unless of course, you're arresting us."

Brad studied them long and hard, and Jake could see Mallory holding her breath. Then Brad waved a hand in the air. "Go on. Get the hell out of here. And don't let me catch you in this hotel again."

Mallory spun around to leave, but her foot twisted on the way around and she stumbled a bit to the left. Brad grabbed her by the shoulder as she fell against him. "Sorry," she said as he righted her.

"Yeah, whatever." Brad said, and stalked over to the doorway and yanked open the door. As he stood in the doorway, watching them exit and walk down the hall, his cell phone began to ring.

Mallory slowed her walk a bit, and Jake wondered what in the world she was doing. She put a single finger to her lips, then tilted her head back toward Brad, who was punching buttons on the cell phone in obvious aggravation.

"Hello. Can you hear me now? Damn cell phones!" The door to the hotel room slammed shut with a bang.

Mallory grinned and stepped around the corner to the elevator. "I should really be more careful when I walk."

Jake smiled. "You are an evil, evil woman."

"I know. It's a beautiful thing, right? Unless he needs to fire a weapon in the next several hours."

Jake gave her a look of mild panic. "Oh shit. I didn't even think about that." He looked back around the corner for a moment, then shrugged. "To hell with him. He probably won't even leave his room, so unless he opens fire on the cell phone, he's safe enough."

Mallory looked at Jake. "Well? What now?"

Jake blew out a breath and ran one hand through his hair. "Damn it! What are the fucking odds? I knew something was wrong about this tournament, but I never dreamed Reginald had got yanked in by a federal agency. I thought he was just having some fun all on his own."

Mallory nodded. "But it explains everything—the players' list, Reginald's anger, and definitely why he'd be willing to cough up ten thousand to me. He runs the risk of losing everything if his dealers can't win. Word on the street is that he owes money to a loan shark in New Orleans. What do you want to bet that he had to borrow part of the money to cover this tournament?"

"We're all screwed," Jake said, "and there's not a damned thing we can do about it."

Mallory thought for a moment. "That's not entirely true. If we're screwed anyway then what do we have to lose? I mean, I guess you still have your job if you walk away, but I won't. I can break in myself and search the room. If I get caught, J.T. will bail me out."

"You're not going in there alone."

"I don't remember asking your permission."

Jake smiled. "Yes, but I have the room key, and short of pulling a gun on me, I don't think you have the equipment to take me down."

"Really? Well, some of us don't have to carry weapons— we are one." She waved one hand in the air. "So what's it going to be?"

The thought of a grappling match with Mallory had Jake's mind bending in a million different directions, some of them not unpleasant. "That's playing dirty."

"Maybe the only way to beat them is to sink to their level. So are you coughing up that card or do I have to tackle you here in the hall? Your friend Brad might get a kick out of it."

Jake stared at her for a moment, then muttered under his breath as he drew the card from his pocket. "Fine, but

I'm going in with you. If I'm going to screw up this bust and lose my job anyway, I might as well go out with a bang." He peeked around the corner, ensuring the hallway was still clear, then hurried down the hall to Silas's room, Mallory close behind. When he reached the door, he pulled the credit card out of his pocket and slid the card into the lock.

Red light.

He looked over at her and she motioned for him to try again. Turning back toward the door, he held his breath as he slid the card in and out again.

Green light. They were in.

Chapter Eleven

Mallory held her breath as Jake eased open the door and stuck his head inside. What if Amy was wrong and Silas hadn't gone to the restaurant? What if Silas was gone but he'd left one of his hired goons behind? A couple of seconds passed and felt like an eternity before Jake looked back out and motioned for her to follow. She let out the breath she'd been holding and slipped into the room, pulling the door closed silently behind her.

"Remember to put everything back exactly as you found it," Jake warned. "We don't want Silas to suspect anyone was here."

Mallory glanced around the room, taking it all in. "Should we start with the luggage?"

"Yeah, that's probably best," Jake said, but a quick inspection of the luggage showed it to be empty. Obviously Silas had unpacked for his week's adventures. "I'll take the dresser and the nightstands," Jake said. "You get the bathroom and the closet."

Mallory nodded and headed for the vanity located off the bathroom. She started with his grooming bag—razor, comb, hair products, deodorant—nothing alarming there. She turned around and slid open the closet door.

There were several suits hanging inside, all top dollar and recently pressed, probably by the hotel valet service. She wasn't likely to find anything inside the pockets, but she searched them anyway, running her hands through every available storage space on the jackets, pants and shirts.

When she was satisfied that the suits were clean, she looked up at the shelf, which held a row of shoe boxes. The man actually traveled with his shoes in separate containers. He probably folded his underwear, too. She reached up, grabbed the first box and pulled off the lid, revealing the black dress shoes inside. She felt down inside of each shoe and turned the box around, making sure nothing was tucked or taped inside or written on the cardboard itself.

Satisfied the box contained nothing of interest, she placed it back on the shelf and moved on to the next one until she was down to the last box on the shelf. It was way too light to be holding shoes, and she'd already seen one empty box on the floor, which she assumed was for the pair Silas had worn to dinner.

She propped the box on her left arm, then pulled off the lid. When she saw what was inside, she gasped, dropping the lid to the floor.

A voodoo doll.

A voodoo doll that looked exactly like her, down to the short black skirt and matching jacket she'd worn the first day of the tournament.

She heard Jake ask what was wrong, but she couldn't find her voice, couldn't make a sound. A second later, he was standing beside her. "What the hell?" he asked, and stared down at the contents of the box. "Where did you get that?"

She pointed to the empty space on the top shelf. "It's a voodoo doll." She looked over at Jake. "Of me."

Jake took the box from her hands and put the lid back on it. "It's bullshit is what it is. There's no scientific proof that voodoo works. It's all urban legend."

"There's no scientific proof for my unluckiness either, but it hasn't changed what I am."

Jake shoved the box on the shelf and shook his head. "It's not the same. God knows, I don't understand any of that paranormal crap, but maybe your situation is as simple as a kind of energy that you can access and the rest of us can't. Maybe you think you're unlucky and somehow your mind creates the energy to make it so."

He pointed to the shoebox. "That is an inanimate object. It has no energy, therefore it can't cause anything to happen. If you fear it, *you're* causing things to happen. Don't you see? It's all in your mind, no matter what."

Mallory looked at him and frowned. "I want to believe that, but a man like Silas . . . why would he bother with something if it didn't work? It can't be the first time. The work on the doll is too perfect, and he had it made too fast. He has a connection somewhere. Someone who was willing to create the doll and deliver it in a matter of twenty-four hours."

"It could have been shipped."

Mallory shook her head. "The service is so horrible, it takes days to get a FedEx here, and if it had been shipped regular mail, Stanley would have opened the package and I'd have known about it sooner."

"Then I don't know how he got it, and I really don't care. It doesn't matter, Mallory, and you can't let it bother you. Do you want me to finish with the closet? You can get the nightstands."

"No," Mallory said, trying to sound like she meant it. "I'm sure you're right. It's all just superstition. I'll finish here." She looked up at him and tried to smile, positive she wasn't successful. He studied her face for a moment, but apparently she'd managed to satisfy him. He nodded once and headed back into the bedroom.

Mallory waited for him to walk around the corner of the vanity, then turned to look in the mirror, watching to see when he disappeared around the corner of the room. When she heard him open the drawer on the nightstand, she stepped to the closet and before she could change her mind, eased the shoebox off the shelf, grabbed the doll and shoved it into the inside pocket of her jacket.

She glanced in the mirror, but Jake was still out of view. She replaced the lid and slipped the box back onto the shelf, making sure it was facing the same way she'd found it. Maybe Silas had the doll but didn't need to look at it, she rationalized. Maybe he wouldn't notice it was gone until the tournament was over and he was packing to leave.

"Aha!" Jake's voice sounded from the next room, causing her to jump.

She smoothed the front of her jacket and stepped around the corner. "You find something?"

Jake held up a deck of cards identical to the ones he was using for the tournament. "Maybe. It might be nothing, but it might be that Silas is palming cards."

"Do you think he could do that without you noticing?"

Jake shrugged. "I'm not sure. But we're going to find out." He pulled a pen from his pocket and began to place a tiny dot in one corner of each card, the black ink hidden in the intricate design—unless you knew exactly what you were looking for. "Check that other nightstand," Jake instructed Mallory. "See if you find anything else."

Mallory stepped around the bed and pulled open the nightstand drawer. She lifted the phone book from inside and found a small leather-bound book beneath it. Pulling the book from the drawer, she saw engraving at the bottom of the cover—"S.H."

"I may have found something," she said, and flipped the book open.

Jake looked up from the cards and smiled, then reached in his shirt pocket and pulled out a tiny pad of paper and a pen. "Make a note of any addresses and phone numbers you find. I'll get my boss to cross-check them with the other information we have on Silas."

Mallory grabbed the pen and paper and jotted down the information in the book, hoping that one of the entries would bring Jake news of his partner's whereabouts. When she got to the fifth page, it was blank. She flipped a couple more pages, but the rest were blanks as well.

"It must be a fairly new book," she said to Jake. "There's only four pages of information."

Jake finished up his deck marking and carefully placed the cards back in their plastic holder. "That's more than we had before. Besides, it only takes one of them to make a difference."

Mallory studied the notes she'd made. "Most of these addresses are New Orleans, and they look like businesses. But this last one . . . I think I know this place. It's an old apartment complex just at the edge of Royal Flush."

Jake looked over at her. "An apartment complex, huh?"

Mallory nodded. "I think it's some sort of affordable housing—you know seniors, disabled, that sort of thing."

"Doesn't sound like the sort of thing Silas would be involved in."

"No. I doubt Silas is involved in anything except things that help Silas."

"I'll have the other agents get on that list first thing." Jake placed the deck of cards back in the nightstand and rose from the bed. "If Silas is using this deck in the tournament, I'll know by tomorrow."

"And what can you do about it? You can't tell Reginald how you know."

"I can always tell Reginald what I suspect. I know he has security cameras everywhere. It shouldn't be impossible to turn one on our table at the right angle to catch the sleeve of his jacket. He's quick enough to fool the naked eye, but running it back in slow motion would clearly show it."

"So you think it's that simple—when Silas couldn't win on the first day, he started cheating? That's why I don't have any effect on him anymore?"

Jake shrugged. "It would explain why you're still affecting the other players but don't seem to have an impact on him." He smiled. "The simplest explanation is usually the right one. That's what they say."

"*They* have probably never been to Louisiana."

Jake laughed. "You get no argument from me there. If you're done in the bathroom, I say we get the hell out of here while our luck is holding."

"All done." Mallory smiled at Jake and felt some of the tension leave her body. Maybe he was right. Maybe it was something as simple as Silas cheating. The voodoo doll was just a desperate attempt from a superstitious man.

It didn't mean a thing.

* * *

Finding the hallway clear—no Brad, no Silas, no other surprises—Jake breathed a sigh of relief. Motioning to Mallory, they crept out of the room, careful to quietly pull the door shut behind them. They slipped silently down the hallway and into the stairwell, then hurried down a full flight before stopping to breathe.

"I can't believe we pulled it off," Jake said, unable to control his elation.

Mallory nodded. "Yeah, but there's a lot of things we're dealing with now—like the whole ATF angle. What are you going to do about that?"

"I don't know and at the moment, I don't care." He grinned at her. "Do you realize that we've got the first lead on Mark that I've had in weeks, and we've most likely figured out how Silas was cheating? We can beat him, Mallory. We will both get what we need out of this."

Mallory smiled back at him. "Yeah, I guess I haven't taken the time to think about the accomplishments, only the new problems."

"Well, stop thinking. We'll have plenty of time to worry later." He took her hand in his and stepped closer to her. "I really appreciate everything you've done for me, Mallory. It would have been so much easier on you to get rid of Silas yesterday and be on your merry way with the money for Harry's business. Don't think for a minute that I don't know that."

Mallory shook her head. "I couldn't let Silas get away. All my life I've heard how bad he was. This is my chance to help get rid of him once and for all. Besides, I couldn't let your partner's wife and kid go on wondering what happened to him. That wouldn't be right."

Jake took another step toward her until their bodies were almost touching. He reached up to touch a tendril

Jana DeLeon

of her hair. "Brave, intelligent and highly principled . . . do you have any flaws, Mallory Devereaux?"

Mallory laughed softly. "You have to ask?"

Jake smiled. "Okay, so one flaw, but at least things are never dull." He lowered his head to hers and murmured, "This should wear off by tomorrow."

A shock wave rolled through his body as their lips touched, almost like an electrical current. Never had a woman's touch made him feel so much, created an ache inside him that had never been there before. He deepened the kiss, mingling his tongue with hers, tasting the sweetness of her mouth. He wanted to touch every inch of her, with his hands, his mouth.

He slid one hand under her shirt, knowing her breasts would be open to his touch, free from restricting garments with complicated openings. She stiffened slightly as his hand slid over her ribcage to cup her breast. He palmed the first one, feeling himself harden as his hand slid over her silky skin. When he rubbed his thumb across the already extended nipple, she moaned, and he almost lost it.

"I want you," he whispered. "Here and now, I want you."

"The others," Mallory argued weakly. "They might catch us."

Jake dropped his kiss to the hollow of her neck, still stroking her engorged nipple. "No one will be looking for us here. Besides, the stairwell is locked. And believe me, this is not going to take a long time. I'm too far gone for you, Mallory. I don't have much self-control left."

Mallory laughed. "And that's supposed to turn me on—admitting that you'll be the five-minute man?"

Jake pulled away from her a bit and smiled. "Knowing what you do to me turns you on. I can see it in your eyes.

176

Consider me a work in progress. After all, if we don't get it perfect the first time, we'll have to keep working at it, right?"

Mallory dropped one hand from his shoulder and barely brushed it across the front of his jeans. "Then let's hear it for mediocrity."

He groaned and locked his lips on hers again, pushing her back against the cement wall.

She broke off the kiss and gave him a playful laugh, wagging one finger in his face. "Oh no. You've been in charge of everything since I met you. It's time for me to call the shots."

Jake laughed. "You think I've been in charge? I must have missed that part, but by all means, Ms. Devereaux, please have your way with me."

She ran one hand across his crotch, this time stronger, with more purpose, then gave him a wicked grin and began to lower herself down in front of him.

As Mallory dropped another inch down the wall, Jake saw the collar of her jacket rising behind her and realized it was caught on something on the wall. He could only see part of the label, but the words "In case of fire" were enough to cause panic. Too late, he reached for her, trying to stop her descent, as a single click came from the wall behind her. Mallory looked up, both worry and confusion on her face.

Then all hell broke loose.

Water rushed out of the spout in the ceiling, soaking them both. A second later, the fire alarm went off and deafened them with its shrill sirens. They both froze for a moment, until the shout of voices all over the hotel set them into action.

"Down!" Jake spun around and rushed down the stairs,

Mallory close behind. "We can't go all the way to the first floor or we'll definitely be caught," he said as they ran. "We'll have to get off on two and find a place to hide."

Above them, the stairwell door opened, and they heard Brad's voice shouting, "That better not be you, McMillan!"

They hit the landing for the second floor, flung open the door and rushed into the hallway, desperately hoping they wouldn't run into anyone they were trying to avoid. A sea of people hurried past them headed for the stairwell.

"There's a fire!" one of them yelled as he passed. "You need to evacuate."

Jake pulled the credit card from his pocket. "Will this work on another room?"

Mallory shook her head. "I don't know. Maybe."

Jake stepped to the first door and slid the card into the scanner. "These rooms are probably empty with everyone evacuating. It's only a one-story drop from the balcony."

Red light.

"Damn!" He slid the card again with the same result. Meanwhile, the shouts on the stairwell had turned from those of frightened patrons to that of a very angry Brad.

"Try again. We're running out of time!"

Jake slid the card again, holding his breath as he watched the indicator.

Green light.

"We're in!" he shouted as he pushed the door open and rushed inside, Mallory right on his heels.

It only took them a moment to realize the room wasn't empty, but the sight in front of them took way longer to register. Reginald St. Claire stood at the foot of a king-sized bed, wearing a French maid outfit, complete with fishnet hose and black FMPs. The woman standing on the bed was barely three feet tall, wearing a black leather outfit and mask, complete with metal studs and a matching whip.

Jake stared at the casino owner, not sure whether to try to explain or pretend not to recognize him at all. Either way, keeping Reginald in the dark about the hotel adventure was going to be impossible.

"Maintenance," Jake shouted, latching onto the first thing he could come up with. "There's a problem with your patio door." He reached back and grabbed Mallory, shoving her in front of him and hoping she didn't stop long enough to look too closely. His hopes were dashed when she ran around him, then came to a screeching halt.

"Oh, my God," Mallory gasped. "I thought they were joking."

Hands on her shoulders, Jake propelled her past the sideshow in front of them and onto the balcony. "I don't even want to know. Let's just get the hell out of here."

Mallory rushed out onto the balcony and flipped over the railing, dropping into the bushes below. Jake crossed to the other side of the railing, casting one final glance behind him as he did. St. Claire and the woman still hadn't moved, both of them staring at him as he let go of the railing and hoped the bushes below didn't have prickly leaves.

He bent his knees all the way down as he connected with the ground, hoping to prevent any long-term damage from their circus flight. Mallory was already out of the bushes and running across the narrow strip of lawn. He started to yell at her to come back when he realized Scooter's battered truck was racing across the parking lot toward them. He pushed himself up and ran behind her. Both of them dove into the bed of the pickup truck, which had slowed just enough for them to jump in. Scooter squealed out of the parking lot and away from the hotel, yelling out the window that he'd gotten to do the Dale Earnhardt thing, after all.

As soon as Scooter exited the main highway, he stopped long enough for Mallory and Jake to climb out of the bed of the truck and into the cab. Even though the leather seats in the back of Scooter's cab were cracked in places and the support sagged in spots, Mallory knew it had to be more comfortable than the bed of the truck. But she was so exhausted by the night's events that she hardly noticed a difference as she slid inside.

Which was a shame, really, when you considered just how much energy she'd had in the stairwell. Apparently, running from criminals and the feds and seeing your uncle in a dress had a way of sapping the strength right out of you.

They filled in Scooter and Amy on the duplicate deck of cards during the ride back home, but neither Mallory nor Jake broached the subject of the ATF, or Jake's partner, and definitely nothing to do with Reginald, or little people or maids. Even her good leather jacket was looking like a great candidate for Goodwill.

It was dark by the time they pulled into the driveway, and Mallory desperately craved a hot shower and a cool bed. Amy had already announced her intention to stay the night for protection, so even if Mallory had any sexual tension left, it was going to have to wait. Not that she was entirely clear who was doing the protecting, either. Because unless they were having a calculus contest, Amy wasn't any match for the people Mallory had run into.

Jake thanked her friends for all their help, nodded at her and jumped in his rental car. Giving Mallory a long lingering look, he backed out of the driveway and waved as he headed down the road to the highway.

Mallory watched until his taillights faded in the distance, yelled good night to Scooter, who was already stepping onto his front porch, and walked toward her own cabin, where Amy had disappeared minutes before.

Amy was sitting on the couch bed, perched on one side and clutching a huge bag of potato chips. "I hope you don't mind," she said. "All this Spies R Us has made me hungry."

Mallory laughed. "I have roast beef in the fridge. Why don't you make us both a sandwich while I take a shower. I think that bush molested me. I'm all itchy."

Amy jumped off the bed. "Supper will be ready when you return."

Mallory slipped into the bathroom and pulled the door shut behind her, turning the lock. It wasn't likely that someone with Amy's upbringing would come barging in on her, but she wasn't taking any chances. She opened the closet door and dug around the back until she found an empty box. Open box on the floor in front of her, she reached inside her jacket and pulled out the voodoo doll.

She wondered how something so simple could bring out such fear in her. Aside from her bad luck, she'd always been a rational person. Why would something so unproven, so bound to superstitions of the ignorant, scare her this way?

She tore her gaze from the doll, closed it in the shoe box, and shoved the box into the back of her closet. Answers weren't going to come standing in her bathroom, and the last thing she needed to do with everything on the line was spook herself. Like she wasn't already halfway there.

A quick pass through the shower and a set of clean clothes made her feel physically more comfortable even if mentally, it hadn't been much help. By the time she returned to the living room, Amy was already propped up on the roll-out bed, clutching a huge roast beef sandwich. She pointed to another plate on the end table and Mallory grabbed the sandwich before plopping down on the other side of the rollout.

"So?" Amy asked as she chewed.

Mallory looked over at her friend and shook her head. "Didn't your momma teach you not to talk with your mouth full?"

Amy gave her the finger and swallowed. "Yeah, she taught me not to do that too. It's a good thing I met you when I did—it was almost too late to reverse all that charm-school learning." She batted her eyes at Mallory and plastered a beauty-queen smile on her face.

Mallory laughed. "If your mother knew half the things you've picked up from me, she might lose a bit of charm herself—at least long enough to shoot me."

Amy grinned. "Now that would be a sight—Mother with a weapon. The closest thing I've ever seen to that was when she used one of her designer shoes to kill a bug. Then she swore me to silence."

"What's wrong with killing a bug?"

"*Ladies* are not supposed to involve themselves in anything rough, even bug killing. She should have called a servant to take care of it."

"Are you sure you weren't adopted?"

"Mom would like to think so, but it was a natural birth, so her memory's real clear." Amy swallowed the last bite of her sandwich and turned on the rollout to face Mallory. "So what else did you find? And no holding back. There were an awful lot of people scrambling in that hotel when the alarm went off, and they weren't all running for the exit. I'm not about to believe that all of them belonged to Silas."

"They probably didn't." Mallory looked her friend

straight in the eyes. "You absolutely cannot repeat what I'm about to tell you."

Amy nodded. "Promise."

Mallory told her what they'd learned from Brad.

"Oh, my God," Amy said when Mallory was done. "What about the box of guns Scooter found in the storeroom. Is Reginald in on the dealing?"

"Brad says no, and I believe him."

"But then why have the guns?"

"I'm hoping to God the guns belong to the ATF, because I don't really want to consider any alternatives."

Amy set down her sandwich and stared out the window for a couple of seconds, then turned back to Mallory. "I just can't believe it. It's so HBO feature film. I mean, you knew he was up to something, but good grief, how many federal agents are occupying the same square footage in a hole-in-the-wall in Louisiana? It's a statistical anomaly."

"My whole life is a statistical anomaly. Why would this be any different?"

"You know, with that alarm going off in the hotel, all those guys are going to be on high alert—the good guys and the bad guys—not that it's all that easy to tell them apart at the moment. I bet none of them chalk it up to coincidence."

"Probably not."

"That ATF guy, Brad, he's going to know it was you and Jake."

"He's going to think it was us. He's not going to have any proof."

Amy sighed. "What a mess. And you tried to tell me, Mallory. I'm sorry I didn't come to you before I signed up."

"What's done is done."

"I guess you're right, but what a disaster." Amy closed

her eyes for a moment, as if in prayer, then opened them again and stared at the ceiling. "Hey," she said finally. "What do you think set off that alarm anyway? I never saw any smoke at all."

Oh there was smoke all right. And fire, but Mallory wasn't about to tell Amy that it had all come from the stairwell action between her and Jake. "My jacket got caught on the sprinkler release when we were hiding in the stairwell. When I moved, it set the whole thing off."

Amy stared at her for a moment, and Mallory was afraid her friend was going to see right through her flimsy story, but she finally smiled, then giggled, then collapsed in a heap over her pillow, her whole body shaking with laughter.

"I'm sorry, Mallory, but that is so you. If there were ever a time you needed to be quiet and unobtrusive, this was it, and instead you managed to evacuate a hotel and put every federal agent and criminal in Louisiana on high alert."

Mallory thought about it for a moment and decided if it hadn't been her, and she hadn't been about to get lucky (so to speak) for the first time in years, it might have been funny in a sad, twisted, how-could-I-possibly-fuck-things-up-more sort of way. Finally, she gave in and laughed along with Amy.

It was either that or cry.

They stayed up a little while longer, talking about Amy's thesis, movies, what they wanted to do for vacation—anything unrelated to poker, criminals, bad luck or men. When Amy finally started yawning more than talking, Mallory reached over for the body pillow and positioned it down the center of the bed between them just as her friend nodded off.

She glanced at her uneaten sandwich but still didn't feel hungry, even though she hadn't eaten since lunch. She was tired but restless, and knew if she tried to force sleep, it would be the kind filled with hectic dreams and frantic situations. The kind where you woke up more tired than before you went to bed. She got up and took a look back at her sleeping friend. Amy's body was curled in a tiny ball, her back pressed against the giant pillow.

The pillow that protected her from Mallory.

Tearing her gaze away from the rollout, Mallory stepped out onto her back porch. The night air was thick with humidity, but a gentle breeze rolling in off the bayou created that nighttime chill that was so common in the spring. She leaned against one post of the porch and watched the tide roll out, the moonlight glittering across its surface like diamonds.

It was better this way, that things between her and Jake had stopped where they did. Breaking into Silas's room was already crossing personal boundaries, especially after a childhood filled with court appearances, Child Protection Services drop-ins and Sunday prison visits. Hell, she'd never even had a traffic ticket, much less done something she could have gone to jail for.

A week ago, if anyone had told her she'd be cooling cards for Reginald and breaking and entering into Silas Hebert's hotel room—with the aid of an FBI agent, no less—she would have accused them of being in the sun too long or trying to outdrink Scooter. But then a week ago, Harry's business wasn't at stake, an FBI agent wasn't missing, and Silas Hebert wasn't at the crux of it all, at least not that she'd known about.

Falling for Jake McMillan was a whole other issue and one she simply couldn't afford. She didn't even know his real name. And what difference did it make when she knew he would be back north of the Mason-Dixon by the weekend, probably vowing to never return to Royal Flush as long as he lived? Breaking the law was something she'd live with, even justify due to the circumstances.

Breaking her heart was not an option.

Chapter Twelve

Jake knew the moment Mallory entered the casino. A strange sensation pulsed through his body, and he looked up at the doorway as she stepped inside. She was beautiful, as always, but even from across the floor he could tell her step lacked the usual energetic bounce and her expression was more thoughtful than playful.

The situation was taking a toll on her, and for that, he felt guilty.

Jake noticed Mallory was careful to avoid his gaze. Probably a good idea. With all his training and experience, Jake could force a blank face if needed, but Mallory's life had probably never called for anything but the truth, something she was used to delivering like rapid gunfire.

Once she'd taken the drink orders and headed off to the kitchen, Jake pulled the first of the cards from the shoe and dealt it across the table. There wasn't any use in waiting on Mallory for the first hand. The other players weren't a threat to him, and Silas had obviously found a way to work around her. A way Jake hoped would surface sometime today.

They were just finishing up the first hand when Mallory returned with the coffee. Father Thomas had managed to play out a rather good hand and had taken a fairly impressive pot to start the day. He beamed up at Mallory as she slid between him and another player to place the mug of coffee in front of him.

"Mallory, my child," the priest said. "Look at the start of the Lord's day—it's rained chips like manna."

Mallory grinned. "Now that would be an impressive trick. And a very dangerous one in this town."

All the other players, except Silas, laughed and even Father Thomas gave her words some consideration. "Perhaps you're right," he said finally. "I shall keep this blessing the Lord has given me to myself. For the safety of the community, of course."

"Of course."

Father Thomas turned to the table and started to pick up his drink when he noticed it was coffee. "What's this? It's already ten A.M. Why did you bring me coffee?"

Mallory moved to the next player and placed another coffee on the table. "Because the casino is completely out of Jack Daniel's—no thanks to you—and there won't be more in until lunch, at which point we'll be about a hundred miles offshore on this floating boat of fun. Add to that, the beer cooler broke down sometime last night, so all the beer is hot. Scooter fixed it, but it will probably take until lunchtime to cool everything off again."

Father Thomas stared at her with a look of dismay. "The plague has come upon us."

"Well, unless you plan on parting the Gulf of Mexico so the delivery truck can drive out here, you're going to have to choose another way to pickle your liver. I brought the coffee to give you time to decide."

Mallory finished up drink service and slid onto her stool, giving Jake a brief nod. She'd done a thorough job touching the players, even Silas, though it was probably a complete waste of time. Still, Jake understood why she needed to try and respected her for doing it.

He dealt the next hand across the table, then reached down to flip up the edge of his cards, hoping for something good enough to keep him in play.

No way!

He stared at the cards, utilizing every ounce of control he had to maintain a blank look on his face. And the royal flush stared back at him in all its glory.

What the hell?

The other men had already made their discards, and he had to think fast. It was tempting to keep the hand, even though he knew there was absolutely no way he could. Finally, he took the ace and king and tossed them into the pile of discards. He dealt the replacement cards and desperately hoped for a miracle.

He held his breath as he pulled the edge of the cards off the table and almost fell over when he saw what lay beneath his fingers—an ace and a king of a different suit. It was as if the first day of the tournament were happening all over again.

As if Mallory's bad luck was back in play.

Mallory watched in amazement as hand after hand went Jake's way. It was as if someone had flipped her switch back on. But how?

Her mind flashed to the voodoo doll hidden in her closet and she drew in a breath. Had that really been the catalyst? Had Silas Hebert held some kind of power over her through the doll? It was the only explanation, the only thing that had changed from yesterday to today.

And it was the last thing she wanted to believe.

Jake appeared normal as he played the hands out, but Mallory knew him well enough by now to know that a confused interior lurked behind that calm facade. Which meant he had no idea why the table had turned, either.

She felt Silas's eyes upon her and shifted on her stool. She'd caught him stealing looks at her several times that morning and felt his stare even more often than she'd seen it, her skin prickling each time.

Did he know? Had he done an inventory of his room after they'd left the hotel and found the doll missing? Or was he simply thinking she and Jake had some elaborate way of cheating and he hadn't been able to figure out how?

Maybe Silas guessed someone had broken into his room, and he'd found the deck of marked cards. Maybe Silas just wasn't cheating any longer because he figured they were onto him. But then if he'd found the marked cards, why in the world didn't he just buy a brand-new deck and proceed as before? The entire situation did not add up, no matter how you sliced it.

She managed to keep her cool until lunch, excused herself from the table almost immediately, and hurried to the ladies' room, hoping to catch Amy before she left for the dining room. The whole voodoo-doll thing was really bothering her, and she needed a second opinion— a rational one, she hoped—before she jumped off the deep end.

Unfortunately, Walter Royal stopped her before she could exit the casino.

"Mallory," he said, with a full-toothed grin, "I've been

meaning to ask you about your truck. That's company property, right? Is that a six cylinder or an eight?"

Mallory grit her teeth and glared at him. "The truck belongs to me, but I'll be happy to remove the Harry Breaux Construction sticker from the door."

Royal looked somewhat disappointed, then brightened. "Oh well, it was an old model anyway. Can't have my new foreman driving around in a beat-up truck. I've got a reputation to protect." He tipped his hat at her and strolled down the hall, whistling as he went.

Mallory stared after him and fought the urge to put an NFL move on the man. Walter Royal gave the term "son of a bitch" a whole new meaning. Trying to block her mind from the potty king and his ridiculous hat, she hurried on to the ladies' room, hoping Amy hadn't already gone to the dining room for lunch.

Amy was just reapplying her lipstick when Mallory burst into the ladies' room and motioned her back toward the lockers. She gave Mallory a surprised look at her frantic waving, but dropped her lipstick in her purse and followed Mallory into the dressing area without a word.

Thankfully, the dressing area was empty, so Mallory whirled around to face her confused friend as soon as they stepped inside. "I am in big trouble, Amy."

Amy's eyes widened. "What's wrong? Is it the ATF?"

"I wish." Mallory reached into her locker and brought out the shoe box with the voodoo doll. She wasn't really sure why she'd brought the doll with her that morning. Her original thought had been to pitch it off the boat somewhere in the middle of the Gulf, but so far, she couldn't bring herself to go through with it.

"I took this from Silas's room last night," Mallory continued. "Jake doesn't know." She lifted the lid off the box and turned it so that Amy had a clear view.

Amy took one look inside the box and gasped. "Oh, my God! Mallory, that looks exactly like you . . . even the outfit."

"I know. Why do you think I took it?"

Amy shuddered and looked away from the doll. "Okay, that's just creepy. Why in the world would Silas Hebert have a voodoo doll of you?"

"I don't know. I was thinking maybe we could find out something about it. I mean, someone had to make it, right? And somehow Silas Hebert doesn't seem the type to sew doll clothes."

"Okay," Amy said, and slowly focused back on the doll. "I can agree with you so far, but how are we supposed to find out anything when we're trapped on this floating wreck out in the middle of the Gulf?"

Mallory bit her lower lip, knowing she was asking a lot of her friend. "My uncle has a makeshift office on the second floor of the casino. He has a part-time bookkeeper or something who uses it a couple of times a week, but otherwise, it should be empty. He's got a computer in there, and I know he has satellite Internet service."

"Can we get to the office without Reginald seeing us?"

"I think so," Mallory replied. Since it seemed that she and her uncle had gone to great lengths to avoid running into each other today, Mallory couldn't imagine Reginald would be out and about during the lunch hour.

"Then let's get going." Amy smiled and shoved her purse back in her locker. "You know, my life has gotten a whole lot more interesting lately. I'm beginning to think hanging out with you more often might have its advantages."

Mallory gave a single laugh and stepped out of the dressing room. "Oh yeah, potential arrests, the risk of crossfire, voodoo dolls . . . I can see why you wouldn't want to miss out on any of that."

Amy just grinned and followed her out of the ladies' room and up the stairs to the second floor. The office was at the far end of the hall, and Mallory let out a sigh of relief when she pushed open the door and found the room empty. Amy hurried behind the desk to the computer and started working her password magic. It didn't even take a minute before she was logged in and ready to go.

"Piece of cake," Amy said, and smiled. "Now hand me that creepy doll. I want to see if there's a tag or something on it. Something that may lead us to who made it."

Mallory hesitated for a moment then passed the doll across the desk. "It looks handmade, Amy. I don't know that you'll find anything that way."

Amy shrugged. "So then I go about searching the long way. I just figured if the person who made this fancies themself an artist of any kind, they might have put their name or at least initials somewhere on the doll."

It made sense, sort of, if you could go along with the idea that an artist would want to advertise he or she was practicing voodoo. "You look for a tag. I'm not touching that thing."

Amy opened the box and stared down at the doll, the doubt on her face clear as day. "Do you know if it works?"

"What do you mean? Of course, I don't know. Not for sure. But if you consider that Silas had it yesterday and won, and I took it last night and now he's not winning, well . . . you have to wonder."

Amy nodded and reached into the box, lifting the doll from its resting place. "Maybe we should test it."

"What? How the hell would we do that? I don't know a thing about voodoo and neither do you." Mallory slid between the desk and the stack of boxes lined against the wall and inched toward Amy.

Amy studied the doll a minute more, then pulled a butterfly barrette from her hair and poked the doll in the leg.

"Ouch!" The pain in Mallory's thigh was so quick, so unexpected, that she yelled before she'd been able to stop herself. Amy jerked back her hand and stared at Mallory, a horrified look on her face.

"Oh, my God! It works, Mallory. This doll works."

Mallory looked down and pulled a metal ruler from in between the boxes. She held the ruler up for Amy to see. "It's just a ruler," she said, secretly thanking God she hadn't tossed the doll overboard as she'd planned. Involuntary suicide was hardly the way she wanted to exit this life and with her luck, she never knew what might happen. "Just get to researching, will you? And no more poking."

Amy giggled. "Okay, but I'm probably going to need to remove the clothes to look for a tag. You might want to turn up the heat in here."

"God forbid," Mallory muttered, and turned her attention to the bookshelves behind the desk, not wanting to watch the dissection of the doll and somewhat afraid of what might happen as Amy dug around for a tag. Deciding not to take any chances, she kicked off her shoes, just in case a heel was compromised, and removed her long dangly earrings with the pointy ends.

"See," Amy said, and held up the seminaked doll, "it's working already."

Mallory looked down at the pile of discards she'd been wearing only moments before and laughed. "Okay, it is sort of funny. But still too weird to be real funny." She turned away from Amy and back to the bookshelf, a picture in the corner catching her eye.

"Hey, look at this," Mallory said. "It's an old yearbook."

Amy nodded but didn't look up from her work. "Yeah,

yeah, then read it or something. I think I found something here."

Mallory tucked the faded yearbook under her arm and sat down across the desk from Amy. "What did you find?"

Amy pointed to tiny initials, "T.H." penned on the foot of the doll. "I bet this is the designer." She reached for the keyboard and began tapping away. "If she does this retail, she might have a Web site."

Mallory shuddered to think of owning a business that helped make others miserable, but New Orleans wasn't exactly known for its most upstanding of citizens. The city defined "weird" in so many ways that Mallory couldn't keep up—voodoo, vampire bars, and probably a whole host of other things she didn't want to know about.

She opened the yearbook and flipped through the pages, hoping Amy found something soon since the lunch hour was starting to get away from them. She smiled at the old-fashioned hairdos in the book. The students looked so prim and proper, like future deacons and elementary school teachers, which apparently wasn't the case if the yearbook belonged to her uncle. That was at least one strike against them already.

She flipped another page and stared at the picture in surprise. Her mother, a much younger, happier-looking version of her mother, beamed up at her from the page. She was wearing a cheerleader uniform and looking quite perky. Mallory stared at the photograph, wondering what had happened to the girl in the picture, because the bitter woman she'd known had never looked this way to Mallory, not once.

"Mallory," Amy's voice cut into her thoughts. "I think I found it. Take a look at this." She flipped the flat-screen monitor around so that Mallory could see the Web site displayed. "This girl, Tammy Howard, is the artist. It says here that she creates the dolls from photos. They are specialty gift items."

Mallory placed the open yearbook on the desk and studied the site, with its pretty pink and purple flowered edging and whimsical gold lettering. No skulls, no blood, no sign of voodoo. "It doesn't look like she's into the whole black arts thing."

Amy studied the site a bit more and shook her head. "No, it doesn't. Of course, this could all be a cover, or she might really be who she says she is and Silas is just using her talent to create the dolls. It wouldn't be any big deal for him to pass off a photo of you as a niece or other relative and pay her a big load of money to put a rush on it."

Mallory leaned back in her chair and blew out a breath. "Yeah, you're probably right. But then who cursed the doll? Obviously it works. What's happening with the cards can't be a coincidence. And besides, if Silas Hebert is spending that much time and effort on something, it must be paying off."

"Or he thinks it does." Amy bit her lip. "I could do some more searching on voodoo. I have a friend who's a religion major at the university whom I could go see tonight. She's doing her thesis on African religions. Surely, voodoo is one of the things she's covered."

"Okay," Mallory said, and rose from her chair. "Give me a call after you talk to her. I'll try to do some research online myself. Maybe we can figure something out."

Amy nodded and looked down at the yearbook. "Did you find a picture of Reginald?"

Mallory looked down at the forgotten yearbook. "No." She picked the book up and showed Amy the picture. "But I found my mother. That's her."

Amy studied the picture for a moment, then looked back up at Mallory. "You look a lot like her—minus that silly hair."

Mallory looked at the picture again. "Yeah, I guess I do."

Amy motioned for her to flip the page. "Is your father in there, too?"

Mallory shrugged. "I don't even know if they went to the same high school. They never really talked about how they met or anything." She flipped through a couple more pages of happy, shiny-faced youths clustered in groups for club photos then entered the section of "Most Likely" shots. She smiled at the "Most Likely to Succeed" photo and flipped the page, but one look at the "Most Likely to Marry" photo made her gasp.

It was her mother again, of that she was sure, but the man with her definitely wasn't her father. The boy in the picture was a lot older now and the youthful expression on his face probably hadn't extended much beyond high school, but there was no doubt in her mind that the boy in the photo was Silas Hebert.

Jake chose a table in the corner of the dining area, some distance away from the rest of the staff and the other players. For a while, he watched for Mallory to enter the room, even though he knew she couldn't sit with him. After a half hour, he gave up wondering where she was and picked up his sandwich. He was halfway through the first bite when Brad sat down at his table.

"I know it was you last night," Brad said. "Don't think I couldn't arrest you on suspicion."

"I don't know what you're talking about," Jake replied, and took another bite of his sandwich.

Brad stared at him, his eyes flashing with anger. "Don't

197

give me that shit. I'm not buying it and you know it." He looked out over the dining area, then back at Jake. "Look, I know about your partner."

Jake stared at Brad in surprise. "How do you know about Mark?"

"I ran into him in New Orleans. He was handling an exchange of goods for Silas in one of the casinos. He told me about the bust."

Jake narrowed his eyes at Brad. "You're telling me a federal agent just walked up to a complete stranger in a casino and blabbed all about his undercover operation? I don't think so."

"Don't be a fool. I met Mark years ago through his wife. One of those damned corporate parties for the bank his wife and mine worked at. He remembered me and what I did. He gave me the heads-up about his job here so I wouldn't blow his cover. I had you pegged as soon as you showed up at Reginald's little event. I figured something had gone wrong and had a friend check with the bureau."

"I can't leave here without knowing," Jake said. "Surely you understand that."

"I understand why this is so important to you, but you're getting in the way of something so much bigger than the loss of one man, regardless of who the man was. Besides, you and I both know that if his cover's blown, there's no way he's still alive."

Jake shrugged. "Guns get into the hands of criminals every day. What the hell difference does one more exchange make?"

"It's not that simple." Brad ran one hand through his hair and scanned the room again. "Look, these guys aren't selling pistols to a bunch of street rats. We've been tracking them for almost six years and couldn't pin anything on them until now. Their distribution in the U.S. is the largest known network, but this latest deal is the one we're worried most about."

"How's that?"

"The deal originated in the Middle East with people who make our street gangs look like a boy's choir. They've ordered everything from fully automatic weapons to much, much worse."

Jake lowered his sandwich to his plate and stared at Brad. "Worse how?"

"Maybe biological. And you didn't hear that from me." Brad rose from the table and looked down at Jake. "There could be millions of people at risk if this exchange happens. So you need to ask yourself if knowing where one man's grave is located is worth all that."

Silas Hebert watched as the two dealers talked and one left the dining area. It was obvious they had disagreed. About what? Silas was tired of questions with no answers, of suspicion when there was probably something simple going on between the two men—like fighting over a woman.

Still, the play today hadn't gone as he'd expected, and there could be only one explanation for it. He pulled his cell phone from his jacket pocket and excused himself from the table. As he stepped onto one of the private balconies off the dining area, he pressed a speed dial number and waited.

The man on the other end picked up on the first ring. "Yeah."

"I need you to check something in my closet," Silas said. "Top shelf—the shoe box all the way to the right. Tell me if the doll is still inside."

There was a pause while the man made his way to Silas's room. Then Silas heard the sound of the closet door sliding open and the rustling of boxes and paper. "It's empty, boss."

Silas nodded and stared out over the bayou. "I figured as much." He stepped away from the balcony and turned back toward the casino. "I'll need another doll. You know who to call. And tell her I need it this evening. You'll drive to New Orleans and pick it up."

"No problem."

Silas flipped his phone shut and stepped inside the casino, wondering where on earth Mallory Devereaux had gotten her balls—because he knew it hadn't been from her father.

Mallory sat on the roll-out couch in her living room, legs fully extended along the length of the mattress, sipping a beer and pretending to watch television. Who, exactly, she was pretending for, she had no idea since there wasn't anyone else there, and T.W. couldn't see or hear the TV anyway. Not to mention, she'd picked the seat on her roll-out couch rather than her normal recliner, because it offered her a view of the road.

The afternoon play had started so similar to the morning that she had to admit it hadn't been a temporary swing in luck—something was definitely up. She'd managed a touch to Jake while taking the drink order that afternoon, which had helped take the edge off him running the table completely, but the day had definitely been his.

She'd felt Silas looking at her again and knew the jig was probably up. If he didn't already know, he'd be sure to check his closet tonight and find the missing doll.

And then what?

And that was the sixty-four-thousand-dollar question. If he'd gotten the first one made and delivered so quickly, it wouldn't be any big deal to get another.

And then what?

They were back to the same question: Did the doll make a difference? Maybe the day before had been a fluke—when Silas had been immune to her bad luck. Or maybe he'd been cheating, as Jake suspected, and hadn't wanted to risk it today. She stared up at the ceiling and sighed. The whole mess was confusing.

Then there was that yearbook photo of Silas and her mother. She'd barely controlled her emotions enough to shut the book and place it back on the shelf without giving anything away to Amy. She didn't understand what she'd seen and wasn't ready to discuss the possibilities with her friend, especially not when they were most certainly grim.

As soon as she could face her uncle without looking away or blushing, Mallory was going to have a serious talk with him.

But for now she sat in her living room, glancing out the window every two seconds, hoping to see Jake's car pull into her driveway. The guilt for taking the doll was overwhelming, and even though she knew he was going to be angry, she had to get it off her chest. So while one part of her wanted desperately to see Jake—and she was fairly certain exactly which part that was—the other part of her hoped he had a flat tire, or a dead battery, or anything non-life-threatening that would keep him from making contact with her tonight like he'd said he would before they left the casino.

The clock on the wall rolled to eight, and she was just contemplating making a sandwich when she saw Jake's car come out from behind the trees and pull into her driveway. Her pulse quickened at the sight of him climbing out of his car, even as her heart dropped, knowing what she needed to tell him.

She waved him into the cabin as he approached the front door, and he stepped inside, a serious look on his face.

"Is something wrong?" she asked. Had he found out about the doll? Surely Amy hadn't told anyone.

"Just frustrated," he said. "I asked for a search of the addresses we found. I kind of hedged exactly how I came about them, and they covered all but one of them today."

"Which one did they leave off?"

"The apartment complex, which was my favorite of the lot." Jake ran one hand through his hair. "They made arrangements with the building owner for a meeting this evening, but there was a kidnapping in New Orleans and everyone got pulled for the case."

"And you can't go yourself because of the risk of being seen by Silas or one of his men," Mallory concluded, now understanding his frustration.

Jake stared at her for a moment. "I'm not *supposed* to search for myself."

"You were going to anyway? Is that a risk you want to take?"

Jake blew out a breath. "I don't know. Yes. I guess I do or I wouldn't be thinking this hard about it, but on the way over here I got this idea."

"What idea?"

"That maybe I could meet with the owner—she's expecting an FBI agent—but if you went with me then maybe if anyone else saw us they'd just think we were a couple looking for a unit to rent. I doubt Silas has passed out photos of us to his crew if he only suspects us of fixing a card game."

Mallory looked at him and laughed. "You're asking me to pretend to be your live-in? What do I get out of the deal?"

Jake looked her up and down and smiled. "We could probably work out repayment when we get back."

Mallory grinned. "Then what are we waiting for?"

Chapter Thirteen

The apartment complex was just off the highway on the outskirts of Royal Flush. Another fifteen miles up the highway was the hotel of Jake and Mallory's infamous breaking-and-entering adventures, and another fifteen miles after that was New Orleans, home to more infamous adventures than you could shake a stick at.

The redbrick apartment building was probably more than fifty years old, but it was maintained well with a new coat of bright white paint on the trim and pretty, flowering bushes lining every edge of the structure and the driveway. There was a midsized SUV parked in front of the manager's office, which she figured belonged to the owner.

Jake pulled in beside the SUV, glanced at his watch, then looked over at Mallory. "The owner's name is Glenda. She's expecting FBI, so you're going to have to pretend to be an agent when we're talking to her."

"Gotcha—agent with Glenda, live-in honey the rest of the time." Mallory grinned. "What an exciting life I lead."

"Just let me do all the talking." He jumped out of the car and looked over at her. "And try not to touch anything."

Mallory laughed and followed him out of the car and into the manager's office.

A bell above the door signaled their entry, and a feminine voice shouted from down the hall, "Be right with you." Mallory looked around the small office, not really sure what she was supposed to be looking for but figuring she couldn't help matters if she didn't bother to try. She was studying an old photograph of the building construction and had just placed her finger on the glass, trying to trace the angle of the roofline when she heard Jake gasp and a voice sound behind her.

"You must be the FBI agents."

She removed her finger from the photo, dismayed to see a single crack in the glass, following the exact same trail she'd traced with her finger. Turning from the photo, she expected to find the manager behind her, but had to drop her gaze a good two feet before the woman came into view.

"Oh, my God." The words came out of her mouth before she could stop them, but even without the leather mask and matching whip, there was no mistaking the tiny woman in front of her. Behind her, the photo on the wall crashed onto the floor.

The woman glanced at the photo and frowned, then took a hard look at Mallory. A couple of seconds later, a blush began to creep up her neck. "Well, this is embarrassing."

Mallory looked at Jake, who had been standing in the far corner when the woman entered the room. His expression was one of pure disbelief, but then he'd probably had an overdose of that since coming to Royal Flush.

"Reginald never told me his niece was an FBI agent," the woman said, "although I guess that would explain you bursting through hotel rooms and jumping out windows."

She waved a hand at the office behind her. "My name's Glenda. You may as well come in and have a seat."

"I'm sorry for the other night," Mallory said once they were all seated. "We didn't mean to barge in that way, we were just . . . well, we were sort of in a hurry."

Glenda smiled. "I bet. You had half a hotel of men chasing you as far as I could see—half feds and half the bad guys. Reginald almost passed out when you jumped over the balcony."

Jake stared at Glenda, clearly surprised. "How do you know half of them were feds?"

"Oh hell, I know all about Reginald's trouble with the ATF. You think I've been seeing the man for twenty years and he doesn't tell me stuff?"

"You're dating Reginald . . . for twenty years?" Mallory stared at Glenda in shock. "But everyone said . . ."

Glenda frowned. "I know the rumors, and they're damned offensive, but Reginald won't let me correct them."

"But why not?" Mallory asked. "Why is your relationship a secret?"

Glenda sighed. "My family comes from old money—I inherited this building and stand to inherit several others that specialize in subsidized housing for the poor, the elderly, the disabled. It's my life's work, helping these people, and Reginald knows if my relationship with him becomes public knowledge, then people will start to poke into his business a bit more than he'd like. My family would probably be the first in line."

"I see," Mallory said. "Reginald is worried that your family will cut you off if they know you're involved with him."

Glenda nodded. "Yeah. The worst part is, he'd finally decided to go legit—after all these years—and damn if the ATF didn't come in and mess everything up."

"I'm sorry for that," Mallory said. "Jake and I are doing everything we can to help win Reginald the money he needs to save the casino."

"I'm sure you are, even though I don't pretend to understand half of what's going on, but enough about all that," Glenda said, and rose from the desk. "I don't suppose the FBI is interested in my and Reginald's bedroom preferences, although it might make some interesting reading."

She gave them a smile, then looked at Jake. "You said on the phone you're trying to track someone down who might have stayed here."

"That's right," Jake said. "Probably within the last six months or so."

Glenda nodded and stepped out of the manager's office and into the hallway of the main building, beckoning them to follow.

"I checked the property records after you called," Glenda said as they walked. "Every one of our residents has been here for more than two years, and all are either elderly or disabled. But there's a couple of vacant units at the back of the building that I've been needing to rehab and just haven't had the time to get around to it. Someone could have stayed there without me knowing, I suppose. It's been months since I've been in any of them."

"Did you go in them after my call?" Jake asked.

Glenda shook her head. "No way. My great-uncle was a district attorney. I grew up on complaints of tainted evidence and mishandled crime scenes. I know better."

Jake grinned. "If only everyone had a district attorney as an uncle."

Glenda pointed to two doors at the end of the hallway and handed Jake a key. "That master key should open both doors. Do you need me to stick around?"

Jake took the key from her and nodded. "If you don't

mind. You're the only person who'll know if something is out of place. Just try not to touch anything."

"Sounds familiar," Mallory mumbled.

Glenda looked back at her and motioned for her to enter. "FBI agents first."

Mallory laughed. "I'm not really an FBI agent—I'm a demolition foreman."

Glenda stared at her for a moment, then smiled. "Hey, whatever role-playing works for you, I'm okay with it."

Deciding an explanation would take too long and would be far too confusing, Mallory just stepped into the apartment after Jake and started poking her head into rooms, careful not to touch anything. As she stepped out of the kitchen into the hallway, Jake emerged from the bathroom.

"Anything?" she asked.

"Clean as a whistle," Jake said, "and the dust is about right for the length of time Glenda claims it's been empty."

Jake locked the door to the first apartment, and they took the few short steps down the hall to the remaining door. Jake unlocked the door and pushed the door open for them to enter. The difference in the two apartments was immediately apparent.

The second apartment was clean. Not spotless but definitely lacking the buildup of dust that should have been present if it had been empty for months. Jake stepped into a bedroom just off the living area, and Mallory slipped down the hall and into the master bedroom. The master bathroom had a few items on the sink—toothbrush, toothpaste and some dental floss.

"Jake," she yelled down the hall. "I got something in here."

Jake hurried into the bedroom, Glenda close behind,

and Mallory pointed to the bathroom. "There are toiletries in there. Looks like they've been used recently."

Jake pulled a clear plastic bag out of his pocket and pulled on a set of gloves. "Check out the rest of the room," he instructed.

Mallory and Glenda walked the length of the bedroom, checking the closet and the built-in hamper, but the remainder of the room was clean. "This is sort of a weird master bedroom," Mallory observed. "There are no windows on this side of the apartment at all."

Glenda nodded. "That was one of the reasons I wanted the rehab. Who wants a master bed and bath with no natural light?"

Mallory looked around the room again. Something about this just wasn't right, but for the life of her she couldn't figure out what. She scanned the walls again, hoping for a clue, something to let her know why this whole situation felt so off and when she reached the open door, she paused.

Frowning, she crossed the room and studied the dead bolt on the bedroom door, a shiny, new dead bolt. "Jake, get over here," she said as the realization of what was wrong with the room hit her full force.

"Take a look at this suite," she said to him. "There's no way out but this door and the dead bolt is on the wrong side." She flipped the door open to show him the hardware. "Whoever was staying here—it wasn't voluntary."

Glenda stared at Mallory, a frightened look on her face. "You think someone was held captive here? Oh, my God, what a horrible thought."

"Maybe not so horrible," Jake said. "It might mean the guy I'm looking for is still alive." He looked around the room then back at the door. "But why didn't anyone hear them?"

Glenda cleared her throat, still looking a bit horrified.

"This building is really old and solid. You wouldn't hear anything through the outside walls, and with the apartment next to this one empty . . ."

"What about across the hall?" Jake asked.

"Directly across the hall is storage and no one's been in there in months. The next door down is Mr. Wilson, but he's darn near deaf."

Jake nodded. "Is it all right if we talk to Mr. Wilson? Maybe he saw something."

Glenda glanced once more at the dead bolt and exited the bedroom. "Come with me," she said as they walked out of the apartment and a little ways down the hall. She knocked on the door, and they heard some rustling about inside. It took a while, but finally the door opened and a man who must have been about a hundred years old stared out at them.

"I ain't buying nothing," he yelled, and started to close the door again.

Glenda placed one hand on the door, preventing him from closing it and said in a loud voice, "Mr. Wilson, it's Glenda—I own the building, remember?"

Mr. Wilson stared down at her for a moment, and Mallory wondered just how bad the mind deteriorated if you had trouble remembering a three-foot-tall person. Finally his face cleared, and he smiled. "Oh yeah. I remember now," he said, the volume on his reply not decreasing in the slightest. "How's that cat of yours?"

"Fine, Mr. Wilson," Glenda said. "I was wondering about your neighbor across the hall. Have you seen him lately?"

Wilson stared at Glenda for a moment. "You want to put Berber in the hall? Well, hell, that's a stupid idea, but go ahead."

"No, Mr. Wilson," Glenda shouted. "Have you seen your neighbor across the hall?"

Wilson looked across the hall at the apartment door and scratched his head. "You mean the cripple? I don't know. Maybe yesterday, day before. That man who tends to him said he was having surgery. I guess he's not out of the hospital yet."

Glenda stared at Mr. Wilson, obviously a bit surprised. "How long has the man lived there, Mr. Wilson?"

The old man stared at her like she'd lost her mind. "Well, how the hell should I know? You own the building." He slammed the door and they could hear him muttering on the other side of the door.

"How reliable is he?" Jake asked.

Glenda considered this for a moment. "Fairly reliable when it comes to certain things. For instance, if he says a cripple lives in the other apartment, then I'm positive he's seen one there. And since that apartment has been empty since before Mr. Wilson moved in, I'd say it's a good bet that he's seen your guy—assuming it was your guy being held there." She shrugged. "Of course, my cat has been dead for over a year."

Mallory looked over at Jake. "If they had him drugged, a wheelchair would be the easiest way to move him. And in a place like this, no one would even think twice about it."

"True," Jake agreed. "I think we've covered everything we can here. I need to make a dash to New Orleans and get this to the lab. They should be able to put a rush on it. Maybe get me some results by tomorrow."

He turned to Glenda and stuck out his hand. "It was a pleasure meeting you. I appreciate all your help."

Glenda took his hand and shook it. "It was a pleasure—*this* time."

Mallory let out a laugh. "When this is all over, Glenda, we're going to sit down and talk over a bottle of scotch—just you, me and Reginald."

Glenda smiled. "Now, that is definitely a plan I can get behind."

The trip to New Orleans took a couple of hours, and it was late before they arrived back at Mallory's cabin. Jake's spirits were running high, and Mallory knew he was hoping for the best concerning his partner. But although she'd been happy with the discovery and the possibility that Mark might still be alive, the drive home had given her too much time to think.

About the voodoo doll.

She knew Jake had other plans once they were behind closed doors, but she couldn't let those plans go forward without telling him. It wouldn't be right.

They pulled up in front of her cabin, and she jumped out of the car and hurried to unlock the door, not wanting to look Jake directly in the eyes, afraid she'd lose control if she made contact with him. She looked back as he climbed out of the car, his dark hair glistening in the moonlight. God, he was good-looking.

And he'll leave town as soon as he catches his bad guy.

She watched him walk across the lawn, admiring the way his T-shirt clearly defined the tone of his upper body. She'd even bet he had the legs to match. Thank God he hadn't worn shorts. If he had legs to match those arms there would be no holding her back regardless of the cost later on. Legs were no small matter.

Smiling, he held open the door for her to enter the cabin, then stepped inside behind her and took a seat in the recliner. "Heck of a day," he said.

Mallory nodded, and decided to wait a while before spilling the beans. After all, this was the first good mood he'd been in since she'd met him. "I forgot to ask earlier if any of the marked cards turned up today?"

"No, so obviously Silas was cheating yesterday." He looked over at her, a puzzled expression on his face. "But I don't get why he backed off. If it worked for him before, why didn't he continue today?"

"Do you think he noticed the mark on the cards?"

"Maybe." He shrugged. "I don't know."

He leaned back in the recliner and blew out a breath. "This entire tournament has tossed me more curves than I ever imagined or was prepared to deal with." He gave her a smile. "I appreciate all your help this evening. You've gone above and beyond in more ways than one."

You should tell him about the doll now.

"No problem," she said.

If you tell him about the doll now, it will just be one more curve he's not prepared to deal with.

"Maybe the alarm situation at the hotel made him nervous," she suggested. "Maybe he wants to buy a new deck just to be sure."

Maybe you're a chickenshit and you're not telling the truth because you don't want him angry at you.

"Maybe. But still, it didn't even feel the same as before. Yesterday, he was confident, almost cocky. Today . . ."

"What?"

"Today, he almost looked puzzled. But that doesn't make any sense. If he was cheating yesterday and not today, then why any confusion at all?"

Mallory rose from the couch and walked into the kitchen. Now was the time. She had to tell him the truth. "You want a beer?" she asked as she opened the refrigerator and stuck her head inside, stalling.

"No," his answer came from directly behind her, and she jumped upright. Before she could turn, he'd wrapped his arms around her shoulders and lifted her hair from the nape of her neck. She could feel his breath, hot and sexy, even before his lips pressed against the sensitive flesh on her neck. "But there is something I do want."

You can't do this without telling him.

"If you keep doing that, you can have anything you want," she murmured.

Traitor.

"Anything?" He ran one hand down over the front of her shirt, lingering over her breast. "That's a mighty bold offer."

She turned slowly around, wrapping her arms around his waist and dropping both hands to squeeze his butt. "In case you haven't noticed, I'm not exactly a shrinking violet."

You're a lying fool.

But at the moment, it simply didn't matter. At the moment, all that mattered was Jake's hands on her, all over her, and returning the favor. Definitely returning the favor.

Somehow they made it back into the living room. It was only a couple of steps away, but when it felt as if your entire body was tangled with another, those three steps were an eternity. As Jake backed into the roll-out bed, Mallory smiled at him and took advantage of his position and pushed him back. He fell onto the bed, a look of surprise crossing his face.

Mallory laughed and tugged her T-shirt over her head, changing his surprised look to a much, much more intense one. As she shrugged out of her jeans with equal enthusiasm, he gave her a smile. "I knew you didn't wear underwear."

"I do on Sundays," she said, and leaned over to unbutton his jeans. "Are you going to just stare at me? Because I had a lot more activity in mind."

Jake kicked off his shoes and shed his jeans and underwear in a flash, taking a few precious seconds to take care of the contraceptive end of the fun and games.

"I'd be happy to help you with that," Mallory teased as he rolled on the thin skin.

"If you touch me now, it's over," Jake said, and grinned.

Mallory laughed and Jake reached up to pull her on top of him. Mallory fell onto Jake in a tangle of arms and legs and hoped like hell the bed would hold. She had intended to be on top, take charge, but Jake apparently had other ideas.

He pulled her down for a crushing kiss, then flipped her over, pinning her beneath him. His breath was short and ragged, and she could feel his heart pounding against her chest—her own heart pounding in her throat. "I want to kiss every square inch of you," he whispered, "but it's going to have to wait. I hope that's okay."

Okay? It was more than okay—it was required. Her skin didn't need kissing, it was already on fire. There was only one thing that would put out the flames they'd started and that was Jake inside of her. "I want you in me now."

He hesitated only for a moment then fulfilled her request, entering her with a swift, hard stroke. Her body had been ready for him, had probably been readying itself for days, and it drank him in deep inside her, making them both gasp. "Don't stop," she said, and dug her nails into his shoulders.

He rose above her and plunged again, over and over until they reached the brink. "I can't—" he started to say.

"Then don't." She raised her hips to meet him, greedily wanting every inch of him deep inside of her when she came. He pushed one final time and she felt his release. She struggled to hold back just one second more but the climax ripped through her like a bullet, shooting pleasure through her from head to toe.

It was several seconds before she could even take in a breath and even then it was restricted by the weight of Jake on top of her. As she sucked in a breath, he rose up on one elbow and smiled at her. "Would you like for me to move so you can breathe again?"

Mallory nodded and took a deep breath as he eased himself to her side. "It wasn't your weight or anything," she started to ramble, "because you're not heavy or anything. I just—"

"Ssssh." Jake placed on finger on her lips. "I'm having a little trouble getting my breath back, too."

"Oh." She smiled with relief that she'd turned things inside out for him. It would have been supremely humiliating if she'd seen fireworks and all Jake had gotten out of it was a smoke bomb.

"I'm sorry things went so quickly," Jake said, and gave her a lazy smile. "But I did warn you at the hotel that my self-control was probably at an all-time low."

"Your timing was perfect. I wouldn't have been able to take another second."

Jake grinned. "I was thinking the same thing."

Mallory propped herself up on one elbow and looked over at Jake. "Do you realize I just slept with you and I don't even know your real name?"

Jake stroked her cheek with his hand and leaned in to kiss her gently. "Ah, but you know things about me that are infinitely more important," he teased. "Let's face it, this was a perfect ending to a perfectly weird day."

"Yes, I think this day was outside of the norm even for me."

"But at least a profitable one, right?"

Mallory felt a dull ache creep up the back of her neck. "Yeah, profitable."

And you still haven't told him the truth.

"All I need is another day of straight play. And with you running a little interference, we'll have this in the bag."

More likely the box in my closet.

Mallory clenched her hands and tried to nod. Oh, she was running interference all right. Jake just had no idea to what extent.

Jake continued to smile. "If he reverts to cheating tomorrow, I'll be able to nail him. I just knew it was something easy to explain."

Unable to stand the lying any longer, Mallory said, "There may be one other possible explanation."

Jake looked her. "Yeah, like what?"

Mallory dropped her gaze, unable to meet his eyes. "I might have taken the voodoo doll." She waited several seconds, but there was no response. Finally, she lifted her gaze to Jake noting the flash of anger in his eyes.

"You. Might. Have. What?"

Mallory sat up in bed and gathered the blanket around her. "I took the doll, all right? It creeped me out, some guy having a voodoo doll made up like me, so I took it. And I'm not sorry I did." She looked Jake straight in the eyes. "I'm only sorry I didn't tell you about it sooner."

"Good God, Mallory!" Jake jumped out of bed, pulled on his jeans, then paced the living room—two steps one direction, two steps another. "Taking that doll could blow everything. Silas is sure to look for it eventually and what do you think he's going to think when he finds it missing? Who the hell else would want to steal it but you or one of your friends?"

"I couldn't leave it there!" Mallory argued. "I just couldn't." She let out a sigh. "I'm sorry for what I risked, but if I had it to do over again, I'd still do the same thing." She looked him straight in the eyes, her gaze unwavering, her voice steady. "Look, when you asked me before if I believed in voodoo, I told you I didn't know because I'd never actually seen any. But now I'm starting to wonder."

"Jeez, Mallory, you know all that stuff is crap. It can't work unless you believe in it."

She stared at him. "Like my bad luck? I spent over half of my life trying to pretend it didn't exist. I didn't believe it was possible, but it was always there. I spent the second half looking for an explanation or a miracle cure. The reality is, I know as much now as I did when I was a child. Nothing."

"Silas was cheating yesterday, and he didn't today. It was that simple. It has nothing to do with anything out of the ordinary, much less out of this world."

"Yeah, then why weren't you so sure of that earlier?"

He ran one hand through his hair and stared out the window. "I am sure. I was sure. The cheating is the answer. Nothing else is possible."

"Yeah, well this voodoo thing scares me more than I'd like to admit, and if you have a problem with that, I really don't give a shit." She rose from the bed, blanket still wrapped around her and walked into the bathroom. "This conversation is over," she said as she closed the door behind her.

She leaned against the bathroom door, the tears already threatening to spill out. Why had she expected someone so narrow-minded to understand her? Why had she even tried to explain her fears? It only made her look weak.

There was silence for what seemed like forever, then finally she heard the front door open and Jake's car back out of the driveway. That was it then. Everything she'd felt when they were together. Everything she'd thought he'd felt. It was a just a momentary burst of emotion that didn't linger once the heart had stopped racing and the skin had stopped burning.

Sliding down the door to the floor, she continued to hold in her tears, knowing that with every breath she grew stronger, more capable.

She'd had a lot of things in her life worth crying over. Jake McMillan wasn't one of them.

Chapter Fourteen

Jake arrived at the casino the next morning full of turmoil. The night before with Mallory had been one of the best and worst nights of his life all rolled into one. Being with Mallory had been everything he'd dreamed it would be and far more, and the depth of feeling he was forming for her scared him.

Then she'd hit him with stealing the voodoo doll, and it had been so easy to use that as his reason to leave. Not that he wasn't angry. Stealing that doll might be enough to make Silas bow out of the tournament before an exchange could be made. It wasn't going to take a genius to figure out who had stolen it, and Silas was no dummy.

But if he really thought about it, and God knows he'd tried not to, he really couldn't blame her for not wanting Silas to have the doll. It *was* creepy. And if a man trained in hand-to-hand combat and weaponry that the public didn't even know about could find a doll creepy, then he imagined it scared the crap out of Mallory.

Then he'd gone stomping out of her cabin like an injured child, which was exactly what he felt like at the moment—the child part, not the injured. Of course, it didn't take long after he'd left Mallory's cabin for her unluckiness to set in, and the emotional injury had come dangerously close to converting to a physical one. The left side of his hip was still killing him, that patch of hair on his leg would probably take forever to grow back, and he was still waiting for a visit from the hotel manager asking what the heck had happened to the stair railing, but none of that mattered at the moment.

The reality was, Mallory hadn't wanted to make him angry, and he knew he'd hurt her with his attitude. Maybe when everything was said and done it was for the best. After all, what possible future could they have? As soon as this was over, he would head back to New Jersey where hopefully, he'd still have a career, and Mallory would pay off the IRS and stay right here in Royal Flush, probably for the rest of her life.

The big plus was the call he'd received from the lab that morning, letting him know that not only did the DNA on the toothbrush belong to Mark, but that the brush had been used recently. Jake had never even held out hope for finding Mark alive, and now all he could think about is where his partner might be. Granted, it was still a slim shot with the tournament drawing to an end and Silas preparing to leave the country, but Jake couldn't help wishing everything would turn out all right.

The sound of the casino doors opening broke into his thoughts, and he looked up to see the players entering the room. He reached for the chips and cards, readying his table for the day's play, and glanced up periodically, checking the doorway for Mallory. As much as she needed the money, there was that tiny bit of worry in the back of his mind that she wouldn't show up to finish the tournament.

Glancing at the doors again, he felt his breath catch in his throat as Mallory entered the casino. She was wearing the required short black skirt, but today she'd matched it with a top of pale green silk, her tanned skin seeming to glow against the lighter color of the fabric. She'd left her hair down for a change and the effect was breathtaking. Long wavy tendrils of black coursed over her shoulder, some lingering just atop her breasts, the rest cascading down her back.

As his gaze rose to her face, she locked eyes with him, but the determined expression on her face never wavered. In that single moment, she'd let him know that Mallory Devereaux would not be swayed or taken by a single night of passion, and that knowledge both disappointed and excited him at the same time.

She gave him the briefest of nods as she approached the table, then pulled out her pad and began taking the morning orders. Once done, she turned from the table and walked across the casino without so much as glancing at him.

It was about ten minutes later when she returned with the drinks. The first hand was still in play, so she started on the far end, passing coffees and making sure she rubbed shoulders or arms somewhere in the mix. But when she got to Silas Hebert, she hesitated, and Jake noticed Silas was staring directly at her.

Jake knew the smile on her face was forced, but she managed to pull it off. He saw her hands shake a tiny bit as she lifted Silas's coffee from the tray and began to place it in front of him, but before she could reach the table, Silas stuck out his hand and took the mug from her, his fingers grazing hers as he lifted the coffee.

Mallory swiftly drew her hand back and started to back away from the table, but Silas placed one hand on her arm before she was out of reach. "Devereaux's your last name, right?" he asked.

Mallory nodded.

"I thought so," Silas said, and gave her a smug smile. "I knew your parents." That said, he dropped his hand from her arm and turned back to the table.

Mallory took two steps back from the table and stared at Jake, a frightened look on her face. Jake tried to blank his expression, tried to pretend that nothing out of the ordinary had happened. It took every ounce of willpower for him to pick up his cards and make the next bet.

What the hell had just happened?

Silas had intentionally touched her—he knew it without a doubt. But why? And why the comment about her parents?

Then there was that smile. That superior smile.

There was simply no reason for Silas to touch Mallory unless he was proving a point. And Jake had a sinking suspicion that the point Silas was about to prove was that Mallory's bad luck didn't affect him at all.

Mallory hurried home after the tournament, not wanting to talk to Jake before she'd had a chance to confer with Amy and find out what her friend had said about the voodoo situation. Because Scooter had eaten with them, they'd avoided the entire conversation at lunch, but Mallory had managed to slip in the fact that Silas had blatantly touched her and was winning almost every hand.

She could tell the information bothered Amy as much as it did her and hoped like hell her friend had found out something useful. Otherwise, this entire situation was about to fall apart and there wasn't a damn thing she could do about it. The only upside was that her uncle hadn't confronted her about the situation at her table at all, making her wonder if Glenda hadn't had a chance to mention their meeting the night before or was waiting for her to work it all out with Reginald before she said anything.

Either way, Mallory was grateful for the reprieve. There was entirely too much going on right now and the last thing she needed was a reminder from her uncle that her entire life was on its way down the crapper.

As soon as she arrived home, she went into the bathroom closet and pulled out the voodoo doll. It looked so harmless lying in the box—still creepy, but harmless. She felt her pulse start to quicken and placed the box on her coffee table, anxious to rid herself of its weight.

She was being silly. It was just a doll.

Granted, it was a doll that seemed to shift things within the universe, but how? And where the hell was Amy?

She was just reaching for her cell phone when Amy's car pulled into her driveway. Amy jumped out of the car, pulling a huge tote bag after her, and hurried toward the house, one shoulder slumped down from the weight of the bag.

"What the heck are you carrying?" Mallory asked as she opened the door for Amy to enter. "A body?"

Amy grimaced and dumped the bag onto the couch then rubbed her shoulder. "Yeah, I killed Patrick and brought him here in pieces. I thought we could feed him to the alligators."

Mallory laughed. Amy was definitely getting over Patrick in a hurry. "So I take it that's the voodoo research?"

Amy nodded and began to pull notebooks, binders and books from the bag. "Yeah, my friend loaned me everything she had. I promised her an exclusive on whatever we turn up with the doll." She looked over at Mallory. "She won't use names. I hope that was okay."

"I don't care. Let's just hope some of this research helps."

Amy pulled a pink notebook out of the stack on the couch and flipped it open. "I've been studying this stuff since last night and making my own notes. Basically, I think the doll was used to put a curse on you."

Mallory frowned. "That seems a strange conclusion to draw when you consider the way my life is naturally."

"I know. That's where my holdup is in moving forward, but essentially, there is no reasonable explanation for Silas to have a doll in your likeness unless he was using it to practice black arts. I mean, you're hot, but I hardly think men are going to run out and have dolls made in your likeness—especially men like Silas Hebert."

"Yeah, I guess not. But if there's a curse on me, what is it?"

Amy opened one of the books to a drawing and passed it to Mallory. "Before you say no, I want you to take a look at this."

Mallory looked at the image, a group of people sitting in a circle, a voodoo doll in the middle. A bright light was beaming down from the sky into the doll. "So?"

Amy took a deep breath. "Those people are drawing the curse out of the doll so that they can identify the purpose. There are instructions for conducting the extraction starting on the next page."

"Oh, no," Mallory shook her head and slammed the book shut. "I'm not doing any woo-woo stuff, especially voodoo."

"Mallory, I hate to point out the obvious, but what other options do you have left? Obviously this doll is a key to everything that's happening. Don't you want to know why?"

Mallory rose from the couch and walked over to the window, staring outside. "You know I want to know why, but voodoo? I mean, it was one thing to play with stuff when we were kids, but now that I know there's something to it . . . well, it doesn't seem like such a great idea."

"Okay, then we'll put that on the back burner for now." Amy grabbed another book from the stack. "This book says that some of the strength of the curse is based on the precise measurements of the doll in relation to the person it's made in the image of." She pulled a tape measure from her purse. "Hold up the doll and let's get some measurements."

Mallory lifted the doll out of the box and held it out in front of Amy, who began to take measurements and jot them down in her notebook. She was just measuring the waist when Scooter walked through the front door.

"Holy shit!" Scooter cried, and took one step back out the doorway. "What the hell are you doing with that? You can't play with that shit, Mallory. It's not a joke."

Mallory shoved the doll back in the shoe box and threw on the lid. "For Christ's sake, Scooter, I'm not an idiot. I didn't make that doll and I'm not happy it's around."

He stuck his head back in the door and looked anxiously from her to Amy. When he didn't see the doll, he took one step inside. "Then if you didn't make it, where did it come from?"

"I took it from Silas Hebert's room," Mallory said. "That night we broke into the hotel."

Scooter stared at her. "Are you crazy? You can't go around stealing voodoo things. Good God, Mallory, if Silas is into voodoo no telling what he might do to you."

"Yeah," Amy said, "that's sort of what we're trying to

figure out here." She waved one hand over the stacks of books and papers.

Scooter looked nervously over the book then back at Amy. "So what are you going to do?"

"Well," Amy began, "I want to try an extraction, but Mallory doesn't like the idea."

Scooter shook his head. "I don't even know what the hell that is and I don't like it either." He looked over at Mallory. "This is bad news. I say you put that doll at the bottom of the bayou and forget you ever saw it."

Mallory bit her lip and looked from Scooter's frightened face to Amy's excited one. "I'm sort of afraid to do that. What if it makes me drown or something?"

"Holy shit, Mallory." Scooter stared at her in dismay.

"Maybe the extraction isn't such a bad idea," Mallory said. "At least we might be able to find out if I can destroy the doll with no side effects."

"Now you're talking," Amy said, and clapped her hands. She grabbed the book from the coffee table and flipped past the extraction image to the instructions. "It says here that we need to do this on blessed ground. Does that mean a church or something?"

"How the hell would I know?" Mallory said. "But if I had to guess, I'd say no. I'd guess they mean ground blessed by a voodoo person."

Amy blew out a breath. "How in the world are we supposed to find voodoo-blessed ground?"

Mallory looked over at Scooter who shook his head, obviously hoping she'd put the idea out of her mind. "I think I might know a place," she said before she could change her mind. "There's a place in the woods . . . a voodoo woman used to live there."

Amy jumped off the couch, grabbed the book and

shoved it into the bag. "What are we waiting for? Grab that doll and let's get going. You coming, Scooter?"

"Hell, no!" Scooter watched as Mallory lifted the box off the coffee table and took one step backward out the door. "This is a really bad idea, Mallory, really, really bad."

"As opposed to the stellar life I have now?"

Scooter shook his head. "Being unlucky is one thing. Curses are something else entirely. This is scary shit—like worse than losing a finger even. You should at least talk to Jake before you do this."

If her mind hadn't been totally made up before, Scooter's last statement had clinched it. "This has nothing to do with Jake."

Jake drove the couple of miles down the dirt road to Mallory's cabin with mixed emotions. He was still frustrated with the position she'd put him in, but the reality was that he would probably have done the same thing if he were her. Besides, he didn't like the distance Mallory had put between them all day. Even though it was obvious that at this point there was little she could do to help, Jake missed the feeling of him and Mallory working as a team.

He was going to get that feeling back—after all, they only had one more day left until the end of the tournament, and he didn't want things left this way.

Mallory's car was in the driveway when he pulled up, but a search of her house produced nothing. He looked out the kitchen window, squinting into the fading sunlight and saw Scooter sitting on his pier, a beer in one hand, a fishing rod in the other. Jake pushed open the back door and walked over to the pier, figuring Scooter probably knew where to find Mallory.

"Scooter," Jake said as he stepped on the pier.

"What?" Scooter jumped up from his chair, dropping both the beer and the rod into the bayou. Quick as lightning, he grabbed a net from the side of his chair and fished the beer out before it sank. "That was close," he said as he poured a bit of bayou water out of the top of the bottle.

He looked over at Jake and glared. "What the hell were you doing, man? Sneaking up on people like that?"

Jake glanced behind him, watched the tip of the rod and reel sink slowly into the bayou and shook his head. "I didn't mean to startle you. I was just wondering if you knew where Mallory was. I need to talk to her."

"It's a little late for that, I would say."

"What are you talking about?"

Scooter threw one hand in the air in obvious exasperation. "Those damn women—Amy and Mallory—I tried to tell them not to mess with voodoo, but they wouldn't listen. I tried to tell them to talk to you first, but Mallory said it was none of your business."

Jake felt his pulse quicken. What in the world had they done? "Where are they, Scooter?"

"They went to the clearing where the voodoo woman's cabin used to be—some shit about 'hallowed ground.' Amy said they were going to 'extract' the voodoo doll. I don't know what it means, but it sounds damn dangerous. But could I talk them out of it? Noooooooo."

Jake's mind raced with possibilities, none of them pleasant. He knew the place they'd gone—the place where he'd kissed Mallory. The question was, could he find it in the dark?

Gesturing at Scooter, he took a step off the pier. "C'mon, Scooter."

"Where are we going?"

"We're going to get the girls before they get into trouble."

"Unh-uh," Scooter said, his voice firm. "Not a chance."

"I thought Mallory was your friend."

"Damn it, why does everyone keep throwing that in my face?" Scooter grabbed his ice chest from the pier. "I'm not going without reinforcements."

Jake shook his head. "Whatever it takes."

Mallory watched as Amy drew a large circle in the dirt with a stick, not sure whether to be disturbed or amused. Surely they couldn't make things worse, right? And that was even assuming the two of them could muster up any voodoo magic at all, which Mallory had doubted from the beginning. Things like voodoo couldn't be learned from a library book—at least she hoped not.

Amy motioned to her to take a seat and Mallory stepped inside the circle and slid down onto the hard ground, thankful she wasn't wearing her new jeans, or shorts.

"Okay," Amy instructed as she sat cross-legged across from Mallory. "Put the doll in the middle, then I'll light the candle."

Mallory pulled the doll out of the box and placed it in between her and Amy, as close as she could figure to the center of the circle. Amy pulled a purple candle and a set of matches from her bag.

"Shouldn't that be black?" Mallory asked.

Amy gave her an apologetic look. "It was the closest I had. I didn't have time to stop by Wal-Mart on the way over."

Hoping the voodoo gods liked purple, Mallory watched Amy light the candle and wave it over the doll. When the wax began to melt, she tilted the candle to the side, waiting for a single drop to spill over the side.

The drop was just about to tip off the candle and onto the doll when a beam of light encased them, causing them both to jump up. Mallory felt her heart beating in her chest as she turned to ascertain the source of the light. A moment later, the light disappeared and she saw Jake's white rental car sitting in the moonlight.

Amy looked over at Mallory with a sigh. "Busted."

Jake jumped out of the car and strode over to where they sat. "What the hell do you think you're doing?" He waved a hand over the circle.

"We're doing an extraction," Amy explained. "To find out what kind of curse is on the doll."

Jake stared at her a moment then looked over at Mallory. "I am having a huge amount of trouble reconciling two women of your intelligence sitting out here in the dark, pretending to perform black magic on a doll, but then things have been more than a bit strange since I got here."

He blew out a breath. "Look, we have to talk, me and you," Jake said to Mallory. "If you want Scooter and Amy to hear it, that's fine, but we got big problems and only one day to try and salvage everything. I know you're mad at me, and I'm not too damned pleased with you, but this is never going to work unless we help each other."

"I'm not mad at you," Mallory said, staring down at the ground. "Not really. I shouldn't have taken the doll—I know that. But the way things look now, if I hadn't, you would have been out of the tournament yesterday."

"You're right on both counts."

She looked back over at him. "So you're okay with me stealing the doll?"

"I might as well be. What difference does it make now?"

Scooter, who had been standing just outside the car door, finally worked up the nerve to take a few steps closer to them. "Well, I'm not okay with it. They're trying to do voodoo, man. You don't mess with voodoo."

"What other options do we have?" Amy asked, her voice filled with exasperation. "Silas wasn't cheating today, was he?" she directed her question at Jake.

"No," Jake replied. "He wasn't."

"See," Amy said. "The voodoo doll is the only explanation. After Mallory stole this one, Silas probably had another made. That's why he was winning again today. If we knew what kind of curse was on it, maybe we could figure out a way to work around it."

Jake stared at Amy for a moment then looked back at Mallory. "You're okay with this?"

Mallory shrugged. "At this point, what could it hurt?" She and Amy sank to the ground, resuming their original positions across from each other.

Jake sighed and stepped into the circle, sinking down on the ground to form a third point. "C'mon, Scooter. Let's get this over with."

Scooter looked from one face to another, obviously waiting for someone to let him in on the joke but no punch line was forthcoming. "Oh hell," he said, and stepped into the circle across from Jake. "You owe me big-time for this, Mallory. It's going to take way more than a six-pack to even this one out."

Mallory grinned at Scooter as he took a seat. "We'll work something out." She looked over at Amy and nodded. "Let's do it."

Amy drew in a breath and reached for the candle again. The purple wax was pooled heavily in the top and it only took a second for it to spill over the side and onto the doll. As soon as the drop hit the doll, Amy picked up the book, and began to chant, "Spirit of the doll, we call you out. Show yourself to us on the hallowed ground. Bring all that you are to light."

As the last words left her mouth, lightning struck the ground in the clearing, and they all jumped. Mallory was fairly certain they all yelled, at least she was sure she did.

The smoke and dust from the lightning strike whirled around not ten feet from them, a thick, cloudy haze that was impossible to see through, and the darkness seemed to close in on them until only the tiny sliver of candle-light remained. The night sounds went away, the insects and birds seeming to be on mute and even the gentle tide of the bayou faded from hearing.

Then slowly a light began to glow and, from the center of the haze, the voodoo woman stepped out.

Chapter Fifteen

Mallory sucked in a breath and stared at the woman, un-blinking. She heard Scooter yelp and Amy gasp. Even Jake scooted a few inches back into the circle away from the woman. It was the voodoo woman, the same in every way as she'd been when Mallory was a kid.

She wore a long black robe with wide sleeves that hung to her wrists, and she clutched a black sack with one gnarled hand. Her skin was the deep, rich brown of the Creoles, and her hair, which at one time would have been a deep black, was now pure silver and seemed to glow in the light. Her dark eyes locked on Mallory's, seeming to look deep into her soul, and Mallory felt a rush of disbelief race through her.

It just couldn't be. Was it really possible that twenty years hadn't changed her at all?

"You're playing around with things you don't understand," the woman said.

Mallory glanced around at her friends, but it was clear from the looks on their faces that if anyone was going to keep the conversation going, it was up to her. "We were just . . . there was this doll . . . and we thought . . ."

The woman locked her dark gaze on Mallory, studying her as a hawk would its prey, unblinking and unreadable. "I know what you were doing, Mallory Devereaux. I knew the instant you stepped onto this ground."

Mallory swallowed and blinked. "You know me?"

The woman nodded. "I remember you as a small child. Your uncle brought you to me, hoping I could remove the curse."

Mallory's head whirled. "What curse? I don't understand." She pointed at the doll. "I just found this . . . what do you mean? It was there when I was a child?"

The voodoo woman shook her head. "That doll protects the man who commissioned the curse on your mother . . . the curse that was put on her when you were still in the womb. There was an anger in him that couldn't be sated. It's still there—an open wound—even after all these years."

"My mother knew?"

"Your mother came to me after the curse was put upon her. The creator had reasonable skill, but nothing that could match my own. I easily removed the curse from your mother, but I told her that I couldn't remove the curse from you until your birth. I told her to call when she was in labor—that I would come and all would be well."

"She never called?" Mallory stared at the woman, a feeling of dread creeping over her. "My own mother? She left me this way on purpose?"

The voodoo woman nodded. "I'm sorry, child, but even your name gives her thoughts away. Mallory is old French for 'unlucky.' "

Jake rose from the circle to stand beside Mallory. "Isn't there something you can do?"

"There is nothing to be done. The curse has been a

part of Mallory for so long that it has a life of its own. In order to take one life, you'd have to take the other."

Mallory stared at her, a faint memory forming in the back of her mind. She was young, not even five, traveling deep into the bayou with her uncle. She remembered the candles arranged in a clearing—in this clearing—and the warm blood of a chicken dripping across her forehead as she lay in a circle drawn on the ground."

"My uncle, he brought me here," Mallory said.

"Yes. He did the best he could. It was simply too late."

Mallory's heart fell at the woman's words. "So there is no hope."

The voodoo woman looked at her, sadness evident in her eyes. "I'm so sorry, child."

Mallory nodded and gestured to the doll in the circle. "What about the doll? Did the same person who put the curse on me put the protection spell on the doll?"

The voodoo woman shook her head. "The protection spell was placed on the doll by the man you took it from. He has very limited skill, but protecting himself from the curse he commissioned is something within his ability."

"And the guy who did the original curse on my mother . . . is he still around?"

"That man passed from this life many years ago in a most unpleasant fashion. He's spending his next life paying for his transgressions in this one."

Mallory stared at the woman for a moment, her mind conjuring up all kinds of visuals with hell and fire and no light. "What should be done with the doll?"

The voodoo woman looked at the doll and motioned for them to step aside. "The doll should be destroyed, but it needs to be done properly. You're welcome to watch, but I need you to step away from the circle."

The four of them backed away from the circle until

they stood about ten feet away. "That's far enough," the voodoo woman said, and she reached into her bag, brought out a chicken and held it up over the doll.

"What the hell is she doing with that chicken?" Jake whispered.

"You probably don't want to know," Mallory replied, and turned just in time to place one hand over Amy's mouth as the voodoo woman drew a knife across the chicken's throat.

Her hand muffled the worst of Amy's scream, but Scooter's "Jesus Christ Almighty" carried across the bayou and probably all the way back to downtown Royal Flush.

Mallory removed her hand from Amy's mouth and focused her attention on the voodoo woman as she shook blood from the chicken onto the doll.

"I don't think PETA knows about this," Jake whispered.

Mallory nodded but didn't take her eyes off the scene in front of her. The air around them was still as death, but inside the circle, the voodoo woman's robes began to ripple. The candle's flame flickered back and forth and the dust stirred around the doll.

Mallory sensed rather than felt the shift in the atmosphere around them as the voodoo woman raised her arms in the air and started chanting. The wind in the circle grew stronger and stronger, until the woman's robe and hair billowed around her in a frenzied dance of black and silver. The flame on the candle whipped back and forth as a roll of thunder echoed around them.

Suddenly, a beam of light came down from the sky, lighting up the circle. Mallory watched as the doll began to glow. The voodoo woman chanted louder and shook the chicken in the bright light.

"Oh, my God," Amy said as smoke began to rise from the doll.

Mallory watched in fascination as the smoke began in a thin stream, growing thicker with each passing moment.

At the exact moment the voodoo woman stopped chanting, the doll exploded into flames, the candle blew out, and the light from the sky disappeared, leaving them in total darkness.

Mallory felt Jake's hand squeeze hers and figured she wasn't the only one who wanted to bolt. Unfortunately, there was the small issue of not being able to see even a foot in front of them. And probably no one wanted to risk running into the voodoo woman . . . or the chicken. Just when Mallory decided she was going to start inching backward until she reached the car, the flame from the candle began to flicker and slowly light crept into the clearing until the entire area was basked in a dim yellow glow.

The voodoo woman still stood in the center of the circle, but the chicken was nowhere in sight and all that remained of the doll was a pile of ash. *Good riddance*, Mallory thought and breathed a sigh of relief. The voodoo woman stepped out of the circle and walked over to stand in front of her.

"*This* doll can trouble you no more, but the man you fear has already replaced it with another that is identical. Its power is weak. The man who owns it is not strong in the craft. Within a couple of days it will be of no concern to you."

"Thank you," Mallory said. "You have no idea how grateful I am. For tonight . . . and for trying all those years ago."

The voodoo woman nodded. "If you need me for anything, I live in a cabin just off the point where you and the other man fish for speckled trout." She reached over and touched Mallory's forehead with her thumb. "Live well, Mallory Devereaux. This is my wish for you."

She glanced at the others and gave them a brief nod

before walking toward the woods, a dim glow surrounding her. She'd only walked fifteen feet or so before the glow faded and she seemed to vanish before their eyes.

Mallory blinked and squinted in the darkness. Where the hell did she go?

"Show's over," Scooter said. "I say it's time to get the hell out of here." He looked over at Amy. "Would you mind giving me a ride home? I figure those two might want to talk."

Amy looked over at Mallory, her expression thoughtful. "If you need anything," she said. "Anything at all, you call me. It doesn't matter what time."

Mallory nodded and smiled at her friend. "Thanks for everything, Amy. You're a great friend and I'm lucky to have you."

Amy smiled. "That makes two of us." She gave Jake a wave and headed to her car, Scooter following close behind.

Mallory watched as Amy backed up and pulled away from the clearing, then she turned to Jake. "Looks like you got a bit more than you bargained for with this investigation."

Jake looked at her, slowly shaking his head. "It's all so unbelievable. Every single bit of it." He glanced back at the circle. "What do you think happened to the chicken? I didn't see her holding it when she left."

Mallory shrugged. "I hadn't even thought about it again. Maybe she had it the bag."

Jake grimaced. "I like fried chicken as much as the next guy, but it will be a while before I indulge in a bucket of KFC."

Jake started to speak a million different times on the drive back to Mallory's house, but there were simply no words that could convey what he felt. Hell, he didn't even know what he felt. He was angry and sad and frustrated and heartbroken, all at the same time. The emotions warred inside him, each canceling the other out and leaving him with nothing to say to the woman sitting next to him.

"I'm sorry" seemed so limited, so futile.

After what seemed like an eternity, they pulled up in front of Mallory's house. He parked his car behind her truck but made no move to exit, instead stared out over the bayou.

"Your parents," he finally started, "where are they now?"

There was only silence for a long time and for a moment, Jake was afraid she wasn't going to answer. Finally, she sighed and said one simple word. "Dead."

Jake looked over at her, a bit surprised by her answer. Mallory's parents couldn't have been very old when they passed, and although her answer meant there wasn't a set of people out there that he needed to throttle with his bare hands, he felt somewhat disappointed that the people who'd done this to Mallory had gotten away with it all.

"My father died in prison," Mallory said, her voice barely a whisper. "He cheated the wrong guy at cards and took a shank in the back. My mother was never the same after that. She wasted away to almost nothing inside of a year's time and finally died in a mental institution in New Orleans."

Mallory turned to face Jake. "She always blamed me, you know. For everything bad that happened to them—their schemes going wrong, my father going to prison. Now I know why."

Jake shook his head. "She was wrong. You didn't bring bad luck on them—they created all that for themselves with the life they chose. You know that."

239

"Maybe. Or maybe letting me become what I am came back on them like some great karmic debt."

"Maybe," Jake agreed. "Although it still doesn't seem like enough." He took her hand in his and squeezed. "I just can't imagine a parent doing that. It's so far from what I know."

"It ought to be," Mallory said simply, then turned to face him. "Tell me about your parents. I want to know something personal about you, Jake McMillan."

"Randoll."

"Huh?" Mallory looked at him, obviously confused.

"My real name is Jake Randoll. I really am from Atlantic City. My mother is a retired schoolteacher. My father was a cop."

"Was?"

"Yeah. He was killed in the line of duty when I was eight."

"I'm sorry," Mallory said, and squeezed his hand. "That must have been hard for you and your mother."

Jake nodded. "It was awful. My dad, he was the best— the best husband, the best father. And my mother . . . left alone with me to raise . . . I don't think she ever really got the chance to grieve."

Mallory reached up to cup Jake's cheek. "He would have been proud of you. Proud of the man his son became. I'm sure your mother is."

Jake looked at her and couldn't help but want her . . . her hair shimmering in the glow of moonlight, her green eyes sparkling as she looked at him . . . her touch so gentle against his skin. Never had he thought another woman could possess the fortitude, the intelligence that his mother had shown all those years, raising her son to be a man. But Mallory Devereaux brought new meaning to the word strength. Her entire life was a testament to that.

Placing his arms around her, he drew her in close to him, lowering his head to press his lips against her. She tasted of raspberry and even though he'd seen her swipe the lip gloss across her lips at the poker table, the flavor seemed so sensual, so Mallory. Unable to stop himself, he ran his tongue across her lips, tasting every bit of the sweetness.

She leaned into him and dropped her hand to his chest, running it along the length of his torso. The light pressure of her fingers brushing against the fabric of his shirt made him start to stiffen. She didn't stop her journey at his waistband as he'd thought she would. When she grazed her hand over the top of his jeans, she almost finished him off.

Surely the voodoo woman was wrong, he thought as he left her lips to kiss the hollow of her neck and down the front of her chest. Mallory wasn't cursed—she was a witch. It was the only way to explain the way he felt when he was with her—as if every nerve in his body were on fire, as if nothing at all mattered any more except touching every square inch of her and burying himself deep inside her.

He moved one hand underneath her shirt and cupped her bare breast, amazed again at her body that was so full and firm at the same time. He grabbed the bottom of her T-shirt with both hands and relieved her upper body of the garment. Breasts that perfect just cried to be free and he wanted to be the man to accommodate them.

He tossed the shirt in the backseat and descended on her chest with both hand and mouth, causing her to groan. She paid him back by opening his jeans and slipping her hand inside, stroking the hard length of him until he thought he would burst from the pleasure.

"I'm going to try to take things slower this time, but I'm not promising success," he said as he tugged at the closure on her jeans, silently willing the tight garment to let go.

"That makes two of us," she teased.

The tiny strip of pink lace posing as underwear hardly presented a logistics problem. They were so damned sexy, he left them on, then threaded one finger around them and ran it down the tiny strip of fabric.

"It's not Sunday," he said, and he pulled the fabric back gently and pressed his finger into her hot, moist center.

Mallory moaned as he stroked her. "Who the hell cares?"

Jake smiled down at her. "You said you only wore underwear on Sunday." He slipped one finger inside of her, still stroking her sensitive nub with his thumb.

Her grip on him tightened and she sucked in a breath. "I promise to wear them every day if this is the treatment I get," she whispered, increasing the pressure and speed of her strokes with every word until he thought he would explode.

He put his hand over hers. "You've got to stop or I won't have anything left," he said as he continued to stroke her.

"But you're not stopping," she tried to protest, but it wasn't much of a fight.

"Yes, but I'm making the rules," he whispered, and leaned over to take her nipple in his mouth. He swirled his tongue around the engorged flesh in complete synchronicity with the stroke of his finger below. It was only a matter of seconds before her breathing quickened, and he felt her body contract around his finger.

She cried out when the orgasm washed over her and dug her fingers into his shoulders. He waited a moment for the trembling in her body to stop before removing his finger and raising his head to look at her.

She gave him the lazy smile of a completely satisfied woman, then pushed him back onto his side of the car and straddled him. "My turn," she said, and lowered herself onto him in a single fluid stroke.

He almost lost it the moment he entered her and had to struggle to regain control. He'd just managed to stave off the worst of the embarrassment when she started her motion, rolling her hips back and forth in a slow, rhythmic dance, and he had to concentrate again on holding himself back.

She dropped her hands to his chest and ran them across his nipples. He was momentarily surprised at the pleasure that shot through him with her touch, and he sucked in a breath as she lowered her head and circled the nipple with her tongue.

"Touch my breasts," she instructed as she increased her hip motion. "Both hands."

He couldn't comply fast enough. Both hands shot up eagerly to encase her breasts and she threw back her head and moaned. Even though he didn't think it possible, her reaction made him even hotter, and he lowered his head to take an engorged nipple into his mouth, suckling on it gently. She responded by tightening her body around him like a glove, increasing the friction and speed until he couldn't hold back any longer.

"Come with me," he whispered, and took her breast into his mouth once more.

"Yes," she replied, and he felt her body begin to spasm, as she took him deeper inside of her.

The orgasm burst through him like lightning, hitting so hard it actually made him dizzy. He could feel Mallory's body around him, growing tight then loose and her legs shook with the strength of their finish. Finally, she became still and leaned against him, her breasts pressed against his bare chest, her heart racing right alongside his own.

He felt the car rumble and the sounds of roaring in his ears and for a second, he thought it was a backlash of previously released energy, but at the sound of the second rumble, he opened his eyes and looked out the windshield just as a flash of lightning lit up the bayou as clear as daylight. "It's a storm," he said.

Mallory rose limply from his chest, a satisfied smile on her face. She glanced out the passenger window. "Looks like a doozy. We'd better get inside before the bottom drops out."

She rolled off him and bounced onto the seat, reaching for her pants on the floorboard. He knew he should be dressing, but instead, he watched her slide into the tight denim, feeling his erection stir all over again. She grabbed her T-shirt from the backseat and pulled it on, her taut nipples protruding easily through the thin fabric.

She looked over at him and shook her head. "Stop grinning like an idiot and get a move on. All of me looks the same inside, I assure you." She reached for the door just as a huge burst of thunder rocked the car, causing them both to jump. Before they could make a move, a single bolt of lightning burst from the sky and struck directly through the hood of the car, spraying sparks of fire in every direction.

Chapter Sixteen

"Holy shit!" Mallory pushed the door open, jumped out into her yard and ran several feet from the car without even turning to look. Jake followed close on her heels, hoping like hell the sparks didn't singe his bare ass as he escaped.

When they turned back to look, the entire engine lit up in flames that quickly spread to rear of the car. Jake stared and shook his head. "My insurance rates are going to hit the roof over this one."

Mallory took one look at the burning car and started to giggle. As the first sound left her mouth, the rain began to pour on them as if unleashed in one big tidal wave. She laughed harder, leaning over at the waist, as the rain soaked every square inch of her.

"Damn it, this is not funny," Jake said, trying to pull her back to the seriousness of the situation. "The car is on fire, there's a flood coming from the sky, and you're laughing."

She raised her head slightly to look at him and he couldn't be sure whether she was laughing so hard she was crying or whether it was merely the rain streaming down her face. Pointing at the car, she finally managed to speak, "I'm not laughing about the car. I'm laughing about your clothes. They're still inside."

Jake stared at the car in dismay, wondering for a moment if he could retrieve them before it was too late.

The explosion that followed settled that question for him.

Pieces of the car burst up from the center and they both crouched down, covering their heads from the shards of flying metal. When only rain continued to pour down upon them, they rose up and looked at each other in amazement.

"I didn't really think it would blow up," Mallory said, "I figured the rain would put it out first."

Jake shook his head. "It must have gotten to the gas tank first. Hertz is not going to be happy about this. Or State Farm."

Mallory started to giggle again, then looked at him and put one hand over her mouth. "I'm sorry," she managed to get out, "but you have to admit, it was a pretty spectacular finish."

Jake wiped the water from his eyes and looked once more at the smoldering car. It *was* kind of funny, when you thought about it in abstract. He let out a single laugh, then another, and pretty soon was laughing as hard as Mallory when the high beam of a floodlight hit them.

"Good God Almighty!" Scooter stared at them for a moment, then brought one arm up to cover his eyes. "We had a deal, Mallory, remember, since that one time with me and the two strippers? No naked people on the front lawn. And this is a guy—I just saw another naked guy."

He stalked back to his cabin, arm still over his eyes,

and ran right into a post as he stepped onto his porch. He wrestled with the screen door for a moment, then slipped inside, the door banging behind him.

Mallory grabbed Jake's hand and pulled him toward her cabin, a huge grin on her face. "C'mon, let's get you inside before you hurt anyone else. I've got some sweats you can borrow and this whole car fire thing has given me an idea about winning this tournament. It's a long shot— I mean miles long—but what the hell, it's better than what we've got now."

Jake hurried along beside her, trying to remain horrified at Scooter seeing him in the buff but too curious about Mallory's comment to stay fixated with one emotion. "Why would the car fire give you an idea about poker?"

They stepped inside the cabin and Mallory hurried to the bathroom and returned with towels. She tossed one to Jake and began to pull off her wet clothes. "The same thing happened before to Amy and me when she let me drive her car," she said as she began to ring the water from her hair.

Jake stopped drying off for a moment and stared at her. "You and Amy were having sex in her car, and it was hit by lightning?"

Mallory rolled her eyes. "Don't you wish. No, Amy was sick with the flu and I had driven her to the doctor. We'd just pulled up into my driveway when her engine started smoking—turns out something was wrong with the fuel line and the whole thing went up in flames. Car was totaled, but I managed to get her thesis research out of the trunk before it was too late."

Jake stared at her, trying to make sense of her line of logic. "And this has what exactly to do with the tournament?"

Mallory grinned. "Amy. Amy has everything to do with the tournament. She's playing the tournament as proof of her thesis. She's developed a method for counting cards that she claims will improve the player's odds by five hundred percent."

"Amy is writing a thesis on poker? I thought she was a computer hacker." Could this get any more bizarre? "What the hell is she majoring in—criminology?"

Mallory laughed. "Well, her minor is political science, which is close enough, but her major is math, and she's a complete prodigy. If she says her method works, I'm sure it does."

"Why didn't you mention this before?"

Mallory shrugged. "I guess it just didn't occur to me until now. In the beginning, it wasn't necessary because I had everything covered. Then we got busy breaking into hotels, finding voodoo dolls and searching apartments . . . I guess I kept thinking we'd figure it out and go on as originally planned. Plus, it took Amy years to develop this. It can't possibly be easy."

She grabbed the phone off the kitchen counter and pressed in some numbers. "We'll just have to hope she can teach you something that will help before tomorrow morning. How are you with numbers?"

What the hell. "Better than with cars."

It only took a couple of minutes for Mallory to arrange things with Amy, who was instructed to hang tight until Mallory had everything in place. Then Mallory hung up the phone and went in search of clothes for Jake. She took another couple of minutes to dig some sweatpants and an oversized T-shirt out of her closet before picking up the phone again.

Jake grabbed the clothes off the couch and pulled on the pants. They were a couple of inches too short but would have to do. The T-shirt, however, was a whole other matter. It was pink, for starters, with the word "Sexy" across the front in glittery silver lettering. "No way," he said, and tossed the shirt back at her. "Give me anything else—Kill Something Season, Fish and Wildlife, Beer Drinking Contest—anything but pink Sexy."

Mallory lowered the phone from her ear and gave him a smile. "That's the biggest shirt I have—I sleep in it." She lifted the phone back up to her ear. "You'll live. And before you even suggest it, you are not going bare chested in front of Amy. She's very innocent and your bare chest is very distracting." She grinned at him and turned her attention back to the phone.

"Scooter," she said, "can you come over as soon as possible? I need your expertise on an electronics matter."

Jake could hear the other man protesting all the way across the room. Mallory rolled her eyes and waited for Scooter's tirade to end. "He's dressed now, I promise," she said. She paused for a moment then shook her head. "Seeing another grown man naked definitely does not make you gay."

A minute or so later there was a knock at the door, and Mallory opened it to an apprehensive Scooter. He took a single step into the cabin but as soon as his eyes locked on Jake's T-shirt, he stepped back outside. "Mallory, you said he was dressed," he protested. "That ain't no way for a real man to dress."

Mallory grabbed Scooter's arm and tugged him inside. "His clothes burned up in the car and that's the biggest shirt I own. And you're smaller than me so don't even suggest it." She walked toward the kitchen, pulling Scooter behind her. "With the way the casino cameras are set up, do you think you can fix something to get a shot of Silas's hands?"

She grabbed a pad of paper and began to draw. His curiosity overriding the insult of his clothes, Jake stepped closer to see a rough rendition of the casino layout on the paper.

"So what do you think?" Mallory looked at Scooter. "Is there any way to install the cameras where Silas won't notice? I figure the table is out because there's no way he isn't looking for that, especially with Reginald hosting."

Scooter flipped the pad around and stared at it a minute, his brow scrunched in concentration. Finally, he shook his head. "I could put three or four cameras in the ceiling with an angle down, but getting a clear look at his hand would still be a long shot. One of them may pick something up . . . say . . . three out of ten times."

Mallory looked over at Jake. "That's a thirty percent better chance than we have right now."

"Yeah, at this point anything is better," he agreed. "Do you think Reginald will let you install the cameras?"

"I think, given the situation, Reginald will be thrilled to let us install some cameras, and we're on our way to talk with him right now." She grabbed her rain jacket from a peg in the kitchen and motioned to Jake. "C'mon, Sexy, let's go find Reginald and get Scooter to work. We'll grab some clothes for you from your hotel room since you wearing my T-shirt appears to be an affront to masculinity. I'll call Amy on the way and tell her to meet us at the casino." She looked at the two men and smiled. "Sound like a plan?"

Jake nodded and followed her out into the rain, wondering exactly how bad things had gotten when he felt better about this tournament right this moment, pink Sexy T-shirt and all, than he had in days.

* * *

Mallory stepped inside her uncle's office and closed the door behind her. Amy and Jake were hovering over reams of paper with numbers and photos of cards on them and Scooter was busy having fun with his new drill again.

With the number of curveballs thrown at him lately, Reginald was probably hunkered down in his office with a bottle of scotch. To his credit, her uncle hadn't shown a single iota of surprise when Mallory had insisted he meet her at the casino, then burst in with Amy, Jake and Scooter and informed him that Silas was a money launderer, Jake an FBI agent and that they knew all about the ATF and their blackmailing scheme. But then she figured with everything the man had endured for the last couple of weeks, he would have bought a story about aliens in the casino.

What she was about to do could have waited—probably needed to wait—but there were too many unresolved items wedged between her and Reginald and she somehow felt that getting it all out now would make things go better tomorrow.

"Uncle Reginald?" she said, and he raised his head from the paperwork on his desk. "You got a minute?"

Reginald motioned to the chair across from him. "At the moment, I got nothing but time, and it's dragging, every single second of it."

Mallory nodded. "I can imagine. It's fairly crawling for me too. We need a lot more of it for our plan to work the best, but at the same time, I just want it to all be over."

"Yeah. It's the 'over' part that I'm most worried about."

Mallory shifted in her chair, not exactly knowing where to start, then finally decided she'd start at the beginning. "I've already told you Jake and I broke into Silas's room, that night I saw you at the hotel."

A fleeting glimpse of embarrassment passed over Reginald's face and he nodded. "I remember."

"Well, I took something from Silas's room—a voodoo doll." She looked her uncle directly in the eyes. "It looked just like me, Uncle Reginald. The hair, the facial expression, the clothes I wore the first day of the tournament. That doll was me."

Reginald stared at her for a moment, then finally blinked, his expression never shifting.

"You knew," she said. "The voodoo woman was telling the truth."

Reginald dropped his gaze to the desktop. "I knew."

"Damn it! Why didn't you tell me? Why did you let me go around my entire life wondering? Why didn't you bring me to the voodoo woman sooner, when something might have been done?"

Reginald looked up at her with sad eyes. "I begged my sister to have the voodoo woman at the birth but she wouldn't hear of it. She said that you were the reason Silas put the curse upon her and you might as well live with it. She said it was karma, or some bullshit, that someone had to pay and it wasn't going to be her."

"But you could have taken me yourself . . . if you knew what was done."

Reginald nodded. "I planned to. As soon as your mother left the hospital I figured I'd get my chance. But she knew. She knew I'd try, and she had some fool idea in her head that if the curse came off you, it would go back on her. So she left the hospital and disappeared."

Mallory stared at her uncle. "What do you mean, she disappeared?"

Reginald held both hands up in the air in frustration. "She walked out of the hospital with you and drove away. I still don't have any idea where she went."

"And my father?" Mallory asked, trying to absorb what Reginald said.

"Was in prison for one of his many visits. Your mother blamed it on the curse, but the truth is Silas Hebert set him up to take the fall in a money-laundering scheme for stealing your mother away. There wasn't anything out of this world about it."

"So my father was telling the truth about the money."

Reginald shrugged. "Maybe he was telling the truth that he didn't know. Or maybe he was in it up to his neck, and he's the one who took the fall. Doesn't matter. He would have involved himself anyway. He wasn't a good man, Mallory. And he was never gonna be."

Mallory thought about Reginald's words for a moment, then nodded. "But why the curse? If Silas loved my mother, why would he curse her?"

Reginald blew out a breath and shook his head. "The line between love and hate is a fine one, but Silas's feelings for your mother were more obsession than love and ultimately, that's what scared her away."

"Then why does Silas hate you so much? I mean, it was her decision to leave him, right?"

Reginald tapped his fingers on his desk. "Not exactly. You see, I knew your mother would never have left Silas on her own."

"So you helped."

"Yeah, I helped. I found out Silas was working for a small-time mob boss out of New Orleans, racketeering, drug running . . . I put the cops onto him and the charges stuck. Silas never had proof, but he knew I had turned him in. No one else but your mother and I knew what he was into."

"So Silas went to jail and my mother got away," Mallory said.

"I convinced her to go off to college, even footed the bill by working two jobs, but in the end it didn't do much good."

"She traded Silas for my father."

Reginald nodded. "And I had to admit that the real problem was my sister, not the men she was with. When she came up pregnant with you, Silas had just been released and was under the impression that she'd waited for him. When she told Silas that she was going to marry your father, he lost it. Blamed the pregnancy for forcing her into marriage. Blamed me for her turning to another man."

Mallory shook her head, incredulous. "So he cursed my mother and me, and set up my father to go to prison. It's too much to believe."

"It's incredibly messed up is what it is," Reginald said, his voice beginning to rise. "In the end, I didn't give a damn about the two of them. They made their beds." He looked her straight in the eye. "I looked for you, Mallory, I swear it. Spent two years and God knows how much money trying to find you before it was too late, but I never turned up a thing. To this day, I still don't know where she went or what she did for money. By the time she came back . . ."

"It was too late to reverse the curse," Mallory finished.

"I'm sorry, Mallory. Sorry for everything."

"My own mother," Mallory said, too numb to feel anything at all. "How could she?"

"My sister was always a selfish person. Even as a little girl I knew she'd never be a good wife or mother. Everything was for her. Your father was the same way, so I guess that's why their relationship worked." He looked her straight in the eyes. "What I do know is that none of this is of your making. You never deserved them as parents, and they sure as hell didn't deserve you as a child. You were better than them, Mallory, and it was apparent from the beginning."

"Why didn't you tell me?"

Reginald dropped his gaze down to the desk. "Why? So you'd know your own mother despised you and blamed you for her ruined life even though it was all of her own making? So you'd be constantly aware that your life was overshadowed by something you didn't ask for and couldn't control?"

He looked back up at her and shook his head. "I'm sorry, Mallory, but I couldn't do it. Harry and Thelma did a fine job raising you. You're my pride and joy even though we've had to maintain distance all these years because of the way I do business."

"Like the distance you maintain with Glenda?"

Reginald looked at her in surprise.

"Jake and I kinda came across her two nights ago when we were investigating a lead on his case," Mallory explained. "She told me about the two of you."

"Yeah, well," Reginald looked down at his desk and thumped his knuckles on the surface. "Glenda's the whole reason behind me going legit. I was almost there before this bullshit with the ATF came up. If I don't get the money to pay back the loan shark, I'll never be able to turn things around."

Mallory shook her head. "That's not going to happen. This is all going to work out right, I feel it in my bones." She looked over at her uncle and smiled. "And thank you, for everything you've done for me. If I didn't think it would break your watch or sprain your wrist, I'd hug you right now."

Reginald rose from the desk and stepped around in

front of her, his eyes misty. He reached down and pulled her up to him, circling her shoulders with his arms and hugging her tight. "It's worth the risk."

Mallory made it back to the casino just in time to get everyone to take a much-needed break. Amy's face was flushed with aggravation, Jake's with frustration. Scooter stood posed at the top of a ladder, drilling a tiny hole in the ceiling and apparently oblivious to the scene beneath him.

"It's not going to work," Amy said. "He's not going to be able to learn all this in"—she looked down at her watch—"seven hours."

"Well?" Mallory looked over at Jake.

He ran one hand through his hair and paced a couple of steps, then turned and paced back to face her. "It's too much information. I'm not doubting her work—she's proven it will fly, but I don't think I can commit it all to memory before the tournament starts again."

Mallory blew out a breath and looked at Amy. "Are there any shortcuts? Anything smaller you can teach him to help, not necessarily the entire package?"

Amy shook her head. "It just doesn't work that way. I narrowed this down to the simplest method possible. But even the simplest method is going to be complicated. We just have to keep working and hope for the best. Maybe enough of it will sink in so that it will give him an edge."

Mallory nodded. "I'll get you both some coffee. Okay?"

"That would be great," Jake said, and gave her a grateful smile as he took his seat at the table again. "Let's give it another try." He shuffled the cards and began to deal.

By the time Mallory got back with two huge mugs of coffee, Reginald had emerged from his office to supervise

Scooter's camera work. Mallory set the two mugs on the card table and went to see Scooter's handiwork firsthand.

"What do you think?" she asked her neighbor. "Will it give you enough of an angle to get anything?"

Scooter looked down from the ladder and nodded. "About as good as I thought. Probably three out of ten times if we're lucky."

Reginald looked from the tiny hole in the ceiling to the card table. "Anything to help at this point." He nodded toward Amy and Jake. "I don't think that's going so well," he said to Mallory, keeping his voice low.

She looked over at the table. "I agree that optimism is at an all-time low at the moment."

Amy dealt the last card for Jake's hand and looked at him. "Three of spades. Stay or fold?"

Jake studied his cards, turned face up for the sake of the training, his brow wrinkled in concentration. "Fold?"

Amy looked at him. "Are you sure?"

Jake blew out a breath. "No. But that's what I'm going with."

Scooter climbed down from the ladder and shook his head. "Man, you're not even close. You're down what . . . two-thirds of the deck and over eighty percent of the face cards have been played? That puts you at a 472 by Amy's counting method, which makes you ripe for an inside straight. You should stay and raise."

Amy sucked in a breath and stared at Scooter in amazement. "Oh, my God, that's right."

Mallory whipped around to look at her neighbor. "Scooter? How in God's name did you figure that out?"

Scooter pulled a larger drill bit out of his toolbox and began to replace the current one on his drill, then shrugged. "It just makes sense. Those numbers Amy's using are like measurements—like building stuff. They all come back around to the same thing eventually." He started up the ladder again and began to drill a second hole, cleverly disguised by a chandelier.

Mallory stared after Scooter for a moment, then turned to look at the others, all looking at Scooter with varying degrees of disbelief. The total ridiculousness of the situation sank in and Mallory started to chuckle.

"I don't believe it," Jake said. "For God's sake, the man has his shirt on inside out."

Which only made Mallory laugh harder.

"I don't see what you think is so funny," Jake said. "It doesn't do us a damn bit of good if Scooter understands Amy's method. He's not the dealer."

"No, he's not a dealer," Mallory said as she flopped into a chair and wiped the tears away from her eyes. "But there's nothing to stop us from putting a camera on your hand and having Scooter watching it and calling the shots."

Jake stared at her for a moment, then shook his head. "Wouldn't work. How would he get the information to me?"

"We were going to work out some method of communication for the thirty percent we were hoping to gain, anyway. We'll just need something more elaborate than hand signals from across the room. You're the federal agent. Surely you can come up with some fancy electronics."

"I can hardly wear an earpiece while dealing," Jake objected. "I think Silas would catch on to that."

Mallory shrugged. "So I'll wear one. Don't tell me the FBI doesn't have something that will pass as earrings. We'll work out a series of signals—something that Silas won't be able to get. I'll take the information from Scooter and pass it to you during play."

Scooter climbed down from the ladder again and

scratched his head. "Does that mean I can't drink beer tomorrow if I'm doing all this numbers stuff?"

Reginald let out a huge guffaw and slapped the other man on the back, moving him about six inches. "Don't worry about it, boy. You help Jake win this tournament and I'll see to it that you never worry about beer again."

"Even Silas Hebert couldn't manufacture enough money to keep Scooter in beer," Mallory declared.

"At the rate my casino business was increasing before all this mess, I won't have to manufacture anything," Reginald said. "I'll be able to run free and clear. Legally."

Mallory looked at her uncle and smiled. "First time for everything, right?"

It was barely dawn when Jake finished fixing Mallory's earring with the earpiece. "You're going to need to wear your hair down," he said. "This is good, but it's not perfect. The earring covers most of the device, but I still have this clear piece that I have to place inside your ear. Otherwise, you'll never hear enough of anything to be of any use."

Mallory nodded and slipped the large gold disk into her ear, then wrapped the thin clear wire around the bottom of her lobe and placed the end piece into her ear. She signaled to Jake that she was ready, and he walked out of Reginald's office with a radio.

She waited for a moment, but nothing came through, no voice, no static, nothing. She was just about to call for Jake when she heard him say, "So what kind of underwear are you wearing right now?"

"A thin string of purple lace." May as well give him something to think over.

There was a pause on the other end, then finally the next question came. "Are all your panties flimsy and lacy?"

She laughed and called out down the hall, "Yes, except my Sunday pair. They're a very respectable white cotton."

Noticing a movement to her side, she looked over and found Reginald standing in the doorway to the storeroom. "I don't think I even want to know the other side of that conversation. I take it the earpiece is working."

"Loud and clear."

Jake rounded the corner and gave her a wave. "Did you get that?"

"Yeah, didn't you hear my answer? I yelled it down the hall."

Jake shook his head and fiddled with a knob on the radio. "No, I was in the lobby."

"You were in the lobby when you spoke to me? That's incredible."

Reginald gave Mallory a thump on her back. "Yeah, and you were busy yelling about your undergarments to everyone in a hundred-foot radius." He walked back into the storeroom laughing as he walked.

Jake grinned. "If it makes you feel any better, I don't think your panties or lack thereof are a laughing matter at all."

"Really?" Mallory gave him a sexy smile. "That's good to hear since I was thinking of giving you a glimpse of that purple lace to signal 'all-in.'"

Chapter Seventeen

Jake pulled out the cards from the shelf beneath the poker table and began to stack them in the shoe. It was a little early yet, but the other dealers were starting to filter into the room. The players wouldn't be far behind. He was just stacking his chips on the side when he looked up and saw Brad standing at his table.

"It's going down today," Brad said. "Reginald is taking the boat in a big sweeping circle. The actual takedown will happen when we're still offshore in order to eliminate the possibility of some getting away on land, but we'll arrive at the docks within fifteen minutes of the arrests. Midafternoon is all you've got to get a money exchange. We'll start the takedown soon after the afternoon break."

Jake nodded. "I appreciate you telling me."

Brad shrugged. "Yeah, well, I asked my uncle about Silas. He gave me an earful and none of it pleasant. Even though what I'm dealing with is a bigger problem, if we could take one more like him off the streets that would be a good thing."

"No disagreement there. I just want this over. Get Silas behind bars once and for all. I'm sure you want the same."

"Yeah, we've got the evidence we need, but it's no small feat to take these guys. The only option for getting them all is doing it at the same time or the rest will run. And the only safe way to get them at the same time is on this boat, where we can be certain they're not carrying weapons."

Jake laughed. "Yeah, the whole thing—the boat, the metal detectors—was really a genius move considering the scope of your arrest. I did have one question, though. What about the players who were cut earlier in the week?"

"The scope of the takedown is really only six people. A lot of them we were watching for an indication of involvement, just in case, and we figured if we put them all in one place, they'd talk. If someone we were watching got cut from the tournament early, we would have had agents on him."

"I see," Jake said. "So this whole setup was as much for the spying as the takedown. Makes perfect sense now that I know the situation, but God, I'm definitely ready to get home. Louisiana is one strange place."

Now Brad laughed. "You got that right. Hell, if I hadn't lived here my whole life, I wouldn't believe the half of what goes on down in these bayous."

Jake stared at Brad. "I thought you lived in New England."

"Hell, no. You think I'm faking this accent? Ain't nobody that good an actor."

"But you met Mark at a party . . ."

Brad gave him a curious look. "Yeah, corporate party in New Orleans. That's where he and Janine lived at the time."

Jake swore his heart stopped beating for a moment. "Mark's from New Orleans?"

"Nah, somewhere in the Midwest, I believe, but he did a rookie stint in New Orleans as a cop, waiting for the FBI deal to come through. That's where he met Janine." He stared at Jake. "You didn't know?"

Jake shook his head and stared down at the table, trying to clear the jumble of thoughts that raged within. It wasn't possible, was it? Could he really have worked with Mark for over ten years and not known what his partner was involved in? But if he were innocent, why hadn't he ever told Jake about being a New Orleans cop? In fact, not once, in all the time Jake had known him, could he remember Mark ever mentioning Louisiana at all.

It was an awful thought, but it would explain so much—why Mark kept trying to file the case away as useless and unsolvable, why Silas managed to slip through their fingers on every setup, why Mark had insisted that it be he rather than Jake who secured a job with Silas's crew.

Jake looked up at Brad. "I need to know exactly when you saw Mark in the casino in New Orleans."

Brad stared at him for a moment, a confused look on his face, then it cleared in understanding. "It was February fifth, a Saturday. I remember because it was my wife's birthday."

Jake did a quick mental calculation. "That was a little over two weeks ago."

Brad nodded. "Exactly how long has Mark missed his check-ins?"

"Including today? Forty-one days."

Brad looked at him, a grim expression on his face. "You've got a big problem, my man."

Jake thought of Janine, waiting in her townhome in

Atlantic City with a five-year-old, praying that Jake brought her good news of her husband. "You have no idea." He clapped Brad on the back as he stepped from behind the table. "If you'll excuse me for a moment, there's a phone call I need to make."

Brad gave him a sympathetic nod as Jake pulled his cell phone from his pocket, walked across the casino and stepped out onto the balcony

"Yeah," his captain said, picking up on the first ring.

"It's Jake. I'm afraid I've got a big problem here."

"It's the last damned day of that tournament, and you still don't have any money to test. Is that asshole Silas ever going to lose enough to buy in for more or was this whole thing a bust?"

If only it were that simple. "That's not exactly the problem I was talking about."

"Well, what the hell is it now?"

"Did you know that Mark worked as a cop in New Orleans before he joined the bureau?"

"I don't know. I guess I read it on his application. Why?"

"When we were building this case, why didn't you ever tell me that?"

"Hell, he probably had his tonsils out when he was a kid, too. I didn't tell you that, either. I'm not in the habit of going over my agents' resumes with their partners. It's your job to know the man you're working with."

"Well, apparently that man withheld information from the beginning. He told me he grew up on a farm in the Midwest and never once mentioned Louisiana or New Orleans. You got any idea why he would exclude that from his life story?"

There was a pause on the other end. "I honestly don't know. Maybe he didn't think it was relevant. Maybe he pulled something stupid working there and didn't want anyone looking too close. I don't get it, Jake. Where is all this going?"

"Somewhere you're not going to like." Jake took a breath and continued. "You know that ATF bust I told you about—the one going down during the tournament?"

"Yeah. Don't tell me you've fucked up their bust. I don't need any problems from the ATF, and I've already gotten more phone calls than I ever cared to take."

"No. Nothing like that. There's an ATF agent here, name of Brad, who met Mark when he was working in New Orleans. Brad made Mark when he was undercover working for Silas in one of the casinos in New Orleans. Mark filled him in so he wouldn't blow his cover."

"Okay. That's a random-chance sort of thing, but Mark did the right thing in telling the guy."

"Yeah. I thought so too—until Brad told me that happened just two weeks ago."

There was dead silence on the other end of the line for what seemed like an eternity. Finally, Jake heard a sharp release of breath.

"Goddamn it!" his captain ranted. "I'm pulling you off this case as of now. You get your ass out of that casino. If Mark's turned, then Silas has known all along who you are."

"Maybe, but if it's as simple as Mark turning, then why was he locked in that apartment? It doesn't add up, Captain."

"Maybe he turned long enough for Silas to get what he needed, and then he was expendable. Maybe Silas only trusts him so far. I don't know and I don't care. The fact is, if Mark were free to roam a casino two weeks ago, having private conversations with the ATF, then he was also free to check in with the office as scheduled."

"Yeah, but it still feels like I'm missing something."

"Maybe the plan was to stage the kidnapping, make it look like Silas had taken Mark and held him captive. Maybe they thought they could release him afterward and Mark could step right back into his job at the bureau. At this point, it doesn't really matter. What I do know is that they're playing you, and it's not safe to remain at the tournament."

"I know that, but I can't leave. Silas may think he's got the upper hand, but his ego keeps him from having the control he thinks he does. This vendetta he has against St. Claire and his family goes back forever. I'm beginning to think this is a whole lot more than a simple money wash. I think Silas is trying to set up St. Claire to go down for the laundering, just like he did Jack Devereaux."

"All the more reason to get the hell out of there. If this is more personal than business, there's no way to know what Silas is capable of."

"If he wanted to kill me, he could have done so already. He's playing with me because he thinks he can win—his final parting shot at the FBI. I still think I can get an exchange. I only need the one."

"It's not worth the risk. We can regroup here and decide what to do next."

"What we can do next is nothing, and you know it. In a matter of days, Silas will be out of the country, probably taking Mark with him. We can't do a damned thing then."

"I don't care. It's likely I've already lost one agent. I don't want to lose another. Don't you make this personal, too."

"It *is* personal, Captain. And it's not just me who's affected by this. I've made promises to other people, and by God I'm going to see that I make every effort to make them happen. I'm sorry, but I can't leave until this is over."

"Even if it means leaving in a body bag?"

"If anything happens to me, get in touch with Brad Johnson at the ATF. Maybe he can help fill in the blanks."

"At least let me send you backup. I can have men at the boat within a half hour."

"There's no time. The boat leaves the dock in a matter of minutes. The ATF bust is going down midafternoon, so I only have five hours or so to pull off an exchange. I'll call as soon as I get an exchange tested."

There was a pause on the other end and Jake heard the captain sigh. "All right then. I trust your instincts. I've got Judge Warner standing by. If you can get an exchange, I'll have the warrant in place when we dock. I'd love to take this bastard down—now more than ever."

"Me too, sir."

"Do not attempt to apprehend Silas on your own. Wait until you dock."

"Yes, sir."

"And Randoll, I don't guess I have to tell you to watch your back."

Jake gave Mallory a brief nod as she approached the poker table while the players took their seats. "Last day, gentlemen," he said with a smile. "The ante goes up to five hundred a hand this morning and will increase again after lunch. Unless anyone wants to quit now."

The men chuckled, except Silas, who gave him a superior look, and Father Thomas, who lifted one hand in the air and said, "God bless this game of which we are about to partake."

Jake looked at the priest, still amused the old bird had held in this long. He probably wouldn't make it until noon today with the chips he had left, but he'd certainly given the words "functioning alcoholic" a whole new meaning. "Well, now that we've been officially blessed, what do you say we play some cards?" He reached for the decks of cards and began to shuffle.

Mallory removed her tablet from her pocket and began to take the morning orders, starting at the far end of the table first. He could feel her apprehension, thick in the air, as she moved closer and closer to the man who had ruined her life, but the resolve on her face was clear—this man was not going to win. What must she be thinking? What would he do in her position?

It was a question he didn't even want to think about answering because Jake was afraid that if he were Mallory those metal detectors wouldn't have kept him from bringing an instrument of death on board. She was serving the drinks, after all. A quick round of rat poison would do the trick and given Silas's reputation, the local police probably wouldn't even look too hard into his death, and Jake would be the last one to point out a discrepancy.

He watched Mallory take Silas's order with the same calm she'd dealt with the other players. This was one woman to be reckoned with. She would never sink to Silas's level and probably wouldn't appreciate Jake's aspersions of death by rat poison. She didn't want him dead. She wanted him in a living hell like he'd put her in. A prison cell for a man like Silas Hebert would be the ultimate in torture.

Mallory made it back with the drink server trailing behind her just as they were wrapping up the first hand. Luckily, his draw had been so bad that a blind monkey could have told him to fold, but that would all change now that Mallory was back to serve the drinks and spread her unluckiness along with them.

He'd tossed in his cards early and spent the rest of the

hand watching the drunken priest make fools of everyone else with his four of a kind. He didn't even try to contain his disbelief when the man turned over his cards because no one else did, either.

The player on the far end clapped Father Thomas on the back and laughed. "I gotta hand it to you, Father," he said, "you've definitely made this God thing work for you. Maybe when I get back home I should attend a Mass or something. Think they'll let me in?"

Father Thomas looked at the man, a serious expression on his usually jovial face. "The prodigal son returns. Always been a favorite story of mine. Until he's eaten by the giant fish." He looked up at Mallory as she served his scotch amid everyone else's coffee. "What about you, Mallory? Do you have a favorite Bible story?"

Mallory thought for a moment, then shook her head. "Can't say that I do, but I'm sort of a fatalist. I like when the rider of death comes in Revelations." She gave them all a smile, then looked directly at Silas Hebert as she slid onto her stool. It was all Jake could do to hold in a smile. Here he'd worried that Mallory wouldn't be able to handle being so close to Silas, so close to the man who'd made her life into the mess it was, and she'd come up with both guns blazing.

He'd never respected a woman more than he respected her at that moment. She was tough and feminine all at the same time. Hard and softhearted. Beautiful and intelligent. She was everything he never thought a woman would be and something he knew he'd never find again.

He set his jaw and began to deal the next hand. He couldn't give Mallory the fairy-tale life she deserved, but by God, he could see that the man who ruined it was behind bars. It was the least he could do.

* * *

When the morning break rolled around, Silas Hebert slipped from the casino and into the lobby, pressing in a number on his cell phone as he walked.

"Silas," the man answered. "Where the hell are you? Don't tell me you're still playing."

"Of course I'm still playing. I have a chance to take Reginald St. Claire for a hunk of money. I'm not letting it pass me by. We're already down one player this morning. That dealer is having a lucky run at the moment, but we both know that will change. He's not the player I am."

"Are you telling me you're going to have to cough up more money to finish the day? Silas, that's a bad mistake."

"Don't tell me how to run my business. What the hell difference does it make if I put up more money? It just means we leave with more laundered money passing through Reginald St. Claire's hands."

"You're crossing lines we never agreed to cross," the man warned Silas. "You need to walk away from that tournament now. You needed to walk away from it sooner. All of this could have been handled the first day Jake Randoll came to town if you'd just let me do my job."

"If an FBI agent turned up missing or dead, feds would have swarmed this place and the entire tournament would have been canceled. I couldn't risk Randoll disappearing before the last day."

"Well, it's the last day now. Forget the laundering. That wasn't the point of all this anyway. The boat is already in position. I can have you out of there in a half hour. You're risking everything over a stupid card game."

"You think I can't beat a Yankee FBI agent at cards? The day that's the case, I'll slit my own wrists."

"It's not just him and you know it. The girl is helping him."

270

"She's nothing but trash made by despicable people. She can't make a difference."

There was a pause on the other end and finally the man spoke. "Is that what this is about? Personal business that should have died a long time ago? You take these chances for nothing. Randoll is no fool."

"Then he'll be a dead smart man by the end of the day."

"And what about the woman?"

"I have plans for her." Silas flipped his phone shut. Oh, did he have plans for Mallory Devereaux. Mallory, who looked so much like her mother.

He pulled an old, faded photo from his wallet and stared it.

Beautiful, unfaithful Marie.

Reginald St. Claire would go down for helping her escape him. He'd know what it was like to sit in a cell surrounded by four gray walls . . . separated from the woman he loved, his entire life changing and unable to do anything about it . . . he'd know with certainty that Silas was responsible for making it all happen

And Mallory Devereaux would become one more dead whore—just like her mother.

Jake placed his cards on the table with a smile. He'd tried to hold it in, but this hand had clinched it. Silas Hebert was out of chips. Even though they hadn't gotten a glimpse of every hand, Scooter's tips to Mallory had definitely given Jake's play that extra edge he needed to beat Silas.

Now, Silas's only option to continue play was to put up more money, and Jake desperately hoped his ego would entice him to do exactly that.

He looked across the table at the man and waved one

hand at the empty table in front of him. "Mr. Hebert, you're out of chips. As this is the final day of play, you're allowed to purchase one round of chips worth ten thousand to stay in the tournament. Are you interested in making that purchase, or would you like to call it quits?"

Silas stared at him for a couple of seconds, not saying a word, and Jake felt moisture begin to form on his brow. *Buy the chips. Buy the chips.* He found himself mentally chanting that mantra and wondering if the whole paranormal thing had finally rubbed off on him and he'd decided to try a mind bend.

Finally, Silas reached into his jacket, pulled out a stack of bound bills and laid it on the table. "I'll take the ten thousand. You're not getting rid of me that easily." He stared directly at Jake, making sure both the words said and those implied were relayed in his gaze.

"I never thought it would be easy," Jake replied as he lifted the stack of bills off the table and placed it on the shelf below. He counted out ten thousand in chips and pushed them across the table to Silas, barely able to contain his excitement. The bastard had gone for it! Now all Jake had to do was continue winning and everything was going to work out.

Silas would go to prison. Mallory would get the money for Harry's business, and based on the dwindling number of players at the other tables, things were looking pretty good for Reginald St. Claire.

As for himself, he'd head back to New Jersey alone—up one huge money laundering bust and down one partner. But when he considered the things Mark had hidden from him all these years, letting go of his old partner would be the easy part. Letting go of his new partner was something he still didn't want to think about.

"Well, gentlemen," Jake said as he shuffled the decks

and placed them in the shoe. "We have about an hour of play left before lunch. What do you say I take all your money and we call this a day."

Silas stared at him and raised one eyebrow, issuing the silent challenge. The Mafia guy smirked and Father Thomas cleared his throat before saying, "This is the poker game that the Lord hath made."

"Then I guess I better get to dealing." Jake placed the final group of cards into the shoe and pushed his ante into the center of the table. "Wouldn't want to disappoint the Lord."

Mallory could barely contain her excitement as she removed the dirty glasses from the poker table and stacked them on the nearby tray. As soon as the door swung shut behind the last player, Jake grabbed the stack of bills he'd gained from Silas and waved it at Mallory.

"I've got to run tests on this," he said, the excitement evident in his voice. "Reginald gave me an office on the second floor with a wall safe to secure the funds. I'll give you a call as soon as I know for sure."

Mallory smiled and gave him a thumbs-up as he hurried away from the table. She glanced at the stacks of chips on the table and couldn't help the feeling of elation that passed over her. It was still too soon to celebrate, but damn, things were looking good.

The Mafia guy and the banker had played out just before lunch, and both had declined the additional buy-in option. Father Thomas only had chips remaining for two more antes. Silas had played well but was already down five thousand of the ten additional he'd put up. All Jake had to do was shut down the table before the ATF bust happened, and she would earn her money from Reginald.

The ATF bust was still a bit of a worry—guys with guns

tended to make Mallory a little nervous, especially when there was no deer or ducks around, but it wasn't like anyone had asked her opinion. And on the plus side, with the boat closing in on land at a rapid speed, there shouldn't be much lag time in between the bust and docking. The FBI had a team of men in Royal Flush waiting for the word from Jake to take their places at the dock, so that end of things was covered, too.

Mallory glanced at the clock on the wall and hurried to the dining room. She needed to eat a sandwich or something before play resumed for the afternoon. She was also dying to check in with Amy, whose table had grown less and less crowded as the morning wore on. Then she still needed to check in with Reginald and Scooter. Make sure everything was all right on their end.

She found Amy at their usual table in the restaurant. When she saw Mallory, a huge smile lit up her face. "I won!" she shouted before Mallory could even make it to the table, then jumped out of her chair and grabbed Mallory's hands, dancing her around in a circle. "I won, I won, I won!"

Mallory smiled back at Amy and allowed herself to be twirled in a circle. "It's a good thing," she said when the twirling finally stopped. "Dancing with me probably just bought you an entire afternoon of bad luck."

Amy waved one hand in dismissal and flopped back in her chair. "Who cares? I've had enough good happen today to hold me over for a long, long time." She leaned toward Mallory as she slid into the seat across from her and whispered, "After lunch, I'm going to Reginald's office to help Scooter give you guys tips. I cleared it with your uncle just before lunch."

Mallory couldn't hold back a grin. Scooter had been

doing a fabulous job so far, but with both him and Amy watching the cards, Mallory knew there was no way Jake could lose. "When this is over, I owe you huge."

"I heard Silas bought in," Amy said, her voice low.

"Yeah, Jake's testing the money now," Mallory whispered.

"When this is over, we are both set for life," Amy said

Mallory was just about to reply when she felt a hand on her shoulder. Knowing that no one she'd want to touch her would dare, she felt her pulse quicken as she turned around in her seat. She almost breathed a sigh of relief when she saw Walter Royal standing there. For the first time in her life, Royal wasn't dead last on her shit list.

"Mr. Royal," she said, trying not to smile. After all, the fool had just ruined his afternoon of play by touching her. "How can I help you?"

Royal puffed up his chest and looked down at her with a broad smile. "Well, I've been thinking about your situation, and I think I can help. You see, I've been needing a route person for the port-a-john plant for some time now. Someone who could manage a big truck and the heavy equipment it takes to lift the johns."

Mallory stared at him in disbelief. "And you think I'd want the job?"

"Well, now you've already met some of my store managers—couple of 'em said you were trying to pick them up in J.T.'s Bar last Friday night. I figured maybe pickins was slim in the construction business, and you might have an easier time finding a man if you were in port-a-johns."

Mallory forced herself to keep from strangling the man. "I think I'll pass, if it's all the same. I'm sure something else will come up."

Royal shook his head. "Hope it comes up fast. The tax

note is going on sale next Thursday . . . just thought you should know." He tipped his hat at her, nodded at Amy and walked away from the table.

"Asshole," Amy said. "God, I can't wait to see the look on his face when you buy that note, Mallory."

Mallory watched the smug owner saunter across the dining area like he owned the world. "Bet I wipe that smile off it."

Chapter Eighteen

Jake stared at the machine in front of him, trying to decide whether or not to kiss it. The money was fake! He had Silas Hebert right where he wanted him and finally the man was going to pay for all his transgressions. If only there were a worse place on earth than jail, he'd gladly recommend the man be sent there for all eternity.

Eager to tell Mallory the good news, he pulled his cell phone out and dialed her number. She answered on the first ring.

"Well?"

"We've got him. It's all fake."

There was a sharp intake of breath and Jake knew her mind was racing with the same emotions as his own, but more, since for Mallory, this entire situation had become very personal. "Oh, my God. I don't think I even know what to say."

"Yeah. I know. It's like the end of a big nightmare."

"Well, maybe not the end, but definitely a conclusion."

Jake felt the breath tighten in his throat at the truth in her words. For Mallory, the nightmare was never ending.

There would never be any justice to right the wrong that had been done to her, but he was going to do everything he could to make things as good as they could get. "Based on the way the play is going, I don't think Silas can hold."

Mallory laughed. "I think you're right on that one, and I have even more good news on this end. Amy cleared her table out, so this afternoon she'll be helping Scooter with the calls."

Jake felt his load lighten even more. "That's fantastic. Good for Amy. Things are looking good for Reginald too, then." Jake carefully removed the money from the machine with his gloved hands and placed it in a plastic bag. "I've got to run. I need to call my captain to ensure everything is in place when we dock."

"Wait, Jake! Exactly what happens during the ATF takedown? That whole thing makes me very nervous. These are not your typical criminals."

"Try not to worry. I think it will go fine. The ATF planned this very carefully, and Lord only knows how many of the staff on board are actually agents. Besides, the bad guys won't have weapons. We'll just pretend surprise like everyone else and keep an eye on Silas so he doesn't slip away."

"You're probably right. I'll see you after lunch then," she said, and disconnected.

Jake flipped his phone shut and walked over to the far wall of the room. He removed a picture of Mallory as a child from the wall and twirled the dial on the safe hidden behind it. The silence in the room made the click of the locking mechanism echo through the room. Smiling, he pulled the door open and placed the stack of bills inside, then shut the door and twirled the combination around and tested it. Satisfied that no one was getting at the money except him or Reginald St. Claire, he pulled the phone from his pocket and dialed his captain.

The captain answered before the first ring was even complete, and Jake decided he must have been staring at the phone with one hand already on it. "Well?" the captain asked.

"I got the exchange, and the money's fake," Jake said, unable to keep the excitement from his voice. "We've got him, Captain."

The captain blew out a breath and Jake could feel his relief over the phone. "That's great news, Randoll, great news. Now, you just keep you head down and stay out of the way of the ATF. We'll handle the rest when you dock."

"No problem. All I've got left to do is win a card game."

"Why? You've got the exchange. What difference does winning make?"

Jake stared at the picture that hid the wall safe and smiled. "All the difference in the world."

Mallory held her breath as Father Thomas considered his bet. "All in," the priest finally said, and pushed his remaining chips into the pot. This was it. Surprising them all, Father Thomas was the last player remaining besides Silas, but apparently even God had his limits when it came to poker.

Silas had already folded, so it was up to Jake to take the priest out. As much as Mallory loved Father Thomas, she prayed that Jake held the hand to remove the priest from the table. Then all his concentration could be on Silas. It was almost time for the afternoon break, and Silas had enough chips for at least two more antes, one more hand worth of chips if he stayed in.

Unfortunately, there was no way they were going to get that hand in before break time rolled around. Damn it. If the ATF made their move right after the break, technically Jake wouldn't win the table. Silas could still leave with his remaining money. Of course, he wouldn't get very far off the dock. Any cash he won would only be forwarded to an attorney, but he still wouldn't lose everything.

Mallory knew if things turned out all right for Reginald, he'd gladly give her the money she needed. But she still wanted Jake to win. Silas to lose. Silas had his voodoo doll, but Jake had Amy and Scooter. Mallory figured that leveled the playing field nicely.

Mallory looked back at the table as Jake pushed a matching bet into the center of the table. "Call," he said, and motioned to the priest.

Father Thomas made the sign of the cross, then placed his hand on the table. It was a good one—three of a kind, but it wasn't as good as Jake's flush. The priest stared at the cards for a moment, then raised his head toward the heavens. "Cards, cards, why hath thou forsaken me?"

Jake smiled. "Sir, you have a single rebuy option if you'd like to exercise it."

Father Thomas shook his head. "I think I'll pass. You're a tad too good for me to risk another ten thousand on, but this has been the most fun I've had in years." He stretched his hand across the table and Jake shook it.

"You played a great game, sir," Jake said. "It was my pleasure."

Father Thomas beamed. "May the force be with you."

Jake grinned. "And also with you."

Jake pulled the chips across the table into his pile and had just placed the spent cards into the shoe when the announcement came for the afternoon break. Silas Hebert rose from his stool without speaking and left the casino.

His frustration had been so clear all afternoon. The crook simply couldn't figure out how he was being beaten at his own game, and it was killing him.

Jake looked over at Mallory and grinned. "It was not nice of you to caress your legs during the signal. I'm supposed to be concentrating on poker, remember?"

"You're telling me a little leg action breaks your concentration on finally busting Silas Hebert?"

"That's *exactly* what I'm saying."

Mallory laughed and pointed to Silas's chips. "He's got enough for two more antes. Do you think we'll have time for two hands?"

Jake studied Silas's chips for a moment and blew out a breath. "I wish to God I knew. Let's just hope he gets something good enough to bet in the first and I get something better. Having Amy in the mix has really helped. Not that Scooter wasn't doing a fine job, but after all, it is Amy's research. She doesn't miss a trick."

"No, she doesn't," Mallory agreed as a glimmer of an idea began to form in her mind. "I'm going to pay them a quick visit right now, let them know how close we're running. I know they're doing everything they can, but maybe there's something Reginald can do to delay the bust until you can beat Silas."

Jake shook his head. "Like what? Reginald has no control over this—you know that."

"Yes, but the engine on this boat has been known to have problems," she said, letting her idea out. "You know, the kind of problems that might not get us close enough to shore until after you've won."

Jake stared at Mallory a moment, then smiled. "You know, you'd have been a hell of a criminal if you'd gone that route."

"With my luck—no thanks." She smiled at Jake and

stepped away from the table. There was only ten minutes left in the break and she had a couple of people to talk to before that ten minutes was up.

She hurried down the hall to Reginald's office, pushed the door open and stepped inside. Then came to a complete halt and stared in shocked silence at the scene in front of her.

Amy and Scooter were sitting in her uncle's office, but they were sharing a chair—and lips.

Mallory sucked in a breath, not believing what she was seeing. That slight noise was all it took for Amy to bolt up off Scooter's lap like she'd been jolted with a million volts of electricity. Then she stood in the middle of the room, staring at Mallory with a terrified expression on her face, as if she'd been caught kissing someone else's husband and not Scooter.

Which brought Mallory right back around to Amy kissing Scooter. Of all the things that had been revealed to her that week, this had to top the list. Hell, even the voodoo curse made more sense than Amy kissing Scooter.

Scooter looked back and forth between Amy and Mallory, the indecision on his face clear as day. Apparently deciding he had no place sitting between two women of questionable mental status, he tore out of the room shouting over his shoulder that he had to go to the men's room. Mallory just watched him hurry down the hall, not even bothering to remind him that Reginald had a fully stocked bathroom not three feet from where Scooter had been sitting.

Amy swallowed visibly and finally blinked. "Uh, Mallory, I can explain."

Mallory raised her eyebrows and stared at her friend. "Really? Well, this I gotta hear."

Amy dropped her gaze to the carpet. "It just sorta happened."

Mallory waited a couple of seconds for her friend to continue, but apparently Amy couldn't explain after all. It was all Mallory could do to hold back a smile. If genius Amy could come up with a logical explanation for this one, Mallory was recommending her for the Brainiac Hall of Fame. "You just sorta fell on top of Scooter and your lips locked together?" she said, unable to keep herself from having a little fun.

Amy looked back up at her and sighed. "Now you sound like my mother."

Mallory just couldn't hold it any longer, and her smile broke through. Amy stared at her for a moment and finally realized that Mallory had been teasing her all along.

"Bitch," Amy said, and giggled.

"Oh, c'mon, Amy. You have to admit it's a pretty shocking sort of thing to see. How was I not going to play with it?"

Amy blushed. "I really don't know how it happened. I mean one minute we're there making poker calls, and Scooter was right almost every time. Then I started throwing in some of the advanced points of my thesis, really minute things that only a small portion of people would even get much less be able to use. He not only got them, he started using them in every hand."

"Uh-huh. So you had to kiss him?"

Amy grinned. "No, I wanted to, and darn if I don't want to do it again. Who would have ever figured?"

"Not me. Hell, no, not ever. But I think it's great. Just think how good Scooter's going to look in D.C. He'll probably park his boat in that fountain in front of the Washington Monument."

Amy giggled. "So he's a work in progress."

"You could always play poker for a living."

"I was hoping for a job with longer skirts."

"And you thought politics was the answer? Amateur."

Mallory scanned the room as she took her seat at the table. Her brief meeting with Reginald had set her uncle into action with the engine idea, maybe buying them another twenty or thirty minutes. That would hopefully be enough.

The room was crowded, and Mallory hoped the noise level dropped when play began. The last thing she needed was to miss a message from Amy and Scooter and since most of the losers had chosen to watch the play rather than hang out in the bar, there wasn't a lot of room left to maneuver the casino floor. Even the kitchen staff had come into the main room to see the final showdown. Since a big lot of the losers and the staff alike were hoping to see a Yankee take down Silas Hebert, the crowd around Jake's table was the biggest.

She gave Jake an encouraging smile as he began to deal and he nodded, his face full of grim determination. Silas lifted the corners of his cards from the table and studied them for a second. His expression never changed, not at all, and Mallory hoped like hell that Scooter and Amy had gotten a peek at his hand. She wanted Silas to lose before the ATF takedown, especially now that all these people were gathered around watching.

Even Father Thomas had stuck around for the finale and stood to the left of the table, clutching a beer and tossing in intermittent prayers. Whether for Jake or Silas or simply that the casino wouldn't run out of liquor before they docked, Mallory wasn't sure, but either way, it probably couldn't hurt anything.

She heard the faint click of the earpiece and grew still, waiting for the instructions that would follow.

"We got a clear look at both hands," Amy said. "There's no way Jake can lose this one, but I doubt Silas will stay in for play. Have Jake raise and Silas will probably fold. That leaves him enough ante for one more hand. Pray that we get a good shot of it, and Jake gets another favorable deal."

Mallory let out the breath she didn't realize she'd been holding, then crossed her right leg over her left—the signal for Jake to up the bet. He never once even glanced in her direction but reached for a stack of chips as soon as her leg began to shift and tossed them onto the stack in the center of the table.

"I'll raise five thousand," Jake said.

Silas didn't even bother to look at his cards again. He simply pushed them across the table to Jake. The mumbling began among the crowd and Mallory knew they were antsy to see how this played out. Even Brad, who'd shut down his table just before lunch, stood off to the side near Father Thomas, studying the game before him and alleviating some of Mallory's worry since she figured the whole takedown wasn't going to start if Brad was watching a poker game.

She caught his eye and he gave her a barely imperceptible nod. That hopefully meant they had at least another hand to go. She looked back to the table and watched Jake deal, silently reciting every prayer she could remember and making up a couple extra along the way.

Jake finished dealing the last card and pushed the shoe slightly to the side. He and Silas lifted the edges of their cards from the table, and Mallory's gaze darted between them like she was watching a tennis match. Except this tennis match was made up of almost no movement and absolutely no expression.

The bet was to Jake and he passed, putting the ball squarely in Silas's court. Mallory figured Jake wasn't positive the hand he held was going to make him a winner, so he was holding back this round in the hopes he had a good hand and signal from Mallory for the final bet. She turned her gaze to Silas, who looked briefly at Jake, then waved his hand across the table. Pass.

Jake tossed in two cards and Silas one. There was no need for a signal on this one since it wasn't costing either of the men anything to draw. Jake dealt the one card to Silas and two to himself and lifted the corner of his cards off the table. Silas pulled the single card toward him, then stopped midway across the table and lifted the end of the card.

Mallory watched him from the corner of her eye, silently willing him to pull the card farther across the table while he still had the edge lifted, afraid that he hadn't placed the card close enough to the rest for it to be caught by the camera. She waited anxiously for a couple of seconds, then fretted a bit more when he pressed the card back flat and dragged it into the rest of his hand, never lifting the cards again.

Jake studied his hand, and even though his face was the usual blank that he wore so well while playing, Mallory knew he was silently willing her to give him the signal. Was it takedown time, or did they have to hope to stretch the play for another hand?

Crap! Mallory reached up for the earring, willing a message to come from Amy and Scooter, caught herself halfway and lowered her hand back to her lap. There were a few mumblings in the crowd as Silas looked up at

Jake, studying him carefully. There were only two options left at this point. He could fold and have half the ante for the next hand—which Jake would play out at half himself, or he could go all-in as he didn't have enough chips left for the bet minimum. All or nothing.

Silas picked up a single chip and tapped it on another, still studying Jake's face, then dropped his hand to the stack of chips and pushed them all to the center of the table. "All-in."

Chapter Nineteen

Mallory sucked in a breath. Where the hell were Amy and Scooter? She glanced over at Jake, knowing he was waiting on the signal from her, and not having any way to tell him there wasn't one.

Just when Mallory had decided that the earpiece had stopped working, she heard Amy's voice. "We've got a problem, Mallory. We couldn't get a look at that final card. Silas was holding two pair, sixes and twos, and there are a ton of them left in the deck at this point. The chance of pulling another is over sixty percent. Jake's holding an inside straight. But if Silas got the full house off the draw then he'll win. I'm sorry, Mallory, but I don't know what to tell you."

Mallory clenched the edge of her stool and took a slow, steady breath. It was her call. She had no way of letting Jake know she couldn't give him an absolute. It was time for a damned good guess and a whole lot of praying. She looked over at Silas. Had he pulled the full house, or was he betting on the strength of the two pair alone since Jake had taken two cards on the draw?

Mallory glanced into the crowd, hoping to catch Brad's eye, but he was no longer standing across from her. Shit. This was all about to go down. She knew it as sure as she sat there. Amy had said there was a 60 percent chance that Silas had drawn the full house. She bit her lip and stared at the cards.

What the hell, she'd been going against the odds her entire life. It wasn't time to get conservative. She leaned back a bit and crossed her right leg over her left, then said a silent prayer.

There wasn't a sound inside the casino. The only noise at all was the steady humming of the boat's engine as it chugged through the Gulf. No one moved a muscle. All eyes were fixed on the table. There wasn't even a murmur when Jake pushed chips onto the table to match Silas's bet. "Call."

Mallory held her breath as Silas flipped his cards over and it was all she could do to hold in a shout when she saw the two pair staring back at her. Jake paused for a moment, staring at Silas's cards almost as if he couldn't believe what was about to happen. Then he reached for his own hand, pulled the cards up from the table and turned them faceup.

Before Mallory could even let out the breath she'd been holding, there was a booming shout at the back of the casino. "This is ATF—no one move!"

Contrary to the order, the entire room of grown men scrambled like a bunch of kids busted at a high school party. Men leapt over chairs and crawled over tables, heading for the nearest exit. The entire lot of them couldn't possibly be guilty of what the ATF was charging, but apparently they were all guilty enough of something to want the hell out of the room.

Mallory watched in amazement as men and women

she'd thought were cooks, dishwashers and waiters pulled weapons from their waists and dashed after the fleeing players. No wonder Reginald had said they were safe on the boat. The place was filled with feds.

A familiar voice shouted out at the table across from her, and she looked over just in time to see an ATF agent handcuff Walter Royal to the table railing. Before she could even wonder what was going on, she caught a glimpse out the window and spun around, hoping she hadn't seen what she thought she had. Shit, shit, shit! Perched on the endless waters of the Gulf of Mexico, she saw a cigarette boat, not fifty yards from the casino. There was no doubt in her mind that Silas had never intended to get off the casino at the dock.

She spun back around to the table just in time to see Silas Hebert slink off into the fray. Jake was standing on a chair, probably trying to figure out if he could assist with the mess. He hadn't noticed Silas leave.

"Jake! He's getting away." Mallory cried. "And there's a boat just off the casino."

Jake glanced outside, then anxiously scanned the room, looking for Silas. "He's headed out the rear doors."

Mallory launched into action as soon as Jake pointed out Silas's exit, kicking off the high heels and skirting the edge of the fray in the casino as she ran toward the rear exit. She could hear the pounding of feet behind her and knew that Jake wasn't far behind. When she reached the rear door, she yanked it open and dashed into the lobby, catching sight of a figure just as it slipped around the corner of the hall to her right. He was headed to the storerooms. And the storerooms had a huge outside exit to allow for freight receipt. It would be a perfect way to get off the casino and onto the getaway boat.

Jake burst through the doors and she pointed down the hall. "That way," she shouted, and took off after him as he sprinted down the hall she'd identified.

"Which door?" Jake asked as they ran.

"Left. There's a freight dock in the storerooms. It's an easy way off the boat."

At the end of the hallway, Jake shoved open the storeroom doors and ran inside, scanning the room as he entered. He could hear Mallory hurry into the room a step behind him. He stopped in the middle of the entryway and put one finger to his lips. Mallory nodded and glanced over to the right, pointing at the freight doors.

Jake was relieved to see the freight doors were not yet opened. Silas hadn't been far enough ahead of them to have exited the boat already, and even if he had, there was no one behind him to close the doors. Based on his earlier talk with Reginald, Jake knew there was no other exit from this room. Silas Hebert was somewhere inside.

Jake ceased all movement and worked to control his breathing. There had to be a noise somewhere to indicate where Silas was hiding, but all he could hear was the hum of the boat's engine. He scanned the room, trying to decipher the most likely place to hide—the most likely place for an ambush since Silas would certainly know they had followed him from the casino.

Finally, Jake pointed to a row of shelves over to the left and motioned for Mallory to follow him. He knew it would be faster if they spread out, but Jake wasn't about to risk Silas getting his hands on Mallory. And Mallory, for all her strength and toughness, was still no match for Silas even if there were no guns involved.

Besides, there was a damned good chance that Silas

had found a suitable weapon somewhere in the storeroom. Plenty of metal and glass could easily be fashioned into something deadly.

Jake took a single step toward the shelves, and Mallory fell in behind him. Step by step they crept toward the shelves, Jake straining to make out any sound that would indicate where Silas was hiding. They were only a couple of feet from their goal when Silas Hebert stepped out.

Holding a gun.

"I'm so glad you could join us," he said with a smile. "Did you really think this was about laundering money or winning a stupid poker tournament?"

Jake drew up short and glanced briefly over his shoulder to ensure Mallory was directly behind him. "I know Mark set me up, if that's what you're implying. He's been working for you all along."

There was movement over to their right, and Mark stepped out from a row of shelves, his weapon directed at Mallory. His partner's hands seemed almost shaky, and as Jake studied the other man's bloodshot eyes, he knew Mark was far from normal.

"I'm sorry about this, Jake," Mark said, and the look on his face was genuine. "But I knew you'd keep looking for answers. We couldn't afford to have you dogging us the rest of our lives. We still have business in this country—and family—we couldn't risk you waiting at the airport every time we came back."

Jake stared at the man he thought he'd known. What had pushed him over the edge? "What happened to you, Mark?"

Mark stared past Jake at the wall. "I had to, Jake. I'm sorry it came down like this, but there was no other way."

"Oh yeah," Jake said. "Says who—the man who kept you locked in an empty apartment?"

Mark flinched and glanced from Silas to Jake. "It was

just temporary . . . until he was certain he could trust me. It was just business."

"Okay," Jake agreed. "So you've got me, but this has nothing to do with her. Let her go."

Silas laughed. "No way. This has turned out beautifully for me . . . my final vengeance on the St. Claire family. She's going the same place you are. And neither of you are walking there."

Mark looked over at Silas. "Your plan never included the woman, Silas. Let's just get this over with and get out of here while we still have a chance."

Silas smiled at Mark. "Oh, we're getting out of here. I just have to lighten the load first."

The shot rang out and Jake involuntarily ducked, Mallory right alongside him. He checked himself for an entry wound, then looked at Mallory, who stared over his shoulder in surprise. Jake whirled around and found himself looking down the barrel of a smoking gun.

Held by Mark's wife, Janine.

One glance over at his partner let Jake know the score. Mark lay on the ground, his chest barely rising, the blood seeping from the center of his stomach.

Janine smiled at Jake, then looked over at Silas. "I told you Mark was too weak. He would have been a liability."

Jake stared at Janine, the woman he'd previously viewed as helpless, trying to wrap his mind around what was happening, when his conversation with Brad flashed through his mind. Janine, who had grown up around New Orleans. Janine, who had worked for a bank.

Janine turned back to face Jake. "Mark was more than a little disturbed that the woman he'd been in love with for fifteen years was a money launderer, especially when he found out that my partner was the man the two of you had been chasing."

She laughed. "Why do you think you never caught Silas? Mark was a carefully selected husband. I knew every move the two of you were going to make before you took one step out the door."

Jake's mind whirled. "So Mark wasn't in on this from the beginning, but he was posing as Silas's employee at the casino. He stopped making his check-ins at the bureau."

"What were his options—arrest the mother of his child? I don't think so. Mark wasn't very smart, but he was loyal, and you know I always came before his job. She glanced over at Mark's body, now still on the concrete. "Besides, who would have believed him if he'd turned me in? He would have gone down right along with me, and I don't have to tell you how prison is for federal agents."

She shrugged and turned away from her husband's body, not an ounce of remorse on her face. Jake felt his skin crawl.

"Oh, well," she continued. "Collateral damage can't be helped. Silas tried to get him on board, but Mark worried too much about everything. He would never have handled the pressure long-term."

Jake stared at Janine, his mind racing to come up with a way out of this and finding nothing. The only option was to stall for time, hoping that he either came up with an idea or someone from the ATF came looking for them. "How did you manage to get guns on board? I thought the ATF screened everyone before entry."

Janine gave him a bored look. "Yeah, but you know how it is—people never look too hard at servants . . . daily help. I've been working in the kitchen the entire tournament, with no fewer than five undercover ATF agents, and no one has even blinked at me. We're invisible. It was a simple matter to come in with the freight one morning and stash the guns in my locker."

She waved one hand toward Jake. "I'm done with the

entertainment portion of the afternoon. Send your girl-friend over here, nice and easy."

Jake felt Mallory stiffen and he knew that if there was any chance of either of them coming out of this alive, he had to come up with something and fast. He looked back at her, saw the fright in her eyes, but knew she wouldn't back down if he called her into action. They would have only one opportunity out of this and that was a one-on-one battle, him against Silas and her against Janine.

He would have given them a decent shot if the guns hadn't been in the equation.

As Mallory walked slowly toward Janine, Jake heard Silas move up behind him. "Don't do anything foolish," Silas instructed. "I'd hate for your mother to arrange a closed-coffin funeral, or St. Claire for that matter."

Jake clenched his teeth. "You won't get away with this. Too many people know why I'm here."

Silas laughed. "You think I care how many people know? You're the only witness who can prove that money came from me. Now, you've got a chunk of counterfeit cash, probably tucked away in one of Reginald's safes, and Janine hid the plates in his storeroom this morning while she was getting more stock for the kitchen. When the FBI gets done tearing this boat apart, the only person left holding the bag will be Reginald St. Claire.

"And do you know what the best part is?" Silas asked. "The best part is it was feds that made all this possible. Without the ATF and their player's list, do you really think Reginald St. Claire would have ever let me set foot on his casino? I've been waiting for this opportunity for thirty years."

Jake looked over at Mallory, who stood just in front of Janine, a gun pressed to the back of her head.

"These FBI guys think they're so smart," Janine said

with a laugh. "Let's get this over with." She grabbed Mallory by the arm and pushed her into a stack of empty crates, then stepped back a couple of feet and took aim at her with her pistol.

"Don't touch her," Silas yelled as Janine grabbed Mallory's arm, but his warning came too late.

A second later, Janine squeezed the trigger and Jake braced himself for the worst, but only a click emitted from the weapon.

"Stupid," Silas ranted. "I told you not to touch her."

Janine studied the gun for a moment, then lifted it again, pulling the trigger back again and again, but the gun never fired.

Mallory glanced at Jake for a millisecond, but he read everything he needed to in her eyes. As she lunged at Janine, he swung around, his fist connecting with Silas Hebert's face. Before Silas could gather himself, Jake kicked the gun from his hand and sent it sprawling across the storeroom floor.

As Jake squared off in front of Silas, he heard a crash behind him and Janine cried out in pain. He set himself up for the second punch, but before he could land it, Silas grabbed a can off the shelf behind it and clocked him in the side of the head.

His ear felt like it exploded from the impact, and his vision blurred. He took a step back, ensuring Silas couldn't connect with him again, hoping his vision would quickly return to normal. Everything was gray and white and seemed to swim in front of him. He could dimly make out Silas's form and he braced himself for another hit, but the form grew smaller and Jake realized Silas was moving away from him.

In the direction of the gun.

He rushed toward the gray figure, his only hope to

tackle him before he reached the weapon, but Jake came up several feet short. His vision cleared just as Silas smiled and leveled the weapon at Jake's head. "I think my business here is done."

Jake looked over at Mallory, who was standing over a somewhat battered Janine. He hoped this final connection between them told her everything he wanted her to know. How much he respected her, how much he had come to love her, need her, and how very sorry he was that things were going to end this way. She stared back at him, her eyes full of the same emotion, and Jake regretted the things he'd never said to her, the future they'd never have.

He heard the shot as it fired and waited for his body to register the bullet's entry, but as he looked back at his nemesis, he saw the look of shock on the other man's face and the blood beginning to trickle out of his side. Silas clutched his side, dropped the gun and turned toward the storeroom door.

Jake ran over and grabbed the gun off the floor before turning to see who their savior was. He blinked in surprise at the sight of Father Thomas standing in the doorway, a pistol peeking from the sleeve of his robe. He heard shouting in the hallway and a second later, Brad and two other ATF agents burst into the storeroom.

Brad quickly assessed the situation and directed his men to handcuff the still-bleeding Silas and a very subdued-looking Janine. He looked around the warehouse, studying their faces. "You all right?"

Everyone nodded, and Father Thomas smiled. "Never better," the priest said.

Brad nodded and motioned to his men, who lifted Silas and Janine from the floor and followed Brad out of the storeroom. Jake watched them leave, then looked at Mallory, who stood staring at Father Thomas, shocked.

* * *

"Father Thomas?" Mallory said. "What in God's name?"

Before he could answer, Amy and Scooter burst through the door, followed closely by Reginald. Amy rushed across the room and flung her arms around Mallory. "Oh, my God, I was so worried. I was afraid you were dead." She released Mallory and sniffed. "Scooter and I saw you on the cameras, running down the hall. We went for help, but it took too long."

Scooter shuffled over next to Amy and gave Mallory a grin. "Gave me a scare, Mal."

"Got that right," Reginald seconded, and pushed Amy aside so he could give Mallory a hug. "I'm glad you're still with us." He released Mallory and looked over at Father Thomas. "You've still got it, you old bird," he said, and grinned.

Father Thomas smiled. "The Lord works in mysterious ways."

Mallory looked from Reginald to Father Thomas. "What the hell is going on here?"

Father Thomas stepped closer to Mallory and placed his hand on her arm. "Don't let it vex you so much, dear. Everything in life is not what it seems. Or maybe I should say everything in life is not always what it seems."

Mallory blinked and stared at the priest in amazement. "You had a gun. You shot Silas."

Father Thomas nodded. "It's only an entry wound. The son of a bitch should be fine to stand trial and hopefully spend a long, long time paying for what he's done to people."

"An entry wound?" She stared at the priest, wondering what manner of creature had assumed the body of the drunk she knew and loved.

Father Thomas smiled. "I spent some of my younger

years serving this country in an, ah, sort of weapons-based role. When I returned to Royal Flush, I spent a great deal of time hunting with your uncle."

Mallory shook her head, trying to wrap her mind around Father Thomas in the military, with weapons, knowing what an entry wound was and exactly how to create one instead of blowing someone away. "But you've been drinking like a sieve. How in the world . . ."

The dismay on the priest's face was almost comical. "Alas, one of Reginald's requirements was no drinking. His bartender has been pouring me only regular Coke." He glanced at his watch. "It's been exactly five days, two hours and sixteen minutes since my last drink."

"Now, that's just not right," Scooter said, and shook his head.

"But you've been drunk," Mallory said, her head swimming with confusion.

Father Thomas shook his head. "Not drunk, just pretending. I was a pretty good actor in my high school days. When Reginald first told me of the ATF situation and asked for my help, I thought it would be better if I went as my usual self—or at least pretended to be." He shrugged. "People will say anything in front of drunks, you know. I gathered quite a bit of information that helped Reginald's dealers and provided a bit of distraction from time to time."

Jake laughed. "Distraction is certainly one way of putting it."

Father Thomas nodded. "Reginald is an old friend who was in a bad situation. I was happy to help. And when Mallory took the job cooling, Reginald and I were both relieved that I'd be there to monitor things—especially with Silas Hebert at the table." He gave them both a smile. "I'm glad I got here before it was too late. Who else could we get to shut down the Yankees at J.T.'s Bar?"

"Unbelievable," Mallory said, unable to stop smiling.

Father Thomas gave her arm a squeeze, then looked over at Reginald, Scooter and Amy. "I think we should give these two a moment, don't you?"

Scooter threw one arm around the priest's shoulder. "Now, you're talking. Let's head to the restaurant. I'm pouring you the biggest damned Jack and Coke ever."

"I'll drink to that," Reginald agreed.

Amy watched the three of them walk away and smiled. "I'll wait for you in the restaurant," she said to Mallory, then followed the others out of the storeroom.

As soon as the door shut behind Amy, Jake gently grasped Mallory's hand and pulled her close to him, wrapping his arms around her. "I thought I'd lost you," he whispered. "Thought I'd lost us, or I guess the us that could be."

Mallory tightened her arms around him and buried her face in his neck, allowing herself to escape, if only for the moment, in the fantasy that she and Jake had a future, a real future. But even as he took her face in his hands and kissed her gently, she knew there was no way she could subject this man that she loved so much to her cursed life.

Chapter Twenty

"How's the business going?" Scooter asked as he slid his rod into the holder on his pier and grabbed another beer from the ice chest next to his lawn chair.

Mallory cast her line into the bayou and leaned back in her lawn chair. "Good. It's been a lot of information to throw at the employees, what with the tax situation, Royal trying to buy us out, then Royal getting arrested. But everyone is happy that things turned out all right."

"And Harry?"

"Harry is especially happy. He barely let the ink dry on the legal papers transferring the business to me before he and Thelma headed to the Bahamas. Apparently they've always wanted to go."

"I'm glad they got the chance."

"Me too," she said and jiggled her rod a bit. "The fish aren't biting so well today, are they?"

"Nah," Scooter agreed. "Too hot. Probably run late tonight."

Mallory looked over at her friend and smiled. "Then I guess only one of us is going to catch any fish today, as lately, you've spent your nights occupied with other things."

Scooter grinned at Mallory and lay back on the pier, holding one hand up to shield his eyes from the sun. "Who would have ever thought, right? Me and someone like Amy. She's, like, the smartest person in the world."

"I'd have to agree with you on that one. The smartest I've ever known, anyway."

"You ought to see the plans we've come up with for the casino. Your uncle is going to flip. Everything is state of the art—built-ins, fold-outs, stuff that rises from the floor and hides in the walls until you need to use it. He's going to make a fortune with this whole casino-of-the-future idea."

"How is Reginald these days? I haven't seen him since the arraignment, and that was a week ago."

"He's good. I met his girlfriend the other day—Glenda— she's kinda cool."

"You're right again. That's two today, Scooter."

Scooter sat up and looked over at Mallory, the smile dropping from his face. "Well, since I'm on a roll, I'm just gonna go ahead and say I think you ought to call Jake."

Mallory looked over the bayou and struggled against the rush of emotions that ran through her every time she thought of Jake. "You know I can't, Scooter. I can't ask him to be with me when I know how things are. Things that will never change."

Scooter shook his head. "That should still be his choice. And if you won't even take a phone call from him, how's the man supposed to plead his case?"

"He's not. That's the whole point."

Scooter sighed and lay back down on the pier. "Fine, but for the record, Amy and I both think you're making a mistake."

Mallory slumped back in her chair and drew in a deep breath. So Scooter and Amy thought she was making a mistake. Well, there was a novel idea. Like Harry, J.T. and Father Thomas hadn't already told her the same thing, some in more polite terms, some in less. Even Brad had weighed in his opinion after the arraignment. It seemed that everyone in the state of Louisiana knew what was best for her.

Except her.

She wanted to call, wanted to answer the calls when she saw Jake's number on the caller ID. But ultimately, she'd been too afraid. Jake may be riding the first throes of romance and love right now, but what about years from now? When disaster after disaster, courtesy of Mallory's curse, affected every day of their lives? Would he still want her then? Still love her?

She didn't see how he could, and was smart enough to know her heart wouldn't be able to take having him for a while, then losing him all over again. It still hadn't recovered from the five days they'd had together. How in the world would she pop back from a year, or two, or ten?

"I knocked on your door." She jumped at the sound of Jake's voice behind her. "I should have known I'd find you two where there was fish and beer." He stepped onto the pier and walked over to her chair, smiling down at her.

Scooter jumped up from the pier and nodded at Jake. "Guess I'll be heading in for a shower." He gave Mallory a thumbs-up and hustled off like someone had just said "last call."

Mallory stared at Jake, wondering what the hell he was doing there. But with the way Scooter had shot off the deck, not looking at her even once, Mallory was afraid the fix was in. She rose from her chair, not liking Jake standing above her. It made her feel she was at a disadvantage, and even though that was probably the case, she didn't need to feel worse about it than she already did.

She looked at him for a moment but couldn't hold his gaze. Shoving her hands in her jeans pockets, she stared down at the pier.

"You've been avoiding my calls," Jake said.

Mallory shrugged and shuffled her feet a bit, still not looking up at him. "Wasn't any use wasting time."

He placed one finger under her chin and tilted it up until she was forced to look at him. "You call what we have wasting time? Jesus, woman, what do you do when I'm not around that's so much more important?"

Mallory sighed. "Jake, you know how I feel, but there's no future for us. Not with the way things are. You'd never have a normal moment for the rest of your life."

"Who the hell said I was interested in normal?"

"You did. Over and over again, when you explained to me how weird Louisiana and voodoo and me thinking I could cool cards was. Remember?"

Jake waved a hand in dismissal. "Old news. The new Jake thinks normal is boring. How in the world could I go back to a regular life when I have a shot with a woman that makes cars explode after sex? Now *that's* something special."

"Yeah, I bet Hertz was thrilled."

"So I'll drive an old clunker and carry liability only."

Mallory stared at Jake and shook her head. "It's not just the car. You know that."

Jake reached down and drew both her hands into his. "What if I told you there was a way around it?"

Mallory felt her heart leap into her throat at his words. "But, the voodoo woman said . . ."

"She said there was no way to take the curse off you,"

Jake said gently. "She didn't say there wasn't a way to protect me from it."

"You saw the voodoo woman?" she asked, trying to control the hope quickly rising inside of her. "How? When?"

"Scooter took me to see her last night. That's probably why he took off so fast when I got here. I think he was afraid you'd come down on him for interfering."

Mallory stared at Jake in disbelief. "Scooter took you to the voodoo woman? I can't believe it. He's scared to death of that stuff."

"That he is, but he loves you more than he's scared. He knew I'd never find her without help and figured you wouldn't take me."

Mallory bit her lip and drew in a breath. "So what did she say?"

Jake reached inside his shirt and pulled out a string with a tiny pouch on the end. "She said that if I wore this, it should protect me—against the curse, anyway. She didn't have a protection against falling desperately in love with you." He placed one hand on her cheek and leaned in, gently placing his lips on hers.

Mallory relaxed in his kiss, every nerve in her body tingling from his touch. "You're sure," she said as he drew back and placed a finger on the pouch. "If this protects you from me, will it work for others?"

"It better not."

Mallory stared at him. "Why on earth wouldn't you want my friends and family protected?"

Jake placed his hand over hers. "I would, but the voodoo woman said this protects me because of the scope of our relationship. I took that to mean in a biblical sort of way." He grinned. "Now if you want to work something like that out with Amy, I might consider it."

Mallory swatted him on the shoulder but couldn't keep from smiling. "You wish." She drew in a breath, trying to absorb everything he was saying. "What about your job? You know I can't leave here—"

Jake placed one hand over her mouth to stop the barrage that was most certainly about to spill out. "I've resigned my position with the FBI, and I'll be relocating to Royal Flush as soon as I can pack up my apartment and schedule a moving truck."

Mallory stared at him in disbelief. "But what will you do?"

"I've been thinking a lot about my work, wondering if it really accomplished what I hoped it would as far as making society a better place. Everything that went down with Mark and Janine kinda clinched it for me. I think I'd rather work with kids—teenagers specifically. Hopefully prevent them from becoming someone I would have arrested."

Mallory smiled. "I think that sounds wonderful. Do you have any idea where you might work? There are a lot of charitable organizations in New Orleans. I know they could use help."

Jake shook his head. "I'm planning on starting my own organization. I have a real estate agent trying to locate a warehouse in New Orleans for me. That should give me the room to start."

A real estate agent? New Orleans? "But, how will you pay for it? Something like that's got to be expensive to get started."

"I've applied for the usual grants. But I have a long-term plan for continual funding."

"What kind of plan?"

"I'm sure you heard about the ATF seizing all of Royal's

assets. Well, I have it on good information that the port-a-john plant is going up for auction here shortly. In fact, the ATF has given me an inside deal. If I can come up with the money they want before the auction, I can buy the plant from them at an absolute steal."

Mallory stared at him for a moment. It had been weeks since the arrests, but the residents of Royal Flush still hadn't quite wrapped their minds around Walter Royal as a gunrunner. The ATF case, however, was solid as a rock. A search of the plant had produced thousands of weapons stored in false bottoms in the port-a-johns. She supposed it made good sense when you thought about it. The port-a-johns were distributed all over the country, and she'd guess no one was going to get overly involved in inspecting a portable toilet, empty or not.

But Jake buying the port-a-john plant? Surely he was joking. "You want to be the King of Crap?"

Jake laughed. "Well, I am planning on living in Royal Flush. If you're going to be King of Crap, this is definitely the place."

Mallory smiled. "Okay, King Jake, any idea how you're going to come up with that capital?"

"Funny you should ask. I hear there's a poker tournament starting up next week in Vegas. I figure with Amy's card shark training and a little help from you, the other players don't stand a chance. And then there's the added benefit of so many wedding chapels."

Mallory drew in a breath. "You want to marry me?"

Jake laughed. "More than anything. But you've got to meet my mother first or she'll kill me. I'm going to have her meet us in Vegas if that's okay with you. I don't think she's quite ready for Royal Flush—I need a little time to prepare her for a visit here, and I would take you to her place in Atlantic City, but she's an artist. She lives and works in her studio and it's probably not the best place for you to meet."

"An artist, huh? What does she do, paint?"

Jake gave her a pained look. "She's a glassblower."

Mallory laughed and threw her arms around Jake, squeezing him hard against her as if there were no tomorrow. "Vegas it is, then."

Gemma Halliday

ALIBI
in
HIGH
HEELS

Baguettes, bodies, and haute couture galore! Shoe designer turned amateur sleuth Maddie Springer is at it again—this time in fabulously fashionable Paris.

When Europe's designer du jour, Jean Luc LeCroix, invites Maddie to show her creations at Paris Fashion Week, Maddie's sure she's died and gone to heaven. That is, until Jean Luc's top model is found dead on the runway, stabbed with a familiar stiletto heel. Sure someone is trying to frame her, Maddie enlists the help of her friends, including the sexy Detective Jack Ramirez.

But as the evidence mounts, Maddie becomes the prime suspect and Ramirez is stuck between a badge and a cute blonde with a tendency for trouble. With her love life on the rocks and a murderer on the loose, if Maddie doesn't uncover the real killer soon, she might be saying her final adieu.

AVAILABLE MARCH 2008!

ISBN 13: 978–0–8439–5835–5